Call Me Daddy

a novel

Kelly Stone Gamble

Call Me Daddy
Copyright © 2016 by Kelly Stone Gamble All rights reserved.
First Print Edition: September 2016

Print ISBN-13: 978-1-940215-82-2
Print ISBN-10: 1-940215-82-X

Red Adept Publishing, LLC
104 Bugenfield Court
Garner, NC 27529
http://RedAdeptPublishing.com/

Cover and Formatting: Streetlight Graphics

No part of this book may be reproduced, scanned, or distributed in any printed or electronic form without permission. Please do not participate in or encourage piracy of copyrighted materials in violation of the author's rights. Thank you for respecting the hard work of this author.

This is a work of fiction. Names, characters, places, and incidents either are the product of the author's imagination or are used fictitiously, and any resemblance to locales, events, business establishments, or actual persons—living or dead—is entirely coincidental.

Dear Linda,
Distance doesn't always make the heart grow fonder...
Hope you enjoy this one!

Kelly Stone Gamble
12/17

For my mother, Vera, who now sings with angels, and for my father, Richard Stone, the only man I'll ever call "Daddy"

Chapter 1

Cass

You would think after killing one man, the second would be easy. Getting rid of Roland was difficult... the shoveling part, anyway. But I guess I didn't mind playing the grim reaper too much. He deserved it. But the guy lying in front of my truck didn't. He just happened to be standing in the middle of the wrong road when my radio went on the fritz and I had to beat on the dashboard to get it working. That explains why I didn't see him before my hood ornament did.

Normally, the only time I drive after dark is when I go out to the Hill because I need to think. Sure, the place where I burned down our house and buried my husband seems an odd choice for me to find peace, but I'm a little odd. The breeze whistling through the trees and the flow of the river are calming to me. Sometimes, I swear I can hear Roland digging in the yard, planting another rosebush.

But tonight, instead of hanging at the Hill, I decided to drive around the backcountry roads and listen to the radio. I imagined Roland in the driver's seat. It felt good for about fifteen minutes, which is about how long a real road trip with Roland would usually last before we started fighting. Amid all that, I somehow wound up in Neosho, forty miles from home. I called Clay to say I'd gotten lost, which he thinks means I'm lost in my own mind. In a way, he's right. I didn't tell him the Roland part. *Watch out for deer*, Clay had said.

So there I was, driving home alone in the dark. Then I suddenly looked out my windshield and saw the body in front of me. Hey, at least it wasn't a deer.

Now, as I sit in the front seat of the truck, I feel a large, wet bump on my forehead. When I pull my hand away, I see the blood, black in the darkness inside the pickup. Figures.

My head is spinning like a warped LP, so I shut my eyes, trying to make the stars go away. I really hope that when I open them, I'll see this is just another of my crazy dreams. I peek out the front glass. He's still there.

Casey Donahew's "Whiskey Baby" suddenly screams through the radio and makes me jump. At least the radio is working.

My cell phone isn't by my side, so I fumble around on the passenger side and finally find it on the floorboard. I hit 1 on the memory dial and wait for Clay to answer. "I got a problem," I blurt out when he answers. "I hit a guy with my truck on 160 outside of Fat Tina's strip club, and I think he's dead."

There are several things I love about Clay, but right now, the fact that he doesn't flinch when I get right to the point is at the top of my list. "Are you okay?" he asks.

I touch the bump on my forehead again and feel it throb. "I hit my head on the steering wheel, but I'm okay."

"I'm on my way. Did you call 9-1-1?" In the background, I hear our front screen door squeak as he opens it, which tells me he isn't wasting any time. Good. It's creepy as hell out here, and it won't take long before the people at Fat Tina's get a whiff of some excitement and start gathering like chickens to feed.

"No, I called you first," I say. Calling 9-1-1 means the police will come, and I'm not too happy about having to see Deacon's chief of police, Benny Cloud.

"Are you sure he's dead?" Clay's voice is calm and steady.

"No, but I'm afraid to get out. He looks dead from here, though."

"You need to check, Cassie. Maybe it isn't as bad as you think."

I was afraid he was going to say that. "Okay, don't hang up."

I slowly get out of the truck and walk to the front. The guy looks as if he lost a fight with a bear. He isn't moving, so I kick his leg. He moans.

"It's bad, Clay, but he's still alive." I move a little closer, thankful for my headlights. The bottom half of his face is covered with blood, but he looks familiar to me. "Clay, I don't recognize him, but it's hard to tell. I'm sure he doesn't normally look like this… Have you crossed the bridge yet?"

I've lived in Deacon my entire life, and I'm very familiar with all the roads leading in and out of town. They've changed over the years, but basically, a road is a road, unless there is a body in the middle of it.

Being out here alone with Half-Dead Harry gives me the creeps. Headlights are coming toward me, and I move to the side so I don't get hit. I don't think Harry notices. As the car gets closer, red and blue lights start whirling on top of it, which isn't doing my head any favors. I sit on the gravel shoulder and pull my sweater tighter around me before putting the phone back to my ear. "Clay? Don't worry about calling 9-1-1. They're already here."

The lights are making it difficult to see, so I turn the other way. I figure it must be Benny Cloud; he seems to have a way of catching me at my worst. Instead, I look at the guy in the road, who isn't looking at anything. I hear the car stop and the door open then the heavy *thunk* of boots on asphalt. When the footsteps get closer to me, I look up. It isn't Benny. It's worse.

Sheriff Rudy Drown kneels beside Harry and mumbles something at the body before pointing a fat finger in my direction. "Don't you move," he yells. I hadn't planned on it. "And put that phone away."

I ignore him and turn toward the back of my truck, grateful to see a set of headlights approaching from behind. Not that I like people much, but I'm glad I don't have to be out here with the sheriff and what's left of the guy I hit. Whoever it is has to be better than Sheriff Drown. Then I see Daze Harper waddling up from behind my truck. I was wrong.

"Clay, I need you out here," I say desperately into the phone.

Rudy has his radio out and is trying to sound all official.

Daze walks over to the sheriff, staring at the guy on the pavement. "Sumbitch! I talked to that fella at Fat Tina's not fifteen minutes ago." He stands in front of my truck and watches Rudy unbutton Harry's shirt. Then he turns to me, smirking while he pulls his phone out of his overalls and starts tapping away on it. "You're in a world of hurt this time, Crazy. Caught in the act by the law. They're gonna eat you alive."

My head hurts, and Daze isn't making it any better. I lie down on the cold gravel and imagine Rudy Drown putting me on a Ritz cracker. I cuddle my phone, somewhat comforted by the fact that Clay is on the other end of the line.

"Harper, get over here and get off that phone! Hold his head steady. Don't let it move. An ambulance is on its way."

"I ain't touching him," Daze says.

"Harper, if you don't do what I say, I swear I'm gonna make your life hell."

I have to laugh. The sheriff obviously hasn't met Daze's wife.

"What are you cackling at? You're in a lot of trouble, lady." The sheriff is standing right over me now, a fat finger within inches of my nose. "Get up," he yells.

I stand up slowly and try to shake the buzz out of my head. The lights from his car are flashing, and more swirling lights are coming down the road. People are running over from Fat Tina's, yelling, and the noise is making my headache worse. I want to grab something to keep me steady, but there's nothing close to me except that fat finger attached to the sheriff.

"It was his fault," I say. Which it was. I was minding my own business, driving and trying to adjust my radio, and there he was. Who the hell stands in the middle of a dark highway and doesn't expect to get hit?

I focus on that sausage of a finger as it gets closer. "When I get done with you—" Drown is cut off by a large hand on his shoulder that spins him around.

I smile. I know that hand.

"You want to talk to her, you'll have to go through me first." Clay pushes the sheriff out of the way and wraps his arms around me as I start to fall.

"It's about time," I say.

"I can arrest you right now, Adams, for assaulting a peace officer." Rudy's chest is all puffed out as though he's Johnny Bravo.

"It won't be my first time in jail," Clay says. "And I got a pretty damn good lawyer on speed dial." He picks me up and starts toward his truck, weaving in between the bystanders. I imagine Clay calling my sister Lola in the middle of the night to tell her that I've killed another one and need the services of her husband, Richard, again. I never had much use for a mouthpiece in a suit until a few months ago, but I'm glad Lola had the sense to marry one. Having one in the family sure came in handy when I got brought up on a murder charge. I can hear an ambulance in the distance, and I know it's coming our way.

"Where the hell are you going?" Rudy yells.

Clay ignores him and talks to me instead. "Where are your keys?"

"Still in the truck." I lean on Clay's shoulder. It's safe here.

He sits me in the passenger side of his truck and checks my body for injuries. My head hurts, but everything else is fine. I don't mind getting frisked by Clay. When he is satisfied that I'm not dying, he kisses the tip of my nose. "We'll have your head looked at in a bit. Stay here." Clay walks to my truck. He says something to Daze Harper and throws him my keys.

Tina is there, staring at the guy on the ground. Benny Cloud is with her, acting as if he's the ringmaster at this circus. And it is a circus. The light from Fat Tina's large pink neon sign mixes with the blue flashes from the top of Rudy Drown's cruiser, giving the whole scene a purple glow. It looks as though everyone in the bar has shown up, including a midget with biceps as big as oak stumps and strippers dressed as sexy pirates, fairy princesses, and angels that would make the Devil blush. An ambulance weaves through the crowd and makes its way close to the body. Tina and Benny stand up and look around, so I lie on the seat of the pickup and try to play invisible.

We are right in front of the entrance to the roadside park, and I need to throw up. I don't think I can make it to the ladies' room. Instead, I open the passenger door and hurl right outside the truck onto the gravel. I'm seeing stars again, and I feel dizzy, so I lie back down on the seat and close my eyes.

That doesn't last long. Clay opens the door, and I sit up long enough for him to get in the truck, then I use his leg for a pillow. He pushes my hair out of my face. "Don't go to sleep until we have your head checked." Damn, that's all I want to do. He dials his phone, and I can tell by the ensuing conversation that he's talking to our insurance company. My old truck isn't much, but it's mine. I sure hope I have coverage for running over someone.

"I lost my phone," I say when he finishes. I'm feeling for it but can't remember if I had it when I got in Clay's truck or not.

"Don't worry about it. We'll get another if you don't find it."

There's a knock at Clay's window, and he lowers it. Benny Cloud's sidekick, Jimmy Ray, is staring in. I guess Jimmy Ray is an okay kid. He brought me pie at night when I was in jail five months ago. Even though I threw it at him, I guess it was nice of him to do it. However, he is still on Benny's side, and since I can't stand Benny, I don't like Jimmy Ray by default. "Go away," I say.

"I need to ask a few questions." He's bouncing back and forth as though he doesn't care to be here in the first place.

Clay pats my leg and tells me to sit up for a sec, which I know means he wants me to play nice and answer the questions. I get up in time to see the ambulance pull away. It's moving away from Deacon, so I know they are going to the big hospital in Joplin. Benny and Fat Tina are talking on the side of the road, and they keep glancing this way. *Crap.* "Start asking," I say.

"What happened?" he asks.

Oh boy. "I hit a guy with my truck." It should be pretty obvious what happened even to someone as dumb as Jimmy.

"I know, but I mean, you didn't see him standing there? How fast were you going? Were you talking on your phone?"

"No. Fifty-five. No. Is that it?" I'm glad he didn't ask if I was trying to tune my radio.

Benny and Tina walk by. Benny glares at me and nods at Jimmy. Good. I was afraid they were going to stop and want to talk too. Tina glances at me then gives Clay a quick smile. I used to work with Tina at the truck stop, and she was okay then. But like everyone else, once Roland moved me outside of town and put me in that prison on the Hill, she quit acting as if she even knew me.

"I need to get the truck out of the highway," Jimmy says. I guess that was all of his questions.

"Daze has the keys," Clay says. "He said he'd wait until you all were done and move it to the rest area until Lucky's wrecker gets here to pick it up." I'm sure Daze isn't too happy about helping with *my* truck, and I'm not thrilled about his fish-stink getting on my seats, either. But like most people in town, he'll do about anything Clay asks him to.

Jimmy nods then takes a deep breath and lets it out. Rudy Drown is coming toward the truck. Rudy moves Jimmy Ray out of the way and is now filling up the window. "What happened out here, girlie? I find it hard to believe you didn't see him standing in the middle of the road." He's snarling and sucking his teeth between sentences.

"Well, I find it hard to believe the citizens of this county keep electing you to office," Clay shoots back coolly. Clay is nice to most people, but he doesn't like the sheriff at all. I don't know much about why, but I do know that Rudy ran with Clay's daddy when he was little, before Clay's daddy up and left town. Maybe that's why he doesn't like the man. Or maybe it's because Rudy's such a dumbass. "Talk to Jimmy Ray. We answered his questions." Clay starts the truck and begins rolling up his window.

I put my hand on Clay's arm. "No, it's okay. I do have something to say. But he needs to come to my side so I don't have to scream." Rudy struts around the front of the truck and stands by my window. I smile, knowing he's standing in a puddle of puke. I roll the window down about halfway.

"What's you gotta say, girlie?"

"Talk to Jimmy Ray. I already answered his questions." I roll my window up and look at Clay, who is smiling. He puts the truck in drive and weaves around the bystanders, back toward Deacon.

Chapter 2

Benny

"Heads up, Benny," Sammie says as she slides me a cold one across the bar—a Diet Coke topped with a red plastic sword stabbing three cherries. She knows I like extra cherries, and I might have thought Sammie had a thing for me if I didn't already know she was into women. I take a big drink and pull one of the cherries off the sword with my teeth, careful not to let any of the juice drip onto my chin. It wouldn't look good for Benny Cloud, Deacon's chief of police, to walk out of Fat Tina's strip club at eleven o'clock at night with cherry juice all over his uniform.

"Thanks, Sammie." I raise my glass to take another sip. It sure would be better with a little Jack, but that wouldn't be very professional, either. I don't come to Tina's to party; I come here to keep tabs on the place and make sure everything stays on the up and up.

Sammie points toward the half-moon stage, which is surrounded by men in half-moon chairs. "Sonja's up." I think Sammie also knows I come to watch the girls. There ain't no harm in a man looking. And looking is all I do. I got a good woman, and Grace trusts me enough that she doesn't say squat when I come out here.

The disco ball above the stage reflects the colored spotlights in all directions. Out walks Sonja, dressed as a schoolgirl. Her long blond hair is pulled up in ponytails, she's wearing a red plaid dress that would get her expelled, and she's carrying a twelve-inch ruler that she uses to smack her own ass. "Centerfold" is blaring from the speakers surrounding the stage, and just like the song says, my blood runs cold. Sonja wraps one oiled-up thigh around the pole as I pop another cherry in my mouth.

Call Me Daddy

One of the bouncers runs right by me, yelling for Tina. It's easy to pick out the guys that work here from the customers because they all wear the same T-shirt—bright pink with a picture of a large woman laughing and a rooster crowing between her spread legs. I try to watch him and Sonja at the same time, but my eyes don't move like that. *Damn.* I take one quick look at the stage—Sonja is kicking off her four-inch-heeled saddle oxfords—then I turn to Tina.

She's standing in the corner, arms crossed in front of her, eyes darting all over the place. Tina is a businesswoman, and she makes sure no one crosses the lines she has drawn for this place. She bends forward as the bouncer reaches her, listening as he screams in her ear and points back toward the door. Tina stands up straight, one hand going to her mouth. She moves past the bouncer, accidentally knocking over a chair on her way, and catches my eye.

I'm off my bar stool before she gets to me. Then my walkie goes off, and I can hear Jimmy mumbling.

"Someone's been hit," Tina yells as she passes me on her way to the front door.

I nod to Sammie, pop the last cherry in my mouth, and take one last glance back at the stage as I turn to follow Tina. Sonja is inching up that pole like a caterpillar on a vine. I head for the front door, pulling my walkie from my side.

Tina may be a big woman, but she sure has speed. By the time I get out front, she's heading toward the highway, where I see two trucks and the familiar flashing lights of a sheriff's vehicle.

Men are streaming out of the club behind us, making a beeline for the highway. I try to get them to stay back, but the crowd pushes forward.

Other than Fat Tina's, there isn't anything out here but a rest area on the other side of the highway. It overlooks the river, and when I was younger, a lot of kids used it for a make-out spot. Since Tina's business has gotten so big, a lot of the patrons use it for overflow parking, or for someplace to park that doesn't fall under the watchful eye of Tina's security team. A steady stream of cars is flowing out of there, riding the shoulder to avoid the accident. I have a feeling they're hoping to make their way out of the cops' radar since Rudy Drown has already set up shop at the base of the entrance.

I wish I could stay out of the radar of some of those cops too—well, the sheriff, anyway. A few months back, I announced my plan to run against him when he comes up for reelection in six months. I've been trying to avoid Rudy as much as possible in the interim. I was hoping the next time I saw him, I would hear him congratulate me on beating him out for his job, not that he would give me that courtesy.

Clay Adams's truck is parked on the side of the road behind the sheriff, and a parade of cars is gathering behind him. Cass's truck is in front of the sheriff, and there is a body lying between them.

Rudy is standing by the side of the road, arguing with Clay Adams, who's holding Cass in his arms. My first thought is that she's dead, but then she gives Rudy the middle finger. Tina squats on the ground next to the body, facing away from me. She is wearing a long green muumuu, and the way it spreads out reminds me of an army tent. Looking over her back, I see Daze Harper near the head of the guy lying on the ground, but there ain't no way I can squeeze by Tina.

I move around so I can come at the body from the other side. His eyes are closed, and his hair is matted to his head with his own blood. Both arms are crossed over his stomach, and one of them looks like it has been put through a grinder. I move my flashlight down his body. His shirt is open, his belt is undone, and his left lower leg is bent at an angle below the knee. I kneel to check his pulse, and as I reach for his neck, he turns his head and coughs, spraying my arm and trouser leg with blood and bits of teeth.

He's not familiar to me, but it's hard to tell with his face messed up. "Do you know him?" I ask Tina. She gives me a confused look, one I can't quite interpret, and sits back on her haunches. I stand up, pulling Daze with me, and point toward the crowd. "Daze, get these people out of here." I wipe the blood from my hand on my shirt. Daze kicks the gravel like a kid but knows better than to say no to me.

I hear the ambulance in the distance and pull my side radio to call Jimmy Ray back at the station. "I'm going to need some help out here, Jimmy Ray." I move further back so I can talk on the radio but still keep focused on the body.

"Almost there," Jimmy says.

Clay walks by without a word, back toward his truck, with Cass still in his arms. I can hear the ambulance getting closer. "Daze, get out there and direct the ambulance back this way," I say.

"Sumbitch!" he yells back but does as he's told.

Rudy turns around as if he just noticed the crowd. "I got this, Cloud. Get your town out of here." He walks toward me, barely glancing at Tina and the body.

"It don't look like you got it." I'm not afraid of Rudy. He may be the sheriff for now, but I intend to be wearing that badge by next summer. He looks me up and down as if I'm a bug then spits on the ground by my boot.

Angus King, one of my auxiliary cops, appears by my side. Angus is a dwarf and takes a lot of crap from Rudy's county guys because of his size. But his stature aside, there aren't many men I know that could carry his stick.

"Angus, get Tina out of the way," I say. Angus's voice is nice and calm as he helps her get up off the ground and out of the way as the ambulance pulls in. I rub my palms together and wish I had my coat. It's colder than Eskimo spit out here, and nobody seems to notice but me.

No one in the crowd is moving. The ambulance parks and silences its siren, but the red and white lights still flash.

Angus is trying to get Tina to go back to the club. "Come on, Tina. There isn't much we can do here." Tina motions for me to come to the other side of the road, away from the rest stop entrance. Jimmy Ray appears at my side, out of breath. I tell him to go talk to Cass. He's not too excited about it, but I wave him off in the direction of Clay Adams's truck and walk toward Tina, leaving the scene behind for a minute. Angus is with us, which is fine. He's Tina's friend, and if she doesn't care if he hears our conversation, then I don't, either.

Tina's lips are all twisted up, and her forehead is scrunched as if she's thinking. "Benny, I might recognize him. Well, I don't know his name or anything, but..." She's a sharp gal, so I wait, letting her figure out what she's trying to remember. "He was at the club about six months ago. He got here at opening time and wanted to talk to Roland." Roland worked for Tina before he died. "He sat at the bar for two hours, waiting for him. Didn't say much to anyone else while he sat there. I remember him because of his red hair. I think it's him."

I'm impressed. With all the blood on the man's head and the darkness of the night, I don't know how she saw that he was a redhead.

"Anyway, when Roland got to work that night, he and this guy talked for a few minutes, then Roland took him out to the parking lot and talked some more." She pauses for a minute, and Angus picks up the story.

"I remember that night," Angus says. "He did more than talk to him. Roland beat him silly. One of the other bouncers had to pull Roland off. I don't know how he did it, but the guy crawled in his car and left. The sheriff showed up and talked to Roland, but nothing came of it."

"Rudy didn't do anything?" Rudy has had a hard-on for Tina's club since the day it opened. I'm surprised by the fact that he had a perfect opportunity to haul Roland Adams off on an assault charge but chose not to. Then again, he is a lazy ass, so I guess it shouldn't surprise me much.

"No." Tina shook her head. "He talked to Roland for a few minutes and then left. Anyway, when I asked Roland about it, he wouldn't say anything. But he wanted to make sure all the other bouncers got a good look at the guy and told them he was barred for life. He said that if they ever saw him again, they should tell him to leave." Tina isn't one to sugarcoat, but she seems to be dancing around the issue.

Angus isn't hearing the same tune. "Come on, Tina, you know what he said. Roland told everyone at the club that if he comes around, don't pull him off, because if that guy ever sets foot in Deacon again, he would kill him." I look to Tina, who reluctantly nods her head.

Hmmm. I don't know all the things Roland Adams was into, but for the most part, folks in this area liked him. Angus never seemed to care for him much, but that might be because Roland had no problem making fun of his size. And of course, Roland's wife, Cass Adams, didn't care for him, either. If she had, she wouldn't have buried him in their yard. "So he isn't from around here?" I nod toward the guy on the road.

"I guess not," Tina says. "But Roland never would say who he was. With him, sometimes, it was best not to ask." Tina has told me before that Roland did a good job for her and kept his private business away from the club. She's a businesswoman, and getting into her employees' affairs is, in her opinion, not her place.

I glance back at the scene and see that Jimmy is heading our way. Rudy is standing beside Clay Adams's truck, and the paramedics are loading the injured man into the ambulance. I see one of the medics digging in the guy's pockets. He pulls out a wallet. I glance back to make sure Rudy didn't see it, then tell Tina and Angus to hold on for a second before I hurry over to the medic.

"You got an ID?" I ask. Usually, a new guy won't give me too much flack, and lucky for me, this one is ready and willing to talk.

He opens the wallet and pulls out a driver's license. "Britt Adam Chandler. Thirty years old, from Dallas, Texas." He turns back and shuts the doors on the ambulance. "He doesn't look too good, either. You gonna notify the family?"

I point my thumb toward Rudy then return to Tina.

Tina is waiting for me; she knows what I was doing. "Well?"

I shrug. "Britt Chandler. Sound familiar?"

She thinks for a minute then shakes her head. We walk back to the club, leaving all of the official cleanup to Rudy and his crew. It's not my jurisdiction, but I have a right to ask questions. And besides, Tina will tell me things she isn't about to tell Rudy Drown.

Rocky Martin is standing inside the door of the club, rubbernecking. Normally, he's in the caged-in office, taking money as people enter, but news travels fast. Even though Rocky knows better than to leave his post, he is obviously dying to gawk. "Somebody got hit? Who was it? Was it bad?" With Tina, Angus, and I filling up the entry area, Rocky goes back into his cage.

"His name is Britt Chandler," I say. "From Dallas. Know him?" Rocky knows almost every man in the tristate area. I guess that's one benefit of being Tina's doorman.

"That little redheaded dude? I checked his ID about thirty minutes ago." He turns to Tina as if he's seeking permission to talk.

She frowns. "Why didn't you tell me he was here tonight after what happened the last time?"

He shrugs. "I had it in my notebook to mention it at the hourly call, but it didn't seem too big of a deal right then. He showed up, and I recognized him. Hard to miss that red hair after Roland made damn sure we all would remember him."

"What did he want?" I asked.

"Roland, again. I told him he had been barred from the club and that Roland was dead. Guess he don't read the papers." At least Roland's murder didn't make the Dallas news. "Then he left. No big deal."

Tina turns to me. "I can print his picture off if you want me to. Everyone who walks through the door gets their picture taken while they talk to Rocky. Security." She nods to Rocky, who starts fiddling with a computer behind him. In less than a minute, I have a nice eight-by-ten of a redhead standing in the doorway of Tina's club. He's not very tall, with a slight build and a thin face. If I hadn't seen his driver's license five minutes ago, I would think he was a teenager trying to sneak a peek at Tina's strippers.

"He must have parked in the overflow across the highway," Angus says. The crowd is starting to file back into the club, and I tell Tina I'll keep her posted if I find out anything.

I hightail it back to my Tahoe and look down at my uniform. I'm covered in Britt Chandler's blood.

So much for worrying about cherry juice.

Chapter 3
Cass

L AST NIGHT, AFTER I DAMN near killed a man, Clay drove straight to Grams's house to have her check out the bump on my head. She must have known we were coming because she was up and had some kind of tea ready for me. After she shone a mini flashlight in my eyes and asked me a bunch of stupid questions, she pronounced me fine and sent me home with Clay. Grams isn't a doctor or nurse or anything, but she knows how to cure a lot of ills, and she's free. She didn't seem too concerned about me but kept checking Clay for some reason. When he went to the bathroom, she said she had a bad feeling and wanted me to keep watch over him. I always do.

Clay and I came home and went to bed, but I didn't sleep very well. I kept having dreams that the guy in the middle of the road last night was Clay, and that's about the worst nightmare I could have. He's the best thing that ever happened to me. I wish I had realized that years ago. I shouldn't have married his brother, but I figured out how to take care of that little problem.

This morning, though, I felt queasy, and I barely made it to the bathroom before I blew chunks. That worried Clay a lot more than it did me, so he drove me to Grams's after deciding I needed a babysitter while he went to work.

"If she throws up again, promise me you'll take her to get checked by a doctor," Clay tells Grams. I know he's concerned. I don't have my truck or my phone, so Clay doesn't want me to be at our house out on the old highway all by myself. In a way, I feel as if he's hiding me from Rudy Drown, as though I did something wrong, which I didn't. I don't mind, though. It's fun to hang out with Grams, and I want to know more about the bad feeling she had last night.

We aren't there five minutes before we hear footsteps on Grams's front porch. "Anybody home?" Maryanne Spencer is standing at Grams's open door. Of course, she knows we're here, and she doesn't wait for an invitation to walk in. Up until a few months ago, she wouldn't have even thought to come on Grams's porch, especially if I was here, mostly because she was sleeping with my husband. But since I killed him, we've become friends again, and she's been pretty steady about visiting Grams. Grams is in her eighties and has a reputation as the town witch, which tends to keep a lot of people away, so I'm okay with Maryanne stopping in to chat with her.

"Come on in," Grams says, but Maryanne is already in. Normally, she would be teaching school today, but it's Halloween, and the school finds it easier to let the little urchins run free rather than deal with them all wearing costumes and acting stupid. Maryanne's hair is mussed, and her smeared makeup looks as if it's left over from last night, so I assume she was hitting the bars as she does. I'm sure that after she heard the news of my trouble, she couldn't wait to hit Grams's door first thing this morning so she could hear all about it.

Clay kisses me goodbye, and I watch him walk away. Maryanne giggles. She knows what I'm looking at. Clay turned forty a few months back, but he's still got the cutest butt I've ever seen on a man. After he leaves, I give Maryanne a quick rundown of what happened. She sits and nods as though she's heard it all already. I'm certain I'm the talk of the town this morning.

Grams is sorting plants and placing them in plastic bags. "I got a call from Benny's wife this morning. Nice girl. Called to check on you and make sure you didn't have a concussion. I told her you were fine and we appreciate the call." Benny called Clay last night, too, asking about me. Grace Cloud is as nosy as her husband.

"Have you heard anything about the guy you hit?" Maryanne looks concerned, and I guess she is. He's a man, and she was born horny. I couldn't care less.

"Grace said he's still pretty bad," Grams says. "Had surgery last night but woke up for a short bit. He's broken in several places."

"Well, he shouldn't have been standing out there in the middle of the road at night," I say. "He must not be very smart."

"It's a miracle he didn't die," Maryanne says. A miracle. Every time something unexpected happens, it's a miracle.

I see things a bit differently. Maybe the so-called miracles are supposed to happen every day, and when they don't, that is something we should comment on—an anti-miracle. I don't say this to anyone, though. They all think I'm nuts anyway.

Besides, I have other things on my mind about last night. I will most likely get a visit from Benny or Rudy today. I'm sure they'll ask more stupid questions. My truck is in the shop, and the mechanic is trying to get pieces of some stranger out of the grille. And I lost my phone. *Damn.* I really liked that phone.

"You ain't sayin' much this morning, girlie. You feeling okay?" Grams always knows when something isn't quite right with me. Maybe she does see a lot more than I give her credit for, or maybe her intuition comes from being around her my whole life.

"Fine. I want to go find my phone."

Grams puts the rest of the roots and plants in the baggies. She brushes the dust from the coffee table into her open palm and drops it into the pocket of her apron. "Well then, let's get it done."

Maryanne and I look at each other then at Grams. "That was easy," I say. "I was expecting you to tell me it's a waste of time looking for it, or that it's too cold, or I shouldn't be playing in the street or something."

"All of that is true," Grams says, "but you're going to do it anyway, so why argue about it for five minutes first? And besides, I gotta stop at the Dollar Store and make sure I have plenty of candy for the trick-or-treaters tonight." Every year, Grams buys enough Halloween candy to feed an orphanage, and every year, all she gets is a bunch of teenagers trying to play pranks on her because of her reputation as a witch. I always stay at her house so that if they get too froggy, she doesn't have to deal with it by herself. This year, I have a surprise for them if they do. I hollowed out a few dozen eggs and filled them with some of Clay's compost. Anyone who tries to mess with Grams this year is going to get egg-bombed with high-dollar worm shit.

"Grams, are you still having those bad feelings about Clay?" I was going to wait until she and I were alone to ask, but Maryanne is antsing to go on our little adventure with us, so I just put it out there.

Grams gazes off at nothing. "I can't quite put my finger on it, but I'd sure like to read his cards."

Some people say there isn't anything to those cards that Grams keeps in her room, but I tend to differ. Sometimes, she doesn't get things completely right, but for the most part, she does okay at figuring out when something isn't perfect. And I like to think Clay is always perfect.

"It's a good thing it's Halloween, then," I say.

"Clay is going to let you read his cards?" Maryanne asks. She knows Clay pretty well since they share a daughter. He didn't sleep with Maryanne to get Shaylene, but he adopted the girl when she was a baby. His brother, Roland, had been too chickenshit to step up. Of course, I didn't know about that until recently.

"Well, we haven't told him yet, but he'll go along." Clay is one of those who doesn't put much stock in the card reading, but it's a family thing we do every year on Halloween. And he loves Grams and will do about anything for her. If she wants to read his cards, then he'll let her, even if he doesn't fancy it. And who knows? Grams has been known to make believers out of those who didn't believe at first. People usually come around if she sees something happy that they want to come true. But the way Grams focused on Clay last night and this morning, I'm thinking she isn't going to see "happily ever after" in his cards. And that makes me want to puke. Again.

The three of us pile into Maryanne's little Honda, and I squeeze in the back. My sister Lola calls Grams's phone on our way out to the highway to make sure I'm okay. In the past few months, since I killed Roland, Lola has become a little more motherly than sisterly, which I guess is okay. Maryanne parks on the shoulder near my skid marks from last night, and I shimmy out of the back before Grams has a chance to raise her seat.

"So I figure this man was at the rest area with a woman last night, or waiting to meet one, and for some reason, he came out to the highway. Maybe she was lost, and he was standing out here so she would see him." Maryanne has her own theory about why that guy was standing in the middle of the road last night, and although I hate to gossip, she has a pretty good one going. We're walking along the shoulder, inspecting the ditch for my phone.

"This is where I was sitting," I say, pointing to the ground. "I think." Grams stayed in Maryanne's car. She said she would be our lookout, as if we're a gang or something. But the truth is that it's cold out here, and she wants to stay warm.

"Of course, he could have been coming from Tina's, but that's no fun." Maryanne purses her lips as she thinks. "Maybe he was out here by himself. And someone saw him, and he ran after them. Or he was with someone, and when they heard the accident, they jumped out of his car and ran into the woods."

In Deacon, the truth is rarely the story that is told, and this isn't going to be an exception. The biggest problem with all the ideas everyone in town is going to be coming up with is that nobody is going to end their tale with the fact that this was an accident. All of the speculation will end with me hitting some stupid ass with my truck and putting him in the hospital. No matter what he was doing out here, it's going to be me running over him that everyone remembers.

I sit on the side of the road, cross-legged, and rest my head in my hands. The highway isn't too busy at this time of day, but a few cars go by, and some honk as they do. I don't even look up at them. I just flip them the bird.

"What's wrong?" Maryanne asks.

"My head hurts, and I'm tired. I'm already sick of the whole thing, and it hasn't even started." I don't like people talking about me. I don't really like them talking *to* me.

"Well…" She stops when we see a big purple Hummer pull into the rest area. It slows down when the driver sees us, and I know Fat Tina is behind the wheel. Everyone knows that Hummer. She rolls down the window and looks at me for a second. Then she turns toward her passenger side. I hear the door open, but I don't see anyone until Tina pulls up the incline toward the rest stop.

I can't help but smile when I see the person who got out of her truck. It's the midget who was at the accident last night, and he's walking toward me. "It must be my lucky day."

"Why do you say that?" he asks in a voice too deep for a man of his size and an accent that sounds like a Kennedy.

"Well, you're a leprechaun, right?" I stand up, and although he's only a few inches shorter than me, he is shorter.

"No, I'm a dwarf, actually, although we prefer 'little people.'" He sticks out a hand and smiles, revealing straight white teeth. "We haven't met. I'm Angus King. You must be Cass Adams."

There's something odd about him, other than the fact that he's being nice. Sometimes, when people talk to me, they keep their distance and look at the ground, as if they are afraid the crazy inside of me is going to jump out and get them. Angus is looking me in the eye and standing close to me as though we are old friends. He seems very sure of himself, but not in a cocky way, and he doesn't seem to mind that I'm asking about his size. I'm not trying to offend him, which is unusual for me, but I am curious as hell. "What's the difference?"

"Well, leprechauns aren't real, and—"

"What about midgets?" I notice Maryanne is walking away. "Hey, Maryanne, where are you going? There's a man here."

Maryanne continues walking along the highway, ignoring Angus and me. "Not my type," she says over her shoulder.

"You don't know what you're missing," Angus yells back. "And yes, midgets are different than dwarfs, and I'd be happy to share the difference, but right now, Tina and I would like to talk to you if you have a minute."

"I didn't do it on purpose," I say.

Angus has several tattoos on his arms, and I figure he must be the guy that owns the tattoo parlor on Military, Little Bit of Ink. I've seen him driving his motorcycle in town and always wanted to stop in that shop. Maybe I should take him one of Grams's Shatner candles next week, and we could talk more about dwarfs and midgets.

"On purpose? Well, no, no one thinks that."

Oh, I'm sure they do. But I shrug and follow him toward the rest area as we keep talking. "Did you know my husband, Roland?" I figure if he hangs out with Tina, he must have known Roland.

He smiles again. "Yes, I did. Interesting fella."

That's one way to put it. "Did you like him?" Roland had his good days, and it seems as though he always put his best face on for everyone else. Nobody but me knew what he kept behind that face.

"Let's say I like his brother Clay better."

Me too.

The last time I saw Tina up close was at Roland's funeral. Since he worked for her at the club, I guess it was expected that she be there. She didn't say anything to me that day, but the whole funeral was kind of weird since I killed him. She's standing behind her truck, digging in her purse.

I've never been good at stuff like this. I guess I should say I'm sorry, but I don't have anything to be sorry about, and I don't know what difference it makes to her anyhow. So instead, I stand there and wait for her to talk.

She pulls a Xeroxed picture out of her purse. "Do you know this man?" The photo shows a young guy with short red hair and light eyes, wearing a plaid shirt with a buttoned-down collar.

"This the guy I ran over?" He seems vaguely familiar, but last night he looked a bit different.

"Yes. Britt Chandler. He was a friend of Roland's, so I thought maybe you might know him too." She's fishing. She has no idea who this clown is.

Angus laughs. "I wouldn't say he was Roland's friend. The last time Roland saw him, he beat the crap out of him and sent him off."

Tina smacks Angus lightly on the shoulder as I look at the picture again.

I don't know why they think I might know the man. After all, everyone knows Roland had a lot of secrets, and most of them were kept from me. He also had a lot of friends I didn't know about, and most of those were women. I give the picture back to Tina. "Nope, don't know him. I—"

My stomach suddenly bubbles over. I cover my mouth and run off toward the ladies' room. I don't make it and barf in the grass. *Damn.* I look around to make sure Maryanne and Grams aren't watching because the last thing I want to do is go see a doctor. I wipe my face with the sleeve of my coat and go back to Tina and Angus as if nothing happened.

"I didn't mean to hit him. I didn't see him." That's all I got.

"I know." She points toward the ladies' room. "Are you okay?"

I touch the knot on my forehead. "Yeah, my head hurts some now and then. And I might have a concussion or something. I hear it makes you puke. But don't tell Grams. It'll go away." Maryanne is pulling the car up the incline toward us, and I'm glad I won't be alone much longer with Tina and Angus. "Why do you care about this guy anyway?"

"Well, like Angus said, Roland and he got into a scuffle when he was here before. This time, he gets hit by a truck, leaving my club. I don't need any more problems than I've already got, so I try to stay a step ahead in case Rudy starts asking me questions."

I can understand that. "I came out here to get away from Benny and

Rudy. They're both assholes." And I need to look for my phone. "Are you sure he was coming from the club? I mean, he could have been doing something else." Maybe I should let Maryanne share some of her theories... On second thought, probably not.

"I wish he was, but I'm sure he was leaving the club. A lot of people park over here when the lot is full. Daze Harper talked to him and so did my doorman. He was asking for Roland again. Thanks for talking to me, Cass. And take care of yourself." Tina moves around to the driver's side of her truck. Grams and Maryanne are out of the car, and they stop Tina to tell her how nice it is to see her and all that. Grams means it. She likes everybody. Maryanne's only saying the words.

Tina gets in her truck and rolls down her window. "Cass, I don't know if his business with Roland had to do with the club or if it was personal. If it's related to my bar, then I'm going to have to deal with Rudy. If it was personal, it's none of my business. One of us is going to be up to our necks in assholes though, so I thought I'd give you a heads up. And if you hear something that I need to know, maybe you could give me a call?"

I nod. Sure, why not? We may not be friends, but we at least have this in common.

Angus introduces himself to Grams and Maryanne. Grams is as giddy as a schoolgirl, and if I didn't know better, I would think she has a crush on Angus. She starts talking about cards and crystals, and Angus is eating it up. "I bet you get a great turnout of trick-or-treaters," he says.

"More like a bunch of punks looking for trouble," I say.

Grams looks as if she is about to wet her pants as she invites Angus to come visit her anytime. He bows to her as though she's the Queen of England. Then he turns to me before getting back into Tina's truck. "Come by the shop. We'll talk about little people."

"You know, dwarves are supposed to be magical," Grams says.

Maryanne rolls her eyes. As Tina and Angus drive off, Maryanne grabs me by the wrist. "Let's get out of here. I'm getting the creeps. And I found your phone."

I get in the backseat, and she gives me the phone. I take it, turn it over in my hands a few times, and smile. Not even broken.

Chapter 4
Benny

JIMMY RAY TURNED ON THE heat this morning for the first time this year, and now my office smells like burnt dryer lint and mildewed electrical wiring. The fire chief, Bucky Crow, has already been sniffing around, giving me mini lectures about the importance of vent maintenance and telling me how many fires are caused by faulty wiring. I tell him that I guess it's a good thing the fire department is attached to the back of the station. Then, just to get Bucky off my ass, I task Jimmy Ray with finding someone to come out and check it over thoroughly.

It's Halloween, not my favorite day of the year. The timing mixed with the smell reminds me of a crematorium. *Dead people. Cass Adams.* The picture Tina gave me last night is on my desk. I'm pretty good with faces, and something is familiar about the man who was hit, but I know I would remember some young ginger hanging around town. Rudy hasn't put his report in yet, which figures, so I decide to do what any self-respecting lawman would do in this situation: Google the man.

Normally, I wouldn't take such an interest in a wreck that isn't in my jurisdiction. I would follow it, but I wouldn't try to run my own investigation unless the sheriff's department asked. And they rarely ask. But this accident has a few components that make it a little more interesting to me.

First, it took place outside of Tina's. Tina and I have been friends since grade school; she's one of the few people I never picked on much. That may be because she was always bigger than me, and I didn't want to know what an arm that size felt like smacking me upside my skull. Or maybe I always liked her... as a friend, of course. That's too much woman for me. But since she opened the club, she's had nothing but grief from Rudy, and although she had nothing to do with Britt Chandler getting run over, I'm sure the sheriff will find a way to make it partly her fault.

Second—the connection between Chandler and Roland Adams piques my interest. The longer Roland's dead, the more I see what an unpleasant guy he was. He had a lot of people fooled, and I won't lie, he pulled me on like a boot. But all these secrets came out when he died: the way he abused his wife, his hankering for different women, and of course, him having a baby with Maryanne Spencer. It's no surprise that Cass killed him—well, buried him. She wasn't convicted of murder, though I still think she killed him. But I'm not sure how.

Which brings me to Cass. Is it a coincidence that she runs over someone her husband wanted to kill? Anything she's involved in turns into tumbleweed, and I don't need any more of her shit on my record leading up to the election. But knowing in the end that it isn't my case makes it easy to follow from the sidelines. If I'm lucky, Rudy will screw it all up and show the voters what a dumbass he really is.

Britt Chandler. Dallas, Texas. It's an odd enough name that I should get some hits. I turn up three articles about a pastor in Milwaukee, an advertisement for an African-American attorney in Provo, Utah, a mug shot of a cute blonde in Fort Smith who was busted with methamphetamines, and a LinkedIn profile of a guy who graduated from Rice University with a master's degree in electrical engineering. I click on the last one, and up pops my Chandler's picture. Yeah, that's him all right. He has an impressive resume for a young guy, and judging by the car he was driving last night—a brand-new Mercedes CLS with plates in his name was parked at the rest stop—he makes a nice chunk of change.

I have enough of the professional stuff, so I decide to creep him on Facebook. I know a lot of people think Facebook is a waste of time, but what they don't know is that a lot of folks— companies looking to hire, prospective boyfriends, lawmen—do a lot of checking up on people on those social media sites. I sure do. In public, people put on a face for everyone else and tell them what they want them to hear. But on Facebook, people spill all. It's a never-ending soap opera with a million characters.

I find him quickly. Britt Adam Chandler is sitting in a fancy bar with a bunch of other drunks, smiling for the camera. I shake my head. They make it so easy.

Most of his posts are private, which tells me he at least knows not to share everything. But some are public. The first one is a note posted today from a Dennis Flynn: "Please keep Britt in your thoughts. He was hit by a car last night and is in critical condition here in a Podunk town in Missouri. I'll keep everyone posted." It was published two hours ago, so whoever this Dennis is, he knows all about the accident and is in a position to "keep everyone posted." There's a ton of comments from well-wishers, so I know Britt has a few friends. Other than that, there's nothing but exercise videos and cat pictures.

Jimmy walks in with a cup of hot coffee for me and puts it on my desk. "What kind of guy posts exercise videos and cat pictures on his Facebook?" I ask him.

"A girlie guy," says a voice from the door. Rudy Drown is filling my doorway. He's got a big grin on his face and doesn't even take his hat off. I hate when he sneaks into the station like this. *Asshole*.

He plops in the chair next to my desk and motions for Jimmy to get him a cup of coffee, as if he's the prince of Botswana or something, and Jimmy scurries off. "I figured you wouldn't be able to keep your nose out of this one, so I'm coming to give you a report," he says. I lean back and cross my arms over my chest. If Rudy is giving me a report, that means he wants something from me in return, and the last thing I want is to do him any favors. "Some guy was calling the hospitals and such last night looking for him, and when he got to Mercy, they directed him to my office." He makes that clicking sound with his teeth that always drives me crazy.

I glance back at the computer screen. "Dennis Flynn?"

He snaps his fingers. "Yeah, that's his name. Anyways, my office told him we needed to talk to his next of kin, and this fella flipped out and said he was the next of kin, but they knew something strange was up and wouldn't tell him nothing. The hospital got a call from the kid's momma later, and she said to let Dennis sit with him until she gets here."

I can't say I agree with the whole homosexual thing. I was raised right here in Deacon, and that didn't happen much when I was growing up. But it's a new world now, and as long as they aren't hurting me or mine, I don't care what they do. I do know that if anyone tried to keep me from Grace if she was hurt, I would be pretty pissed off. "So who is he, Rudy? I know you talked to Roland about him once before."

He glares at me, as if I'm supposed to be scared. Jimmy comes back with his coffee and sets it on the side of my desk near Rudy. The sheriff spills a little when he picks it up and doesn't bother to wipe it.

"Like I said, Chandler's momma called the hospital this morning." He raises an eyebrow. "Her name is Stefanie Adams."

"Adams?" That name keeps popping up.

Rudy clicks his teeth again. "You ain't as dumb as you look. Picked right up on that, didn't ya?"

I want to slap the smile right off his face. "What's the connection, Rudy?" I'm getting tired of his games.

He lets out a slow breath. "I got this Stefanie lady's number from the hospital and called her back. She's in Los Angeles and is married to Freddy Adams. He goes by Rick now, but yeah, Freddy Adams. Sound familiar?"

Something clicks into place. Freddy was Clay and Roland's dad. I vaguely remember Freddy Adams from when I was young. He and Rudy and my dad terrorized this town for a long time. That is, until Freddy disappeared one night about thirty-five years ago, never to be heard from again. Even though Clay and Roland's momma, Donna Sue, filed a missing person report, she told her sons that he died in the war. I don't know how old Clay and Roland were when they found out her story wasn't true, but it had to hurt. Finding out your daddy wasn't a hero is one thing, but not knowing exactly who or where he was is completely another.

"So Britt's a half brother to Clay and Roland," I say. It's starting to make sense now. The fact that Britt is a gay engineer from Dallas might have been enough for Roland to kick his ass. Throw in the fact that he's his long-lost brother, and it was a sure bet.

"You do math real good, Benny." Rudy takes another drink of his coffee and plunks the mug back on my desk. "And it's best if we don't say much about it and let this guy get well enough to go on back to Dallas. That's what Roland tried to tell him the first time he was here."

"Clay has a right to know." *Even though it's something he's probably not going to want to hear.* It's bad enough that Clay is going to find out he has a brother he didn't know about, but to find out his dad has been in Los Angeles with another family for basically his entire life will be a whole different cupcake. Sooner or later, secrets all come to pass. "So what about Freddy, or Rick, or whatever he's calling himself now?"

"He's dying, according to the wife. In a hospital in LA. She's there with him, but if the kid isn't better by tomorrow, she's going to get on a plane and come here."

Yes, Clay is definitely going to find out. *Damn.* This could be an episode of *Days of Our Lives.* I'm not sure anyone would believe it's the truth.

The phone rings, and Jimmy quits eavesdropping long enough to pick it up. "Chief, it's Harvey. He says it's important." I tell Rudy to hold on for a second. If one of my patrolmen says it's important, it damn sure is. And I like to make Rudy wait.

"Benny, I caught a pair of teenagers trying to walk out of Archie's with a couple of pints of whiskey under their shirts. They're already half lit, and Archie is pissed."

I stifle a sigh. It's too early for this. "Arrest them or call their parents. Hell, Harvey, it's Halloween. Might as well get ready for a long day and night."

"Archie's done called their parents, and I have two mommas on their way here, but I'm not so sure that Archie isn't going to take a bite out of their hides himself." Harvey's a good cop, but he isn't much for getting involved in family drama.

"Okay, I'll be there in a few." I hang up the phone and look back to Rudy.

"Everything okay?" he asks, smirking.

I'm not going to give him the satisfaction. He knows it's Halloween, and he also knows what that means to a small-town cop. "Fine. So what do you need from me on this Britt Chandler thing?" As I said, I know Rudy, and I know this visit isn't a social call.

He finishes his coffee, stands up, and adjusts his belt. "Well, like I say, it's best if the kid hightails it out of here, but I know you aren't smart enough to let it go. So if you can't let it lie, then I'm tasking you with telling Clay Adams. I don't want no part of it."

I want to inform him that he made himself part of it when he didn't say anything the first time the guy came to town, but I'm focusing on the telling-Clay part. "Why me?"

"Well, the fact that Cass ran over the guy looks real suspicious, and I thought about investigating that. But I figure it wasn't on purpose, so I'm dropping it."

That's not the Rudy Drown I know. Usually, he would jump at a chance to crawl over someone like Cass Adams's tail, or at least look as if he's doing his job. But dropping it altogether?

He sucks his teeth again. "And there is one other small detail that makes it a little uncomfortable for me."

"And that is?"

"I knew Freddy was in California."

I'm on my feet and in front of Rudy before he hits the doorway. "You knew for all these years and never said anything to Clay? What the hell, Rudy?" I'm standing my ground on this one. My dad, Tenesy, may have been a shitty dad, but at least I had one. Clay didn't have the chance to know what an ass his father was.

"Not the whole time. I found out twelve, maybe thirteen years ago. From Tenesy. He *has* been in touch with Freddy the entire time. Also, by the way, so was Clay and Roland's momma, Donna Sue." Rudy smirks again. "Now, get out of my way and keep your nose where it belongs. There's a lot more to the story than you or Clay care to know. Let's keep this where it is for now. If we're lucky, Freddy will die before he gets a chance to screw up anything else."

I step to the side, anxious for Rudy to get out of my office. After he leaves, I stand there for a full minute, trying to decide how I'm going to mention all of this to Clay. I guess the best way is to put it out there and let the chips fall where they may. I grab my hat and my coat off the rack and tell Jimmy to keep this between us. He nods, and at least I know I can trust him.

My watch reads two o'clock. The Halloween shenanigans have already started, and it seems as if one of Clay Adams's ghosts is about to come back a-haunting.

Exercise videos and cat pictures. Sometimes, I hate this job.

When I get to the liquor store, there's a small crowd out front. Archie, my patrolman, Harvey, and a dozen bystanders are watching a woman swing her purse at her teenage son. She's making some decent contact about every third go-around. He's twice her size and trying to duck and cover, but she gets in some good licks. I hate to break it up. I'm of the notion that a kid will remember a good public ass-kicking from his momma a lot longer than a trip to juvie.

"You want to press charges, Archie?" I ask. Harvey has a big smile on his face, as though he is enjoying the purse beatdown a lot more than he should.

"No, the other boy's momma paid me before she hauled him off," he says.

The kid takes a solid one to the side of his head, which makes me flinch. That one's going to leave a knot big enough for a calf to suck. I catch his mom's purse in midair and step in between them.

"Get them all out of here, Harvey. And wipe that grin off your face. It's Halloween, and this is just the beginning."

I get back in my Tahoe and see Clay Adams's truck in the parking lot, which makes sense because he works next door to Archie's at the hardware store. I think about getting this whole telling thing over with. But instead, I put the Tahoe in drive and head toward Joplin. There isn't any reason why I can't check on this guy in the hospital first and talk to Clay later.

I can't say I keep many close friends in town, but if I were to call someone a friend, I guess I would say Clay Adams. Sure, we haven't hung together or anything in the past few years, but back when we were younger, we joined the army together on the buddy plan. Although things didn't work out the way either of us planned, we still have that bond. The thing is, I don't look forward to telling him the news, but I would damn sure rather it be me than Rudy.

Clay is a man's man, loves to work, loves his worm farm, and for some reason, loves Cass Adams. But he also has a soft heart, and I don't know how he's going to handle the news about his dad and his half brother, or the fact that Roland knew about it all six months ago and didn't say a word.

I thought about not mentioning the Roland part—why open old wounds? But the truth is, there's nothing I hate more than half a story. No, I'm going to lay it all out for him, and he's going to have to deal with it all at once. I don't want him to find out something later that he should have known up front. I'm not Rudy Drown, keeping secrets and not giving two shits about who might get hurt.

Damn. The force of it hits me. Rudy knew where Freddy Adams was and never said a word. He claims Tenesy knew, too, so I realize that means my momma probably knew as well. But the big clincher is, *Clay's momma* knew, according to Rudy. That makes me wonder if there's more to the story since she filed a missing person report. Or maybe Rudy is lying.

Nope, that's not for me to figure out. It's not my sideshow.

When I get to the hospital, I park my Tahoe in the lot marked Visitors and walk to the front entrance. It's chilly out, and if I'm lucky, it will get downright cold by tonight and keep some of the trick-or-treaters off the street.

I get in the elevator with a pregnant woman and an elderly man in his hospital gown, who is pushing an IV pole. "Stairway to Heaven" is playing in the elevator, a light, instrumental version, and I think how inappropriate it is for this song to be playing in a hospital elevator. The other two don't seem to notice, though, and when the elevator stops on the third floor, I wait as the man exits. He doesn't seem to care that his tighty-whities are showing out the back of his gown. I guess he has other things on his mind.

When we stop on the seventh floor, I get out, leaving the pregnant lady all alone with the watered-down Led Zeppelin classic. This floor smells like urine and oranges, and I have to stop for a minute to get my bearings. A big waiting-room sign is posted ahead, and when I get to the doorway, I see a young man.

He's muscular, with tattoos on both shoulders, and he's wearing a white sleeveless T-shirt and Levis. His face is puffed up like a melon, and his eyes are red. He stands when he sees me. "Sheriff Drown?"

I've been called a lot of things, but nothing makes my stomach turn like someone thinking I might be Rudy. "No. Benny Cloud. Deacon Chief of Police." I'm a guy with no jurisdiction, just a curiosity that might get him in trouble. Hopefully, I'll be out of here before Rudy shows up. Granted, I don't have any business here, but I figure if I'm going to be the one responsible for spilling the news to Clay Adams about his half brother, I should at least know what kind of shape he is in.

Dennis Flynn introduces himself and shakes my hand. I feel the strong roughness of a workingman. I hate to stereotype people, but this is not what I expected. "It's a pleasure to meet you, Chief Cloud. I was expecting Sheriff Drown. I didn't realize this was multijurisdictional." Fancy words. He must know a bit about the law.

I nod toward the ICU floor behind us. "How is he?"

"He's in bad shape, and I'm not used to all the medical terminology," Dennis says. "They let me stay in the room for fifteen minutes on the hour, and I guess I understand. But Britt and I have been together for five years. That's longer than a lot of marriages. I want to be there with him."

I may be a good old country boy, and I don't claim to understand why a man would want to be with another man. I'm also a Christian, and I know some of my brethren won't do squat to support these guys because it's a sin. And it is, at least that's what my Bible says. But it also says to show compassion, and to do unto others as you would have them do unto you. And I know how I would feel if someone tried to keep me from Grace. I would have gone off by now and not stayed as calm as Dennis is. I have to have respect for that, even if there isn't much I can do.

"What do you do, Dennis?" I figure I'll make small talk, because I honestly don't know what else to do at this point other than be nice.

"Do? Oh, I work campus security at A&M. Dispatch. I'm working on my degree." He runs his fingers through his hair and looks around the room.

I nod at his hands. "Those ain't the hands of a dispatcher."

"Oh yeah. I worked in the oil fields for several years. Not much for manicures." He smiles nervously.

I'm thinking Dennis must know more about the Adams family than anyone, and he can give me some insight from a perspective I can't get anywhere else. I hate to take advantage of that, especially when he's under stress, but I'm going to have to talk to Clay sooner or later, and anything I can find out will help. You wash my back, and I promise not to drop the soap.

"What about his mom? She on her way?"

"She's waiting for an update. She'll have to fly into Springfield and then drive here. It's not an easy trip from LA."

A voice from behind us startles me. "What the hell are you doing here?" We both turn toward the door, and there's Drown again. Damn, I hate when he sneaks up on me.

"I got this, Rudy." I don't even introduce him to Dennis.

"You ain't got nothin'." He pulls a piece of paper out of his pocket and gives it to Dennis. "Here. This is the info for where we hauled his car. Now, do whatever it is that you guys do. Maybe it will get him well and outta here faster." Dennis takes the paper and walks toward the door without saying a word.

"He's in the ICU, still not fully conscious, Rudy," I say. "They're not going to discharge him this afternoon and send him on his way." I'm not too happy about having to break this news to Clay, but I damn sure don't believe sending this Chandler boy home and letting it all lie in the basement is a great idea, either.

Rudy adjusts his belt and throws his shoulders back. "So whatcha waiting for? Shouldn't you be telling Clay Adams all the gossip instead of nosing around here?"

Dennis is standing at the door, watching Rudy and me. "Clay Adams?"

"Yeah. He's a friend of mine. Rudy here has decided it's my job to let him know what's going on," I explain.

Dennis slowly nods. "Can I ask… What about the woman that hit him? Is she okay? Did she say anything—"

Rudy starts laughing and sweeps his hand in my direction. "Yeah, you got this, Benny. Go right ahead and tell him all about Cass Adams."

"Adams? Cass?" Dennis's face scrunches up in a look of confusion, anger, and disgust. "Wait, isn't that the woman who was married to the other brother? The one who killed him?"

"She lives with the other brother now." I walk toward Dennis. "Come on, I want to check on the kid myself before I go see Clay." Dennis starts to say something to Rudy, but I shake my head, and he takes the hint. *Don't stir the pot. Let him go.*

I hate to be here when it should be just family, but Dennis understands. Besides, my other option is to go chase trick-or-treaters for a while and run down Clay Adams so I can stab a knife in his gut. I would like to see what kind of shape Britt Chandler is in myself, and yeah, see what kind of information I can get from Dennis. I'm curious as hell, or maybe I'm putting off what I know I need to do.

We walk down the hallway. Fluorescent lights illuminate tiled floors, which reek of some foreign cleaning agent. Dennis walks absently into an empty gurney. It turns, and the steel bars on the end crash into the white wall. A nurse whips around at the sound as if a major mishap has taken place. "Sorry," he says. The nurse gives her best fake smile and turns back to her desk. Dennis moves fast, and I have to step up a notch to keep up.

"He's right down the hall." Dennis opens the double doors located under a sign that reads "Intensive Care Unit." I keep walking, careful to avoid the wheelchairs, gurneys, and other medical equipment lining the hallway.

Curtained-off cubicles cover one side of the room. I look around, listening to the *beep beep* of machines, not knowing which space Britt is in. Dennis walks, and I follow. We stop at curtain number two, and I'm reminded of *Let's Make a Deal*.

Britt's left leg is in a cast, hanging from the top of the bed by a mini trapeze. His right arm is also in a cast, while his left arm is tied to the side of the bed with tubes running from it to an IV bag hanging on the side. Both of his eyes are black and swollen, and his head is entirely wrapped in a bandage that is stained orange and red. His mouth looks like that of a giant red fish, wide open and stuffed full of bloody gauze. I'm taking Dennis at his word that this is Britt Chandler. Anybody could be lying here. A nurse stands on one side of the bed, writing down numbers from all the machines on her clipboard.

"Oh, Britt," Dennis whispers. Britt slowly opens his eyes and tries to say something, but it comes out as nothing more than a muted sound from his throat. Dennis slowly maneuvers his way around the equipment into the small room and puts his hand on Britt's left shoulder. "Don't try to talk, honey. It's okay." Dennis tries his own fake smile, which is a bit more genuine than the nurse's.

Britt keeps trying to talk, and he's fighting the restraint that holds his hand to the bed. Exhausted, he finally gives up.

"We can talk later," Dennis says. The chair next to Britt's bed creaks as Dennis lowers his frame onto it, not taking his hand from Britt's shoulder. Britt's not a very big man. Dennis appears much taller, although it's difficult to tell from this angle, and he has at least fifty pounds on him. The redhead seems even smaller, lying in this bed.

"He needs to rest," the nurse says.

"He's going to be okay, isn't he?" Dennis asks.

"I'll have to let the doctor talk to you about that. He took quite a beating, but he's a tough guy." She finishes scribbling on her clipboard and bounces toward the curtain.

"Yes, he is," Dennis whispers. Britt opens one eye and looks at me. It closes then reopens in a slow blink and focuses on Dennis, who stands, leans over, and kisses Britt on the shoulder. It's the only spot on his body that isn't either covered with a bandage or black and blue.

Britt makes another sound, and even though it isn't words, Dennis seems to know exactly what he's trying to say. "I love you too," he says. Britt shuts his eyes and seems to relax.

I stand there for a minute, watching them and listening to the machines. Whatever they have, it seems to work for them.

"So, the woman that hit him was Cass Adams," Dennis says as Britt falls back asleep. "Who was married to Roland Adams, but killed him, and now lives with the other brother, Clay?"

"Yeah, that's about it."

"Did she know about Britt? I mean, the sheriff said he's investigating, but if she knew Britt was Roland and Clay's half brother, she might have done it on purpose."

Investigating, my ass. "I doubt she knew. Coincidence." I would like to say that Cass doesn't have it in her to kill some guy because he's bringing bad news. After all, she did kill her husband, so who am I to assume she's innocent of trying to kill Britt too? But I don't believe she knew about Britt; she's not much for keeping her mouth shut.

Dennis focuses on the machines. "It's crazy," he says.

Crazy is right. He has no idea.

He wipes his cheeks and lets out a slow breath, as if composing himself. "So what do you want to know?"

I sit down in the chair by the foot of the bed. "Well, if you don't mind..."

Dennis nods. "I know you must be curious. And besides, he isn't real talkative right now."

I don't know where to begin. There's a lot I want to know, and not much of it has to do with anything police related. "What was he doing out there?"

Dennis looks off again, as if trying to decide where to start. "How about if I tell you a story about his dad first?"

I nod. I would love for him to start there.

"According to Britt, he and his dad were very close when he was young. His dad and Stef, Britt's mother, weren't married. In fact, they only got married about ten years ago, so Britt has his mother's name. Chandler. She gave him the middle name Adam as a nod to the sperm donor, I guess.

"Britt got a scholarship to Rice and went to Houston for college. When he graduated, he came out to his parents. Stef was okay with it, but his dad—jeez. Told Britt he was dead to him and to never come home. So he didn't. He got a job in Dallas, we met three years later, and his dad never talked to him again until last year."

I nod. I know what it's like to have an asshole for a dad. But even Tenesy wouldn't tell me to get lost. He likes to torment me too much.

Dennis continues. "Rick, his dad, has cirrhosis. He's been on and off the transplant list for two years."

"Why did his dad start talking to him again last year?"

"He realized he wasn't Superman and was going to die. Decided it was time to make amends so he could ask for a liver from his family. He's off the transplant list for good now—couldn't stay sober long enough to meet the criteria. So his family is his only chance. I told Britt it was insane."

"Well, maybe he had a change of heart and wanted to accept Britt after all those years. You said they'd been close once." I hear people do that, make amends when they are on their deathbed. Maybe they are sincere, or maybe it's their way of bargaining with God, but it's not unusual.

Dennis shakes his head. "No, he wants someone to donate a liver. And Britt can't, even though he wanted to. He's diabetic. And besides, it wasn't Britt he wanted to make amends with. It's Clay and Roland. So he told Britt that he had two brothers. Told him all about his other life. Britt never knew. What kind of a monster leaves two kids when they're little and never looks back?"

That's a good question, and one I can't answer. "So Britt never knew he had two brothers until last year? Damn." *Damn.* Clay has no idea what's about to hit him.

"Mr. Adams tasked Britt with finding Clay and Roland and getting them to come see him so he could apologize. And to see if they were a match for his liver, of course. Britt believed if he did it, his dad would accept him, and…" He stops and grits his teeth. "It doesn't work that way. His dad is a manipulative bastard. And besides, it wasn't Britt's job to do that. His dad should have done it himself years ago."

No shit.

"But Britt is a bit hard-headed and was curious. So he did a little research about these two brothers, tracked them down, and six months ago, came to see them. Well, he saw one, got beat up and threatened, then came home. I told him. I mean, what would you say to someone who shows up and says 'Hey, I'm your brother, and Dad wants to see you after he left you when you were a kid. And by the way, he'd like a piece of your liver.'? But he wanted to come back here once more because I guess his dad is pretty close to dying now."

"But after what happened the first time, why would he try to go see Roland again? You'd think after getting your ass kicked, you'd at least try the other brother."

"Britt said he wasn't going to let some redneck intimidate him. Oh, sorry. No offense."

Maybe a little taken, but I wave it off.

"So I came with him, but he made me stay in the hotel. He went to the club and found out that Roland was dead. He called me and said he was coming back to the room and would try the other brother in the morning. Said he hoped he wasn't an ass too."

"No, Clay's a good man. It's a shame he didn't talk to him first." I guess when you're in that situation, you have to roll the dice and hope you don't crap out. Britt Chandler rolled the wrong number.

"Figures," Dennis says. "After he called me last night, I Googled Roland and read all about him and his wife. Dude was a piece of work." That's an understatement.

I look at my watch and see that it's six o'clock. I need to go home, eat dinner, and get ready to turn Clay Adams's world upside down. I stand up, and Dennis follows.

"I'm going to talk to Clay tonight. It ain't gonna be easy on him."

"I can imagine," Dennis says.

I reach in my billfold and pull out one of my cards. "If you need anything, give me a call. I will do what I can." I nod toward Britt. "I'm sorry about all this. It's a mess."

Dennis sticks his hand out, and I take it. "Thank you. I wish I could tell you more, but when Britt is better, I'm sure he'll answer any questions you have."

"No, I'm good. The sheriff might be nosing around, but speaking of assholes..." We both smile.

"Thanks again, Chief Cloud. It means a lot." Dennis seems like a solid guy, which makes me think Britt must be too.

I walk down the hall toward the elevator, thinking about Britt Chandler. Here he is, trying to win his dying daddy's approval, and he may not survive himself. I think about Clay and even Roland.

Freddy fucking Adams. *How many lives do you have to ruin?*

Chapter 5

Cass

It's eight o'clock in the evening on Halloween. Grams and I are sitting in the living room, watching reruns of Wolfman Jack's *Midnight Special*, and trying to work our way through a big bowl of Twizzlers and bite-sized Snickers. It happens every year, but I still can't get her to stop buying candy. Trick-or-treaters aren't coming to her house. Period.

Clay seemed restless tonight. He went home after work to check on his worms, came to Grams's for dinner, then—about an hour ago—went out to check on the Hill. It's the first Halloween since I buried Roland, and there are so many stories flying around town about me, Roland, and the Hill that we're pretty sure the Hill is going to be a magnet for ghost hunters this year. I wanted to set up a haunted house out there and make some money off of it. But Clay said to leave it alone, so I did. Besides, it would be my luck that Roland *would* show up, and I don't want to be seen arguing with air. Clay should be back any time, because it's almost time for Grams to read our cards.

The doorbell rings. I grab my loaded eggs and run to the back door, ready to sneak around front and bombard the little asses trying to be cute by messing with my Grams. I learned how to hollow eggs out when I was a teenager, and we used to load them with oatmeal. This year, I borrowed some of Clay's worm droppings. I've gotten to use them once already tonight, and boy, were those kids pissed when they realized my eggs weren't loaded with oatmeal. Grams said I was being mean, but I saw her smile when she turned around.

"It's okay, Cass," Grams calls before I get out the door. "It's that nice Angus man from the rest stop." Damn, I wanted to worm-shit somebody.

When Grams opens the door, two fat kids dressed as superheroes yell "trick or treat," and Grams about falls over. Fat Tina's kids are standing on the porch. I can't remember their names, but I would recognize those two chubballs anywhere. They're both covered in freckles, and Tina keeps their hair shaved so close, it's hard to figure out what color their mops are. Behind them are Angus, dressed in a cop's uniform, and a tall blond woman dressed in a Little Red Riding Hood costume. Grams fawns over the boys and shovels candy into their sacks—as if they need any more—then invites them all in for a drink of her special punch.

I just let it happen. Grams loves kids, even the bad ones. I wish my sister Lola or I could have had one or two for her and given her someone to play with, but it never worked out that way. I wish the people in this stupid town knew what a wonderful woman my Grams is and that they would quit treating her like some scary old witch. Sure, she has some oddities, but don't we all?

Grams and the kids are engaged in a lively conversation about their costumes. I grab a handful of candy and hold it out to Angus. "Cute costume, little guy. Where's your bag?"

"It's my uniform. I'm on the police auxiliary, and Benny has everyone out tonight to watch out for troublemakers." He looks at the eggs in my other hand. "Don't know any troublemakers, do you?"

I set the eggs on the coffee table as Wolfman Jack howls. "None that I can't handle." I look at the young woman with him in her Red Riding Hood outfit. "Is that a uniform too?" She twirls around like an eight-year-old and does a curtsy.

"Cass, this is Sonja. Sonja, Cass Adams." She's tall and probably has a good twelve inches on Angus even without the four-inch heels she's wearing.

"Hi. I'm Sonja," she says. I already knew that. "Gus said you were Roland's wife. I liked Roland. He was *so* nice to me."

Grams is talking in a lower voice, and I know she's listening to this conversation more than the one with the kids.

"I bet he was." I'm trying to be nice because I appreciate that Angus brought the kids over for Grams, but it's hard. Angus winks at me.

Sonja lowers her eyes and sticks out her lower lip. "And I'm sorry for your loss. I'm sure you must miss him."

My hands are on my hips, but Grams is between Sonja and me before

I can say a thing. "Miss Sonja," she says, "would you join me and the boys for some spooky punch? I have some cherry cobbler too."

"You have cobbler?" the biggest kid cries and takes off for the kitchen.

Sonja smiles at Grams. "Sure." They follow the kids to the kitchen.

"Is she really that dumb?" I ask Angus.

"She's had a rough life. Took one too many hits to the head from a boyfriend that should have met your shovel. She stays with me, and I try to look out for her."

"And she's a stripper."

He holds both hands out with his palms up and shrugs. "The world is not a perfect place."

This guy is too nice, and I know better than to trust his kindness because people haven't ever been that nice to me. Except Clay. Yet I can't help but like Angus. Maybe my sessions with Dr. Button are paying off, or maybe he is magical, as Grams says, and he's trying to cast a spell on me.

"So why are you here?" I find it hard to believe that he and Sonja the stripper are out making social calls.

"Sonja and I took Tina's boys trick-or-treating so she and Harlan can work. And your grandmother has a crush on me, if you haven't noticed. It's good for the ego."

I try to picture Grams and Angus dancing around to her Doors music. Wolfman Jack howls again. *Exactly, Jack.*

"And I wanted to ask you a question," he says.

I laugh. Of course there's something else. I sit on the couch and cross my arms in front of me. "Okay, shoot."

He sits in the chair next to the couch. "If you're interested in selling your land outside of town, I'm interested in buying."

"What for?" Of course, I know why someone would want the land, and Clay and I have talked about it. I am having a hard time giving it up. It's my quiet place, even though when Roland shows up with the other guy that haunts me—Old Man Booker—it's not too quiet.

"I want to build a house so I don't have to live above my shop anymore, and I love the view."

"I'm not sure it's for sale," I say.

"Oh. Clay suggested I talk to you about it. I figured..." He lets the thought trail off, and I turn toward him.

"Truth is, it has ghosts. It's haunted." A few others have inquired about the Hill, and this revelation seems to scare them away. It's not a lie, either.

He nods. "Let's see… Mr. Booker and Roland Adams, I suppose."

"How did you know?"

He smiles that smile again. "Dwarves are magical, haven't you heard?"

"No, really, how did you know about Booker and Roland?" Old Man Booker owned the Hill long before Roland and I did. He had a house that sat on the same spot where our shack stood. Rumor has it that he turned the entire house into a giant still, and when it blew up, there weren't any chunks of Booker to be found.

"I read a book once that said ghosts tend to haunt the place they died. As far as I know, those are the only two that have met their demise on that hill. Are there more?"

I shake my head.

"If you do want to sell, I'm very interested. And the ghosts don't bother me. Give me someone to talk to."

I stop. "You talk to them too?"

"Oh no. I was… You talk to them?"

"No. That's crazy. I don't know why I said that."

He touches my arm lightly. "It's okay. I won't say anything. There are a lot of people that can talk to ghosts. It's not crazy at all."

"How do you know that?"

"I read about it. Is that why you don't want to sell? You enjoy talking to them?"

I've never even told Clay about the ghosts, and here I am spilling to Angus King. "Yes," I say.

"If I bought the land, I promise you would be welcome anytime. Promise. It's fascinating, and now I want the land more than ever." He smiles, and it seems genuine.

I want to believe he means it. "So that's why you're being nice to me? You want my land?"

"Oh no! I like you. You're an interesting person, and you make me laugh. Besides, once your Grams and I make our relationship official…"

I have to laugh. "Yeah, I don't know if you can handle her."

"Besides, it's hard enough being pregnant. Maybe you need another friend right now."

"What did you say? I'm not pregnant." I look down at my stomach and wonder how he knows. Hell, I'm not even sure myself.

"I saw you protecting your stomach last night, and then you threw up this afternoon, and you have this glow about you."

"I threw up because I hit my head." At least that's what I've been telling myself, but that doesn't explain why I've been nauseous for the past week, even before the accident.

He raises one eyebrow. "You haven't told anyone, have you?"

The doorbell rings at the right second. I jump off the couch, and before I open the door, I turn to Angus. "Don't you say anything, either. I don't know for sure."

"Trick or treat!" It's Maryanne, dressed in a short, tight blue dress, wearing a blond wig.

"Who the hell are you supposed to be?" I ask.

"Cinderella! And I'm out looking for my prince!" She bounces in the door and sees Angus. "Oh, you again. Maybe Snow White would have been more appropriate."

Angus gets off the chair. "Don't flatter yourself."

Grams and the crew come in from the kitchen, and Sonja's eyes light up at Maryanne's outfit. "Oh, that is a fabulous outfit! Are you a stripper too?" It just keeps getting better.

Maryanne rolls her eyes and turns to Grams. "I came to pick up the tiara you said I could borrow, Ms. Shatner."

"I put it in Cass's old room on the dresser for you, honey. And I think you look beautiful."

"Thank you." Maryanne stomps off toward my room at the back of the house. "Tell me when your company is gone."

"Why do you have a tiara?" I ask Grams. I know everyone thinks I'm nuts, but tonight, I feel like the normal one in the room. Grams waves a hand at me, as if everyone has a tiara lying around.

"Well, we need to go. I'm going to take the boys back home, and Sonja and I have to get to work." Angus kisses Grams's hand. "It was a pleasure, Ms. Shatner." She hugs both of the kids and Sonja and makes them all promise to come back and visit. I smile. It's good to see Grams so happy.

"And Cass, take care of yourself." Angus winks at me. I wonder if he has some kind of tic.

"Already do. And you're wrong."

He smiles and herds his three charges out the door. Grams and I stand and watch them pile into Tina's Hummer.

"Wrong about what?" Grams asks.

"He thinks I'm pregnant."

"And you said…"

"I told him to eat worms."

Grams nods. "So… maybe." Her face is lit up like a Christmas tree.

"Yeah. Maybe. But please don't say anything to Clay." Not yet. Not until I know for sure, and especially not until I know how I feel about it.

Chapter 6

Clay

After dinner at Babe Shatner's, I drove out to check on the Hill as I had promised Cassie I would. After all, it is Halloween night, and with everything that's happened out there, I expected it to be swarming with teenagers and others looking for something creepy. But it was all quiet. Nothing out there but bad memories and ghosts.

Driving back to Babe's, I pass a few small kids out with their mommas. A boy dressed as a pirate pulls the crown right off a girl about eight years old and runs away with it. She chases after him. I watch for a minute then have to smile. He could easily outrun her, but he's going slowly on purpose. He wants to be caught. The moms holding their candy bags chat while they wait for the game to be over. It reminds me of when my daughter Shaylene was young. I sure miss that. Now Shaylene's running around the University of Kansas, not much of a little girl anymore. And I'm sure if some pirate tried to tear her crown off, she would rip him a new one.

Maryanne is leaving Babe's, dressed like a slut, and a shovel is stuck in the ground in the front yard. I park the truck and grab the shovel on my way to the porch. Cute, Cassie, but some people won't find it funny at all. As I enter, the smell of fresh-baked cherries makes my mouth water. Babe and Cass are whispering in the kitchen like two teenage girls. Whatever they are talking about must be good because they don't even hear me come in. It must also be a great secret because the second they notice me, they shut up like two hunters that spotted a prize buck.

Babe motions toward the oven. "I made your favorite—Cherry Delight. It's fresh out of the oven."

Growing up, and until the past few months, I was always scared of Babe

Shatner. I guess after hearing rumors about her my whole life, I tended to believe them. But now that I've gotten to know her, I've found she's one of the nicest gals I've ever met. She's a little hard to understand at times, with her visions and seeing auras and everything, but she means no harm.

While Babe dishes me a big bowl of dessert, Cassie casually mentions the "family tradition" about getting our cards read on Halloween. She knows I don't care for that stuff, but she also knows I'm not going to make a fuss in front of her grandmother.

Babe has sets of cards for all of us and says it's best to do it closer to midnight. I pick up my set of cards and flip through them, looking at pictures I don't understand. Kings and queens adorn the cards, but they're not like the face cards in a regular deck. I stop on a card with three girls, all holding cups in the air as though they are making a toast. Babe is watching me and probably making a mental note of what I'm looking at, but I don't say anything. I put my deck back on the table. I don't know what a bunch of cups could say about me.

The doorbell rings, and Cassie grabs a carton of eggs off the counter, while Babe goes to the door. "It's Benny Cloud," she yells.

Cassie lets out a loud groan. "What the hell does he want?"

It isn't a secret that Cassie and Benny don't care much for each other. They have a history that goes way back. In grade school, Benny was a bully, and he picked on the wrong girl one day. Cassie beat him like a stale cake mix, and after that, he steered clear of her—that is, until she buried my brother Roland in her yard.

"I'm sure it's procedure," I tell Cassie. "Paperwork stuff. No big deal."

Cassie rolls her eyes and sets her egg carton back on the counter. We walk into the living room as Benny comes in, takes off his hat, and nods to us all, keeping his head down. Babe's forehead crinkles up like a dishrag, and she sits on the couch with her hands in her lap.

"Is everything okay?" I ask her. Something I've discovered about Babe is that her intuition is pretty spot-on. If she isn't talking, it usually means she's feeling something bad, and looking at her now makes my stomach turn.

Benny motions for us all to sit. He doesn't give us so much as a "howdy do," no smile, nothing. Cassie plops in a chair in the corner, and I sit directly across from Benny. Babe starts to get up, saying she's going to busy herself in the kitchen, but Benny asks if she would stay.

He slides a picture across the table to me. "Britt Chandler. Do you know him? Ever heard the name?" I look closely at the young face in the picture. It's a little grainy, but I can see him. I shake my head. No, I don't recognize him.

"I've never seen him, either," Cassie says from the corner. "Except last night. But he didn't look like that."

"You might want to at least look at the picture," Benny says.

Cassie crosses her arms over her chest. "I saw it today. Angus and Tina showed it to me. Still don't know him."

"You saw Angus and Tina?" I asked. With Cassie, I have to ask the right questions. She'll answer me, most of the time with no filter, but only if I ask her exactly what I want to know. For instance, instead of asking her if she was feeling better, I should have asked her what she did today. She hasn't talked to Tina in years, and I didn't even know she knew Angus King. Now I know different.

"It wasn't a big deal. I went to search for my phone. They saw me there and stopped to ask if I knew the guy. I like Angus. He's funny. Tina's still kind of uptight, but—"

Benny holds up a hand to stop her. She growls at him but quits talking. "His name is Britt Chandler. He's pretty torn up. Rudy was going to investigate the whole wreck." He nods toward Cass.

"For heaven's sake, why can't people leave my girl alone? There's no reason in the world that she would intentionally run over a man in the road." Babe is wringing her hands again, and I feel as if I'm in a conversation where I'm the one who doesn't know the inside story. Cass pulls out her phone and starts dialing.

"Put the phone down, Cass," Benny tells her.

She ignores Benny and begins talking to someone. I can tell by her conversation that she is speaking with Richard Warner, her sister Lola's husband. He was her lawyer when she was arrested for killing Roland, and he's probably the best call to make right now.

"Gotcha," she says and closes the phone. "My lawyer said to tell you to kiss off. I told him it was my pleasure."

"Benny, why in the world would Rudy think this was intentional?" I ask. "She didn't know him. She had no reason to run him over." I know Cassie has a history. I mean, it's hard to bury your husband in your own yard and not have a bit of a reputation. But she did have her reasons for that.

"Because Roland knew the guy and had some beef with him, so the dumbass sheriff thinks I must have too," Cassie says. She makes a motion that looks as if she is zipping her lips. Then she crosses her arms and leans back in the corner.

"How do you know all this?" Benny shakes his head. "She's right. About six months ago, he came to see Roland. But you missed the key word in what I said before you all jumped into defense mode. I said he *was* going to investigate. He dropped it all this afternoon, said there wasn't no evidence to go on, so you're in the clear."

I don't claim to be the smartest man, but I think if I could get this story from the beginning instead of the middle, I might be able to understand it better. And from the way Babe is wringing her hands, I know there is more to this than Benny's letting on.

"Benny, why don't you start talking and tell me what the hell is going on. If I want to dance, I'll turn some music on." I'm normally a patient guy, but damn, everybody's on page ten, and I just opened the book. Yet somehow, I feel as if this has more to do with me than Cassie.

Benny clears his throat. "This is going to be hard to hear, Clay. I want you to know, I'd rather be here to arrest somebody than to tell you all this. And there's probably much more to it that I don't know, but I'll give you what I got." Babe gets up, stands behind me, and puts her hands on my shoulders. Cassie must sense something, too, because she takes the seat Babe was in and doesn't say a word.

"This Britt Chandler came to see Roland about six months ago. Roland beat the crap out of him and told him if he ever came back, he'd kill him. Well, he came back this week, found out that Roland's dead, then he got hit by Cass's truck, walking back to his car at the rest stop." He pauses again and looks at the ceiling as if he's trying to figure out what to say. "The thing is—why he came to see Roland…" He takes a deep breath and lets it out slowly. "He's your half brother. His daddy—your daddy, Freddy Adams—is in a hospital in Los Angeles, dying of a bad liver. He wants to make amends. Roland apparently wasn't interested the first time Britt came to see him, but from what I take so far, your daddy's pretty close to the end now, so Britt decided to try again." He sits back in his chair. The only sound in the room is the steady hum of the floor furnace. Babe squeezes my shoulders, and it's like a shot.

I stand up, but my head is spinning, and I sit back down fast. It's hard for me to even think of Freddy Adams as my dad. His name is only a memory. "I…" I don't know what to say.

Cassie says it for me. "Oh crap." I reach for her hand, which is shaking as badly as mine.

"Roland never said… I…" My face is hot, and I want to throw up. I bang my fist on the table and stand again. I'm the kind of man who wants everything to be laid out in front of me so I can take it all in before I decide how to react. That's how I feel most of the time. But this… It feels as though I'm back in the army on one of our training missions, but instead of the enemy popping up in a doorway, they've surrounded me, and I'm not sure who to shoot first. Except this isn't training, and Benny is firing live bullets. I let go of Cassie's hand and run mine through my hair, holding on to a chunk of it.

Roland, you son of a bitch. Why didn't you tell me? And Freddy Adams? My *father*.

Benny is standing now, as if he's ready to catch me if I fall. I'm not going to fall. I pull my truck keys out of my pocket and cut a path to the door. I'm done talking. I need to think. I need to get out of here.

"Clay, wait." Cassie is moving toward me, but Babe catches her wrist and holds her back. Babe nods toward me, giving me the go-ahead. Sometimes, a man needs to be alone so he can decide what to do, and right now, there's only one thing I really want to do. But I don't think driving to Los Angeles to kill a dying man is a great idea.

Most women assume that men are hotheads by nature, and instead of thinking or reasoning anything out, their first instinct is to resort to anger. Sure, we get angry, but we also get hurt. Since we've been told all our lives that men don't cry, we don't always have any other way to let that hurt out. But we do cry. We don't always let anyone else see it.

Women, at least the ones I've known, like to talk about everything. I don't, at least not until I've had some time to decide what I'm going to say. Benny's words hit me like a sledgehammer, and as much as I know Cassie wanted to be with me, I need to be alone—to think, to cry, to be a man.

But anger comes first, and when I leave Babe's and get in my truck, I am shaking so bad, I have to hit my fists on the steering wheel until they hurt. The feeling doesn't pass until I'm halfway to Tulsa. That's when I realize that Los Angeles is a long drive, and he isn't worth the gas.

I turn around, knowing I would be better off with a handful of worms, and start for home. How am I going to deal with this mess?

I've tucked things away for so long, and I can tuck this away, too, and carry on. But this is my whole life. Everything I've ever known has turned out to all be a lie. I want to blame Roland for not telling me in the first place. But maybe he was an ass because he didn't have a father, either. So maybe it wasn't his fault after all.

So I have another brother, a half brother, one who came looking for us, or at least came looking for Roland. Why him and not me? To fulfill the dying wish of our father? *His father. Not mine.*

I decide there is no way I'm going to give the bastard the satisfaction of apologizing to me for what he did to my momma, Roland, or me. No way. He's dead. At least he's dead to me. It may not be that simple, but it's going to have to be.

The streets of Deacon are usually empty by this time of night except for a few strays coming home from Tina's or the casino. Tonight, there are a few more out since it's Halloween. I drive past Babe's and see that all of her trees have been toilet-papered. All the lights are out, and Babe's car is gone, so I figure Cassie has borrowed it and gone home. I park and get rid of the toilet paper. I don't want Babe to wake up and see it. Then I head out to the old highway, where I've lived my entire life.

As I get closer to home, all I can think about is a handful of worms, something that might take my mind off of Freddy Adams. Normally, I would pull the worm hatches into the kitchen to ride out winter. Their boxes are insulated, but it doesn't take much for the little guys to freeze. I guess I should have built a hothouse for them years ago, but I never thought the time would come when my kitchen was being used for cobbler-cooking and candle-making instead of worm-storing.

Pulling into the drive, I see Babe's big pink Cadillac parked in my spot. That's not a big deal to me, except that we all get used to our space, and Cassie has been very good about respecting that. I think for a second about not saying anything, but then again, if I don't, maybe she'll keep parking there, then it won't be mine any more at all. Oh hell, it's a parking space, and I have other things to worry about right now. So I pull up on the gravel at the side of the house and get out.

It's getting colder by the minute—one of those nights when you can feel winter getting ready to hit. No stars are in the sky tonight, probably covered by dark clouds. I pull my coat closer to me and walk around back to check on the worms. What I don't expect to see is a fire burning and Cassie sitting at the picnic table, focused on the tree line. "I figured you'd come to the back first," she says.

A small bonfire glows too close to the house. I check it and make sure it's safe then sit with Cassie at the table. I know she wants to talk. Women all think we need to talk, but I don't want to. Maybe if I don't say anything, she'll understand.

"Roland never told me much about your daddy," she says. "Only that he left when you were kids and didn't come back." Cassie and I both had dads that left us when we were little kids, and truth is that we never talked about it much to each other. She has her demons, I have mine, and we've always left it at that. But now the subject has been broached. And here she is, wanting to know more about my dad. "How did he leave?"

Yes. We're going to talk about this. *Fine.*

"What do you mean? He just left, I guess. I was a kid, Cassie." I think people try to keep some memories tucked away as much as possible because it hurts too badly to let them rise to the surface. I've done a pretty good job keeping this one down, mostly because nobody talks much about it. But I'm forty years old now; I'm not a boy anymore.

"My daddy is in St. Louis," she says. "When I was little, I always wanted to go find him, but now, not so much." In the light of the fire, she looks like a rabbit that has been caught in headlights. You see, Cassie's mind works a little differently than others. I know she knows I don't want to talk, but she feels if she shares with me, it will make it easier. It won't. But I know this hurts her, too, so I put my arm around her and pull her close. She keeps talking.

"I don't remember much about him. I was a baby, so I'm not sure if I remember at all. Grams told me everything I needed to know. He lived with us when he didn't have anywhere else to sleep, then one night, he and Momma got into a fight and he said he was leaving and never coming back. And he did. That's about it. I don't even have a picture of him, not like the one you have in the bedroom of your family. It's like he never was." She shrugs. "Maybe he didn't exist. Maybe he was made up. I don't know. But I know he went to St. Louis. Lola tells me he's still there. I don't care."

I start to get up. I have worm tending to do, but Cassie grabs my coat collar and pulls me back. "Now your turn," she says.

I take a breath, then another. "He went out a lot, and one night, he didn't come home. Momma looked for him, had Percy, the chief of police back then, searching for him. Rudy and Tenesy came by a lot, but my dad was gone."

"Rudy? Why the hell would he come around?"

"Before he cleaned up and ran for sheriff, he and my dad were friends. Used to run the bars with Tenesy Cloud." I used to think Rudy was the giant chicken on the Saturday morning cartoons. Even now when I see him, with his chest all stuck out and calling everyone "boy," he reminds me of Foghorn Leghorn. That was his name. Tenesy, on the other hand, talked loudly and twitched a lot. He was pretty scary to me.

The flames from the fire dance in a perfect circle. "When I was little, my dad used to light a fire almost every night, summer or winter. Didn't matter whether it was hot or cold. It used to make my momma so mad, but he didn't pay her any mind."

"What was he like?"

I focus on one bright star peeking through the clouds. "Well, what I can remember, he was always making jokes. He must have been funny because the adults always laughed. He'd wink at me, like we had a secret, and I would smile." Roland used to do the same thing when he got older, but I didn't find him funny.

"Your momma was always so serious," Cass says. "I can't see her with someone who is playing tricks."

I tried to picture Momma, how she looked when I was young, but for some reason, it wasn't easy to remember her. "Maybe she was taking care of business, while he had all the fun. Before he left, she used to laugh a lot too. After, not so much." I start to get up, hoping Cassie is done talking about this, but she isn't.

"What about the night he left?"

"Cassie, I don't want—"

"Please."

It hurts. I hate to admit that. I'm a grown man, but maybe, if I get it over with, she won't ask again. I take a deep breath. "I was a kid, but I remember him tucking me into bed, and then he left. That wasn't anything unusual. He'd go out damn near every night, and Momma would scream at him the next day. But that morning, I woke up way before sunup, and they were fighting."

I look up at the sky again but can't find my star. "Then he left again. And never came back. I'm not even sure she cared. Hell, she didn't call the cops for almost a week. Maybe she thought he'd come back, or maybe she was glad he was gone. She told me and Roland some story about him going off to fight a war. I knew better but never said anything because Roland didn't know any different."

"Are you going to go see him?" She looks at me, then off into the yard, then back to me.

"Would you, if it was your dad?"

She laughs. "Hell no. But I'm not you. I don't give two shakes about my dad. But I know you feel different."

"I don't feel different." I hold her face gently and turn it toward me so she has to look at me. "He's gone. He's always been gone. I don't think about him and don't intend to start. Momma raised us, and we turned out okay. I'm not going to see him. He's already dead to me. Okay?"

She nods and doesn't say a thing. I get up and get the small space heater and tarp off of the back porch. Cassie sits on the picnic table and watches me while I arrange the worm hutches in a circle, put the space heater in the middle, and cover them with the tarp. When I'm done, I get the shovel on the side of the house so I can put some dirt on the fire before it gets any bigger.

"Wait," Cassie says then jumps up and runs in the house. She comes back with two clothes hangers, a loaf of bread, and a pack of hot dogs. "No use letting a fire go to waste." She unravels one of the hangers and puts a hot dog on the end for me. I'm so hungry that even a roasted wienie sounds good. I stick it in the fire and turn it until it bubbles black and crispy, just the way I like it.

"And you're lying to me, but that's okay," she says.

"What?" I turn so fast at her words that my wienie falls in the fire. *Damn.*

"You look at that picture of him on the bedside table every day, Clay. You do think about him. A lot."

Chapter 7

Cass

Sometimes my head gets full of things, and the only way to clear it out is to go to sleep for a while. It's as if I have a brain fairy that picks through all the rubbish and leaves the important stuff. After last night, I definitely needed the brain fairy.

When Clay left, I was upset because he didn't want me to go with him. I knew he was hurting, and I wanted to make it better, but I didn't know how I was supposed to do that. Grams told me that men feel better when they want to anyway, and I shouldn't let it get to me. She said that once he calmed down, he would come home and play with his worms, then he would be better. She was right. That's exactly what happened.

A lot of mornings, when I wake up, Clay is next to me, watching me sleep. But this morning, he's out cold and facing away from me. I watch his back move with each breath, and I hope he has figured out what he's going to do. Hell, I already know what he's going to do—he'll be in Los Angeles before the week is over, one way or another. My bigger problem right now is what I'm going to do.

Once Grams and I were alone again last night, we considered my problem. I've been sick for about a week, and I might have briefly considered that I could be pregnant, but it wasn't real until Angus said something. How had he known?

"I told you, a lot of little people have the sight. And Angus seems real special to me." Grams's eyes had a spark to them when she mentioned his name, a look I haven't seen in a long time. She pressed her palms into my temples and shut her eyes. Then she smiled. "Honey, you need to get one of those sticks to pee on. See if it turns blue."

"Okay, let's stop," I said. "It's a maybe. I've been sick, but I might have the stomach flu." I can't get pregnant. I'm thirty-seven years old, and Roland and I tried to have a baby for almost twenty years.

"You haven't said anything to Clay?" She looked at me dead on, probably trying to see if I was going to tell her the truth. I always do.

"He doesn't monitor my periods. And don't be giving him ideas. He's got enough going on right now on his own."

Finally, we agreed: if I puke this morning, I'll pee on a stick. If not, we'll leave it alone—at least until I start puking again.

Clay rolls over and kisses my forehead. "Whatcha thinking about?"

"A foot-long cheese coney with lots of onions and maybe some candy corn on top." He laughs and heads for the bathroom. I prop the pillows up against the headboard and wait for him to come back.

Next to our bed, we have two tables. Mine is always cluttered with junk, fingernail polish, receipts, scraps of paper, and candles that look as if they are crawling up the walnut-based lamp that sits in the middle. It seems whatever I walk in here with, I drop on the nightstand to put away later. But later usually doesn't come until I throw it all in the trash.

Clay's side is different. All he keeps on his side is a lamp that matches mine, his alarm clock, and two pictures in matching frames. One is of him and me, smiling and holding hands at his momma's funeral. To this day, I can't remember what we were smiling about. The other is a picture of his mom and dad, standing together in front of a slick red Chevy Camaro, with four-year-old Clay standing in front of his dad and two-year-old Roland on his momma's hip. I'm holding that picture in my hand when Clay comes back from the bathroom.

"You all look real happy," I say. Freddy, Clay's dad, has his arm around Donna Sue. Clay is already tall, up to his daddy's belt.

Clay lies back down and takes the picture from me. "I guess we were. That's the day my dad got his new car. I loved that car. Used to sit in the driver's seat and play like I was in a race, turning the wheel, going 'round and 'round the track. Even got to sit on his lap a few times and steer when we were outside town. Yeah, I guess we were happy that day."

The smiles on their faces make them look like the happiest family in the world. But like everything else, what appears on the outside isn't always so. Less than a year after that picture was taken, Freddy Adams just up and left one night and never came home. Clay places the photo back on his table, making sure it's straight.

"What are you doing today?" he asks. It's Thursday, and Clay is off work, so as long as I don't puke, I don't have any plans other than to spend the day with him.

"Whatcha got in mind?" Some days, he'll make breakfast, and we'll stay in bed most of the morning. I like those days a lot.

He's playing with my hair, but he's got a frown on his face. I trace his lips with my finger and try to force them up into a smile. "I'm going to go see him. Will you come with me?"

Well, I figured as much. Clay acts tough, and he is when he needs to be. But he has a soft side, a forgiving side that is wonderful if his charity is for someone deserving. Personally, I don't think Freddy Adams deserves squat.

"To Los Angeles? I've never been." I've never been much of anywhere. And I don't want to go to California, but I do want Clay to be happy.

"No, not *that* him. The guy in the hospital. My half brother. It's not his fault, and I want to see him. Talk to him. I..."

Oh well, Joplin I can handle. I rub the side of his face with one finger, trace his jawline to the chin, and continue down his neck. Then I feel my stomach turn. I roll over and sit on the side of the bed before he has a chance to notice that I don't feel well. "Sure, I'll go with you." *But first, I have to puke.*

Clay said he wasn't hungry, but I knew he needed to eat. He loves onion rings, well done, from Sonic, so I made him stop there on the way to the hospital. At least he would have something in his system. And I could get my foot-long cheese coney with lots of onions, but no candy corn.

Benny called while we were driving. I assume he wanted to see how Clay was feeling this morning. It's none of his business, and he should feel guilty about spilling all that crap on Clay last night, anyway. I bet he enjoyed it. Clay told Benny he was fine and that we were on our way to the hospital to see this Britt guy. I don't want to see him. I already met him once, and things didn't work out very well.

"It's fine, Benny. I want to meet him... Yes..." He turns to me. "Trust me, it will be fine." I know Benny is worried because I'm with Clay. *Asshole.* "Okay, do what you need to," Clay says and hangs up.

It's almost noon, although I wouldn't know by the sky. Everything is gray, and the sun is hiding behind the clouds. I turn the heat up in Clay's truck and keep eating my coney.

"Benny said Britt has his boyfriend with him. I don't understand that, but I assured him that I just want to meet the guy." He is clutching the steering wheel so tightly that his knuckles are white.

"So Britt is gay," I say. Big deal; so is Clay's daughter, Shaylene. "And you told Benny I'd be on my best behavior."

He glances at me, and one corner of his mouth rises up. "He also said he sent Angus over there to check on Britt, so you'll have a friend to play with."

Damn. I do like Angus, but I don't want him to say anything to Clay about our talk last night. I don't think he will if I tell him not to. Did I tell him that last night? I don't remember. "Can you stop at the drugstore for me before we get there?" I promised Grams I would pee on a stick, and I figure that will give me something to do while Clay is meeting his half brother.

"You feeling okay?" His smile is gone, and his forehead is all bunched up.

"A little heartburn." That is true, but my coney dog is so good that I don't want to stop eating it.

When Clay stops, I run in and grab some Tums and a home pregnancy kit. I throw the kit in my purse and pop a few Tums in my mouth. Candy corn is half off at the counter, so I grab a bag of that too.

We ride the rest of the way in silence, which is fine. Like Grams says, men don't want to talk much about their problems. I'm sure Clay is thinking about a lot of things right now. I have my own mind jumble going on.

The parking lot at the hospital is full, and we have to drive around and wait for someone to leave before we can get a spot. A guy wearing a deflated sumo wrestler costume with a white bandage wrapped around his head crawls into a beat-up yellow Honda and pulls out. Clay squeezes his truck into the guy's spot. As much as I hate hospitals, I'm thinking that hanging out in the emergency room on the day after Halloween might actually be entertaining.

When we get to the seventh floor, I go straight for the waiting room.

Clay goes off to find the almost-dead guy. I don't want to see him, but I'm happy to wait. Besides, I have something else to do as soon as I know Clay is occupied.

But when I walk into the waiting room, I see Angus sitting with a blond woman. I figure she must be Britt Chandler's mom, Freddy Adams's wife. She doesn't look at all like what I expected.

Clay's mom was never what I would call a pretty woman, even in her younger days. Donna Sue was sturdy. I guess that's the best way to describe her. She wasn't fat, but tall and thick. I never saw her wear makeup, and her prematurely graying hair was always tied back in a ponytail, with pieces of it sticking out like a game of Kerplunk. The woman in front of me is small, not much bigger than me, and her hair is long and styled as if she just walked out of a beauty shop. I bet she spent more on makeup than on breakfast this morning, and she makes jeans and a T-shirt look good. Angus winks at me, and I walk right over.

"I'm sorry I hit your kid. I'm glad he isn't dead." I'm not one to lie, but Grams told me that sometimes I have to be polite and say things to people that I don't mean. I don't understand that at all because how is lying polite? But telling this woman that her son was a dumbass for walking out in front of a truck on the highway doesn't seem like the right move. So, I'll try it Grams's way.

The woman's eyes get wide, but her forehead doesn't wrinkle. In fact, she doesn't have any wrinkles, and she has to be close to sixty. "Oh, you must be Cass Adams." She turns back to Angus, and he nods.

"Yeah, that's me. But it was his fault, you know." Grams also says I don't know when to shut up.

Angus interrupts, which is probably a good thing. "Stef was telling me about Rick, her husband. They gave him a year to live, but he has fooled them out of another year so far. Tough guy, wouldn't you say, Cass?"

Tough guy, my ass. I would say he's a chickenshit, and I don't care if he lives another day. He was nothing but a thorn for Roland and an ice pick for Clay.

I sit in one of the green upholstered chairs across from them. "Rick?" Another one of the things Grams has taught me lately is that if I can't say something nice...

Stef dabs at her eyes with a Kleenex. "Fredrick. He went by Rick. I hear he went by Freddy years ago. He never told us about the boys. He told me and Britt after he was sick. I'd have done something if I'd known, but I didn't know." She raises her chin up as though she's proud of herself.

I start laughing. "Bullshit." So much for Grams's rules.

"Excuse me?"

"I call bullshit. You never knew that he had a wife and two kids before you? How long were you together?" I lean back and cross my arms over my chest.

"Thirty years. But no, I never knew. He kept it all a big secret and—"

"No. That only happens on TV. In thirty years, you never met any of his family, never went back to his hometown with him, never even asked about his life before you met him? I don't believe you." She's one of those women whom I can tell has a little money and thinks everyone should treat her like a queen. But my sister, Lola, is also one of those women, so I know for a fact that they are as insecure as everyone else, maybe more so. That's why they try to act important all the time. This woman doesn't mean shit to me.

"I don't care what you believe," she says. "From what I hear, you didn't know everything about your husband, either." She attempts a smirk but pulls her resting bitch face back together. She's probably afraid her cheeks will crack.

"But I'm crazy, and my husband kept me doped up for twenty years. You don't look crazy. Maybe you do drugs."

Her mouth drops open, and I want to stuff something in it before any more of her crap comes out.

Angus is up and in between us, acting as though he's afraid there's going to be a throwdown. I show him my palm as if I'm a crossing guard stopping traffic. Then I grab my purse and walk to the door, but I turn back before I leave. I have one more thing to say.

"You see, I don't care that you moved in with a married man and had a kid. You must have loved his sorry ass because you stayed with him this long. So I get that. But damn, don't lie about it. That makes you no better than him. And here's a news flash—your husband is a piece of shit."

I walk down the hall, searching for a bathroom. Angus catches up with me. "That went well," he says.

"Screw her." I open my purse and show Angus what's inside.

"You're doing it here?"

"It's a hospital, isn't it?" I ask as he walks with me to the ladies' room. "You can't come in, you know."

"Yes, I know. But if you don't mind, I want to know if I'm right or not."

Just like a man. I shrug and take a deep breath.

He stops me before I open the door. "And Cass? You were right. That story is bullshit."

Chapter 8

Clay

DENNIS SQUEEZES WATER FROM A sponge and sprinkles a few drops of powdered soap onto it that the hospital gave him to use. He says he prefers giving Britt his bath instead of having the nurse's aides do it, and he says Britt is happy he's doing it as well. He starts on his face, the parts that aren't bandaged, and is very careful around Britt's mouth. Some of his teeth are gone, and a small disc holds his mouth partly open. A thick, clear tube is sticking out, helping him breathe. His lips are swollen and purple with bruising, and Dennis dabs them lightly.

"Can he hear us?" I don't know if Britt is sleeping or in a coma, and to be honest, I don't know the difference. I do know that when Dennis says something, the numbers on his machines go up. If that means he can hear us, I don't want to upset him.

"I sure hope so, or I'd look pretty stupid talking to myself. He's drugged up, but he wakes up every now and then and tries to talk." Dennis moves the sponge over the light stubble on Britt's chin, down his neck, and to his hairless chest. I know he's thirty, which means he was born five years after my dad left us, but he looks much younger.

"I'm sorry this happened. Cassie is sorry too." In her way, she is. But she has a weird way of expressing herself. I hope she's behaving in the waiting room.

Dennis smiles. "I read about her and your brother. And Chief Cloud told me about you two. She sounds like a real firecracker."

I shift on my chair. "It's a long story. And Roland was an ass. But I guess you already figured that out."

He cleans Britt's right leg then moves to the other side of the bed to do his arm, avoiding the cast and the trapeze that holds his broken pieces off the bed. On both casts are two big hearts with "Dennis" signed in the middle in black Sharpie marker. "After Britt came here six months ago, I wanted to come myself and take care of this Roland dude. I mean, come on, Britt was trying to tell him something, and he shot the messenger. But Britt wouldn't let me."

He puts the sponge in a small plastic bowl, grabs a towel, and starts drying Britt's body. "When he said he was coming back, I insisted he let me come with him. I told him to forget about that guy and to at least try to contact you first, but it was late when we got in. He figured the strip club would be open. He's normally a smart man, but I guess his emotions got the better of him."

"Roland never told me that Britt was here." Of course, Roland never told me about a lot of things, and one of his greatest pleasures in life was making me suffer, so it doesn't surprise me. It does piss me off, but I've been pissed at Roland for so many years, it almost doesn't even faze me. I thought once he was dead, he couldn't affect me like that anymore. Boy, was I wrong.

Dennis puts a clean gown on Britt, covers him up, and sits in his chair. "Well, I'm glad you came. Britt will be anxious to meet you when he gets better. You have a lot in common, it seems." I look at Britt. Other than the same sperm donor, I don't know what we could have in common.

"About eight years ago, when Britt came out, his dad told him that he wished he was dead and said he never wanted to see him again. It hurt. But when Great King Rick summoned Britt to his bedside, he went running, assuming he would be forgiven. Britt thought by bringing you and Roland to see him, it would somehow absolve him in the eyes of his dad. It doesn't work that way, but he wanted to make peace with his dad. He misses him."

"Well, I'm not gay. And I don't give a shit about Freddy, or Rick, so I don't see how Britt and I are alike." I can tell Dennis doesn't think too highly of Britt's father. Maybe it's Dennis and I that are more alike.

"He deserted you both. Selfish bastard if you ask me." The numbers on Britt's machines start moving. Yeah, he can hear us.

I run my hand through my hair and try to keep my anger in check. "Did Britt play ball when he was a kid?"

Dennis looks confused. "Well, he's fairly athletic, so I would guess so. I know he liked to go fishing. His family traveled a lot. I don't know."

I feel my face heating up as I think of my father taking his new wife and kid on vacations, while my mother scrimped to raise us on her own. I force myself to take a deep breath. *Not this guy's fault*, I remind myself. *I'm not Roland.* "My dad left the week before I started kindergarten. The first day, I remember drawing a picture of him and me and asking my teacher to help me write the words 'I miss you, Daddy' at the top. No daddy came to my ball games. I fished alone, and the only airplane I've ever been on was an army transport." I nod toward Britt. "I was *deserted*. They had a disagreement." The numbers on the machines are all over the place, and I walk outside the curtain. Damn, I have to get this under control.

Dennis follows me. "I'm sorry. I didn't mean to assume… you're right. I can't imagine what that had to be like." Two nurses are watching us from their station, and Dennis nods to them and gives them a wave.

Down the hall, Cassie is standing with Angus. "I gotta go, Dennis. Will you let me know when he wakes up?" I do want to meet him. Maybe I'm grasping at something that isn't there, but… hell, I don't know.

"Sure. His mom is here. Would you like to meet her? She's pretty awesome."

I shake my head. My mom was pretty awesome too.

Dennis's hand is on my arm. "Thanks for coming. It'll mean a lot to him." He pauses for a second but doesn't remove his hand. "Can I ask you something? Are you going to go see Rick? He doesn't have much time left, so…"

"No. I won't give him the satisfaction." He wants to apologize to me? For what? Everything? No, that isn't going to happen. Dennis lets go of my arm, and I walk down the hall toward Cassie.

"You have to tell him," I hear Angus say when I walk up to him and Cassie.

"Tell me what?" I ask. Cassie turns, and her mouth drops open when she sees me, as if I've caught her trying to steal candy from a kid.

She looks at Angus then back to me. "I need to talk to Grams."

Chapter 9
Cass

CLAY AND I DON'T TALK much on the way home. He tells me what the boyfriend said, and I tell him the mom was a bitch, and we leave it at that. When we get home, he kisses me and goes into the house, and I leave for Grams's.

Grams always wanted a big fancy car, but she and Grandpa Jack never made that kind of money. Ten years ago, some lady in Joplin died and left her grandkids a big pink Cadillac that she got by selling makeup. The car was already ten years old at the time, and they didn't have any use for it, but Grams wanted it badly. She bought it for a song, and it usually sits in her driveway with a cover over it. Since my truck is still in jail, she let me borrow it. I feel like I'm crawling into a vat of bubblegum every time I get in. But it's transportation, which is perfect because I need to talk to Grams, and Clay wanted to play with his worms.

She doesn't see me when I walk through the front door, but I can see her. The Doors are playing from her bedroom, loud enough to make the candles on the coffee table flicker. Grams is in the kitchen with her back to me. She is washing dishes in the sink and shaking her behind like a teenager, while Jim Morrison screams "light my fire."

Grams may be in her eighties, but she acts much younger. Maybe she does see a lot and knows that being old is no fun. Maybe she has painted her house different colors to protect her from things like aging.

I stand in the doorway and watch her for a second, trying to mimic the way she moves her hips. "I never could do that," I yell over the music.

She turns around and dances her way toward me, grabs my hips, and makes them sway. "Sure you can, honey."

She's in a good mood, and I hate to change that. "I need to talk," I say.

She makes her way to her bedroom and turns the music down. When she comes back in the kitchen, she's holding a lit candle. She sets it in the middle of her dinette and drops into one of the chairs, motioning for me to sit in the other.

"Don't do it," she says.

I haven't said anything yet, and already, she's telling me what not to do. I guess she assumes that if I have something serious on my mind, it must mean trouble.

"I haven't even said nothing yet," I say.

"Okay, say what's on your mind. Then I'll tell you not to do it."

I reach out and grab her hands in mine. Blue veins are thick over thin skin, but I know her hands are strong. "I'm not doing anything, Grams, but I need your help."

"Are you feeling okay, honey?"

I take a deep breath. "I felt better before that pee stick turned blue."

Grams claps her hands together as if she can't hardly wait to get her new toy. Given that I'm the one carrying the toy around, I can't say I am as excited.

"Don't tell Clay," I say.

"What? Cass, he is going to be so excited."

"Please," I say. "I don't want him to know. Not yet. He's got a lot on his mind right now, and so do I."

"Have you called Lola? She'll be so excited."

I shake my head. I'm sure my sister will be as giddy as Grams about me having a baby. I need to tell Lola. And Maryanne. The more people that know, the realer it becomes.

Grams gets up and gives me a big hug. "How about some cobbler? I've got blackberry, your favorite."

"I'm not real hungry."

"Well, that would be a first. You're eating for two now."

I've always hated hearing people say that. I'm not eating for two. I'm eating for one, and there happens to be something inside of me that's taking a little bit. Hell, I don't even know if it likes cobbler.

"This wasn't supposed to happen, Grams." Despite all those years of trying to get pregnant, I never thought much about what kind of reaction I would have if I *were* to get pregnant. Once, when I was eighteen, I thought

I was, but it wasn't because I was having any morning sickness or anything like that. I don't remember feeling anything. I simply woke up one day and decided I was pregnant. Roland married me on the spot, which was fine. Thinking back, maybe I was trying to get him to say "I do."

But this is different. I'm sick. I don't want to eat blackberry cobbler, and all I can think about is how much I would like another foot-long chili coney dog from Sonic with lots of onions.

"Honey, things happen in their own time. Yours is a little later than we expected. But it will be fine. You're healthy, and you have a good man beside you. Everything will be just fine."

I'm a little worried about Clay. I mean, he's got one kid, and Shaylene is a grown woman now. We're talking about a baby here, an itty-bitty person that we will have to take care of all the time. Clay's forty. And I'm crazy.

"I've never even had a puppy, Grams." I always wanted a puppy. When I was a child, Grams and Grandpa Jack never brought it up. Once I was with Roland, he told me he wasn't about to take care of a dog, and he was sure I would forget to feed it. He may have been right. But still, I always wanted one.

"A baby is a lot different than a puppy," Grams says.

Yeah, I know that. But if I never had a chance to practice on a puppy, who knows what I'll forget with a baby?

"How is Clay feeling today?" Grams loves Clay. It's hard not to. I tell her about our visit to the hospital this morning, and she hangs on my words. "Why don't I read your cards?" Although we were supposed to do our readings last night, we never got to them with all the excitement. I know Grams loves doing them, and she doesn't get to as often as she used to. Once in a while, one of the ladies from town will sneak over in the evening, when there isn't much chance of anyone seeing her, and ask Grams to read her cards. It makes Grams happy.

"Okay." I don't care if she does or not, but I do like to see her happy.

She gets up from the table and goes to her bedroom. When she gets back, she pulls the worn cards from their pack. The deck is familiar to me, but I'm not quite sure what the pattern on the cards is called. It always reminded me of purple stars with big sunflowers in the middle. The cards are thin, and the colors have faded with age. Grams shuffles them twice and sets the deck in front of me. I cut them a little less than halfway off the top.

She turns the top card over and lays it in front of me. "The Moon!" she says. The card shows two wolves, standing on either side of a small pond with a giant lobster in the water. She studies the card for a minute then starts to nod. "Well, I guess that makes sense."

"What do two wolves and a lobster have to do with me?" There are also two towers in the background. I don't get it at all.

"Well, honey, this card is pretty common for those of us that have the sight. It means your visions are going to be a lot stronger for a while, which makes sense, since you're pregnant."

"That's it? Great." My sight, as Grams calls it, is seeing a few dead people, usually Old Man Booker and sometimes Roland. Nobody knows that except Angus, and I'm not too happy about seeing the ghosts any more than I already do.

"See those towers in the background? They represent choices. You've got some to make, and with the Moon, you might do some things you're okay with at the time, but later, you will wish you hadn't. It's a tough card for you. Your mind will be playing tricks on you. Don't let it fool you."

The thing about Grams's readings is this: I know she sees a lot more in the cards than she shares. I know every card has a light side and a darker side, but she tries to find the good to tell people. If the good part of the Moon card is my mind playing tricks on me, I'm not sure I want to know what else it could mean.

Grams flips two more cards. The first is a woman sitting between two pillars, one black and one white. She resembles a female pope with a moon on her head, and she is reading a scroll. The second is a king holding two cups.

Grams taps the second one and smiles. "The King of Cups! That's Clay, and he loves you dearly, but we already know that. This card also means he wants a family and he is going to be the best daddy in the world. Oh, this is such a wonderful card to get. Wonderful."

"What about the one in the middle, Grams?" I know the name of the card: the High Priestess—another woman in between me, the wolves howling at the moon, and Clay, the king with two cups.

"That's another decision card. See the two pillars on either side of the priestess? Choices. But it's more about holding off on any decisions. Remember, the Moon says, if you do something rash, you may regret it."

She pauses for a second and looks at me with a funny expression. "Cass, you're going to have a baby. I think you're right to hold off on telling Clay for a bit. Maybe you need to wrap your own mind around it first."

"I wish Clay was here. I'd like to see his cards." He's acting funny, which I guess can be expected. I know I haven't been very supportive, but I have my own problems, and I know he'll figure out what to do with his. He always does. And besides, I already know he'll end up going to Los Angeles. I sure hope he doesn't want me to go too. It was hard enough holding my tongue with the plastic Barbie at the hospital. I doubt I would fare too well with Freddy Adams.

Grams smiles. "Well, give me a minute." She picks up the cards, puts them back in their deck, and takes them back to her room. When she comes back, she has another deck with her. She opens them up and lays them on the table.

"Remember when Clay was fumbling with a deck last night? I knew he didn't want me to read his cards, but I wanted him to touch the deck anyway." She takes the top three cards and places them face down in front of her.

"So you tricked him?" That isn't like Grams, but I have to admire her efforts.

She dismisses the thought with a wave of her hand. "It's all right. It was Halloween. Tricks are part of it."

I don't think it works that way, Grams.

She flips the first two cards over. The first is a man sitting on a throne with two rams. The man is holding a scepter and a globe. The throne is on top of a mountain—not a pretty green mountain, but an empty, lonely one. It's the Emperor—I know that card—and it's upside down. The second shows two children playing, with six cups around them. It's upside down too. Grams is studying them with a funny look on her face. I can see that one deep line, what she calls her thinking line, in between her eyebrows.

"What's wrong, Grams?"

She's slowly tapping her finger on the upside-down Emperor. "Oh, nothing, honey. Just considering."

I know she's trying to make light, but I think I know what's wrong. I tap the Emperor. "I know this card, Grams. This means a male figure, and it's upside down. I know it's somebody rotten, so it's Clay's daddy." That wasn't very hard. Maybe I should start reading cards too.

I tap the next card, the one with children playing around the cups. "What about this one?"

"Well, it usually means childhood memories. It's upside down, too, which means bad childhood memories."

"Yep, Clay's daddy again. Grams, he says he doesn't want to see him, but I know he does, although I can't figure out why. I mean, I sure as hell wouldn't. I can't imagine that Clay would forgive him after all these years."

"Clay's a good man, honey. You have to remember, you ain't him. Whatever he feels he needs to do, you need to be there to support him. He'll make the right choice." She taps the last card with a crooked finger. "One more card."

I nod my head, and she turns the last card up. A bunch of naked men are rising up from graves, and Gabriel is blowing his trumpet overhead. I know that card too.

Judgment.

"This is a strong card for him right now. He's making some life-changing decisions and finding some peace with his past so he can move on." Grams seems satisfied with the card, but I'm not so sure. It seems too easy. And I know from experience that "easy" never is.

Chapter 10

Clay

THE BLACK CAT CLOCK IN the kitchen screeches a meow, and I damn near drop the casserole I just pulled out of the oven. Cassie saved the clock from her house before she burned it to the ground because it had been my mother's. It was a thoughtful thing to do, and I'll never let her know that I hate the thing. It used to scare me when I was a kid with those eyes looking all around as though it knew what I was doing, that tail that never changed pace, and that loud screech on the hour. It reminds me of Roland.

Cassie asked me about Britt on the way home, and I replayed the conversation I had with Dennis. She spent most of the drive gazing out the passenger window. She had something on her mind. I hope she isn't worried about me, because I can handle this. I just need to figure out the best way to do that. I was glad she wanted to go see Babe the minute we got home because I wanted to be alone for a while. She probably sensed that too.

I started packing up castings to fulfill some of the orders I've gotten this week, but even the worms reminded me of my dad. Instead, I decided to cook dinner, something special so when Cassie got back from Babe's, we could eat a nice meal, maybe watch *Top Gun* or something, and relax by a fire. I want to forget about all this stuff for the day, but I don't know for sure if I can.

It would be nice to know the full story, though, at least the story from Freddy's point of view. It's funny how people can justify their actions, especially after years have gone by. It would be interesting to hear how he does that. I know Momma's side—hell, I lived her side. No, there isn't much he could say to justify the pain he caused her.

I wonder if he told Britt anything much about it? Dennis seems to be an all-right guy, and I hope that Britt is innocent in all this too. I want to know why he sought out Roland first and not me. I'm the oldest. It should have been me. But even if he had, I still wouldn't have wanted to see Freddy Adams. I refuse to call him my dad any more.

This afternoon, as I walked past the visitors' lounge in the hospital, I glanced in and saw a blond woman that must have been Stefanie Adams. She may be great, as Dennis said, but I don't want to know. Cassie told me about their brief interaction, and I'm glad she spoke her mind. I've heard the rumors that my dad left town with some blond woman, but I don't know if that woman was Stefanie. If it was, she knew about my momma, Roland, and me, and I don't like her for that at all. If he didn't leave with her... Hell, there are so many ifs and so many questions, it's making my brain hurt. If I want to know, I'm going to have to open myself up, not something I do much. And do I really want to know?

The phone rings, and I hope it's Cassie, saying she's on her way home. But it's a Texas number, and I know it must be Dennis. I hit the answer button, put it on speaker, and lay the phone on the dining room table.

"Clay, I didn't mean to offend you when you were here this afternoon. I'm sorry if I did. You're right. Your situation and Britt's are completely different. But he's not the bad guy, and he doesn't want to be a stranger to his own brother."

"How's he doing?"

"About the same. He's waking up more but not saying much. He's going to be hurting for a while, but everything will eventually heal."

I take a breath. "Dennis, I have a lot of questions."

"I know you do, and I wish I could answer them. I wish Britt could answer them. But in reality, there's only one person who can. And there's no guarantee he's going to tell anyone the truth either way."

I know he's right. No matter how many bits and pieces I pull together, in the end, only Freddy Adams can speak for his own actions. I used to tell myself that he was dead, and strangely, that made me feel better about him not being around. As I got older, I believed that in some way. He left, so why else would he never come back? Either he didn't care two licks about Roland and me, or he must be dead. If he was dead, he had an excuse I could forgive him for, so that's the theory I always went with. Now that I know better, he has no excuse, and the thought of seeing him brings out feelings I've had tucked inside for a lot of years. I'm angry. I want to kill him, and I have to get that under control.

I clear my throat. "Yeah, but I'm not giving him the chance to explain. That's what he wants, and I'm not giving it to him."

"He wants a lot more than forgiveness," Dennis says.

Forgive him? Not a chance. There isn't anything he could say that would make me forgive him for what he did to his family, *my* family. And what could he want more than that?

I hear Cass pulling in outside, but I'm not feeling very hungry any more. "Thanks, Dennis. I gotta go, but keep me posted. I do want to meet Britt." And that's true. Maybe it's curiosity, or maybe I'm grasping at a brother I never had. I don't know.

"Something smells good." Cassie walks in, throws her purse on the couch, and gives me a kiss on the cheek. Her eyes are red, and her face is puffy.

"You been crying?" I grab her by the waist and pull her onto my lap. Her hair smells like strawberries, and I bury my face in it and breathe it in.

"I'm tired and hungry. And I want to take a nice long bath."

I wish it were that simple. "I don't want you to worry about me, if that's what's making you upset. I can handle this." I don't want her to feel bad. *Damn you, Freddy Adams.*

She fidgets on my lap then relaxes. "I know you can." Her attention moves to the black cat on the wall.

I don't try to imagine what goes on in her mind, but I can usually tell when she's struggling with something heavy.

"Is there something else, Cassie?" I can feel her shaking, and although she isn't one to spook easily, she seems scared. I just don't know about what.

She lays her head on my shoulder. "I never had a dog when I was a kid. Never."

That's not what I expected. I wait, expecting her to say more, but she swats at something imaginary in the air and jumps from my lap. "Let's eat and try to get some sleep. Tomorrow is going to be a big day."

I'm not quite sure what she means by that. With everything that's happened in the past two days, I can't imagine tomorrow being any bigger.

Chapter 11

Benny

THIS MORNING, THE TEMPERATURE WAS a decent fifty degrees. The sun was shining, not a cloud in the sky. But now it's eight o'clock in the evening, windy, and the temperature has dropped twenty degrees. I would like to say this is unusual for November, but in Kansas, the unpredictable is almost expected. I turn the heat up in the Tahoe and drive down Nineteenth Street toward my mom's house. I sure hope it doesn't decide to start snowing before I can get back home.

My mom is the kindest person I've ever known. But that doesn't mean she's soft. She's not at all. She's a petite woman and always has been, but she was raised with seven brothers on a farm in southeast Oklahoma, and she is stronger than some men I know. Hell, she's in her sixties, and I still wouldn't bet on a wildcat against her. I'm not even going to say she wouldn't kill someone. I've seen her as mad as a hungry bear, and I imagine in the right situation, she would take a life to save her own… or to save mine. Hell, she would even do it to save that no-good Tenesy.

Mom was also a friend of Freddy Adams, and I figure I should let her know what's going on. Rudy said Tenesy knew all along where Freddy was, but that doesn't mean my mom knew.

I drive by the road that leads out to the airport. It's dark, and not much goes on out this way anymore, especially at night. There was a time when this road was hopping, back before the Amvets bar caught on fire when the mines were still in operation. But now it's just an empty road that takes you out of Deacon and into Oklahoma. The woods to my right are dark, but I look anyway, maybe expecting a ghost to jump right out at me. But none do.

When I was a kid, we lived in a small house on Seneca Road, west of Military Avenue and south of Twenty-second Street. Our road was basically the last street in town. We had a nice house, not run down or anything, and Tenesy kept it fixed up. It was old, and after I grew up and moved away, it got older.

After Tenesy went to jail the last time, Mom sold that house and moved into a brand-new doublewide. Her trailer sits on land in Oklahoma, just outside the city limits of Deacon. I hate that my mom lives out here by herself. I tried to convince her to at least get a place in town, where she would be closer to Grace and me.

"I can handle this place until Tenesy gets back," she had said. I didn't have any doubt about that. She's a tough lady, and I pity anyone who crosses her. "And I want your dad to have a nice home waiting for him when he gets out," she had added. That, I doubt. The getting-out part, that is. His original sentence was for thirteen years, and he wasn't expected to serve more than four. He's now been there for eight years. My dad has found ways to get into more trouble in prison than out.

As I cross the Oklahoma state line, I turn left on the road that leads to my mom's trailer. It's even darker down here. One streetlight turns everything an eerie yellow. Damn, I wish she would move back to town, but she won't. She has taken to being out here where it's quiet and nobody is in her business.

The road to her trailer is winding, and I have to drive slowly to avoid the potholes and watch for any wildlife aiming to be roadkill. It's paved for the first half mile, but the last quarter is gravel. It's a bitch to navigate in the dark or when it rains and damn near impossible when it snows hard.

Still, there's no missing her trailer. It's as lit up as a drunk on Saturday, and Rudy Drown's car is in the drive.

Rudy is standing on her front porch with his arms wrapped around her like a bear.

I barely get my truck in park before I'm out the door. "What in the name of all things holy is going on?" I yell.

They step back from each other, as if it makes any difference.

"Benny, stop," my mother says. "Rudy came to let me know about Freddy. It's horrible."

I'm on the porch with them, and I'm breathing hard. I'm so close that I can smell Rudy, and he smells like fried chicken. I stick my finger so close to his nose that if he sneezes, he'll lose a nostril. "You stay away from her."

He laughs, and it's all I can do not to slap him off the porch. "Josie and I are friends. Good friends. Ain't that right, Josie? And besides, her house being outside the city limits, and me being the sheriff and all—"

"Rudy, I don't care if you are the king of Kansas," I say. "This is Oklahoma. You stay away from my mother."

"Excuse me, boys." Mom has her hands on her hips. "Rudy, quit making it sound like we are more than friends. You'll ruin my reputation." I swear she winks at him, which makes me want to hurl right there.

"And you"—she turns to me—"I am a grown woman, and you will not decide who can and cannot come to my house. Both of you—a man is about dead, and all you can do is fight with each other. Benny, you are more like your father—"

I hold a hand up. "No."

Rudy is off the porch and moving toward his car. "Benny, you're digging in an empty hole, but hey, go ahead. Remember what I said, Josie. I'll see you soon."

I watch him get in his car and make sure he is out of the driveway before I turn back. I follow Mom inside and stand in her living room, too worked up to even sit. There's a photo album on the coffee table and two empty glasses.

"What was he doing here?" I know Rudy and my parents were friends years ago, but I did not know that Rudy has been visiting my mom while my dad has been away. I'm a tad pissed about that, considering he's the one who busted Tenesy to begin with. But I'm more pissed that my mom hasn't told me they still carry on.

"Oh, sit down. He came out to let me know about Freddy. Honestly, I'd expect my own son to do that, but I guess you were too busy." She picks up the glasses and takes them to the kitchen.

I shed my coat and sit on her couch. "I am here to do that. But I *have* been a little busy, doing my job and everything."

When she returns, she has two cups of coffee and a plate of warm peanut butter cookies. She puts the plate on the coffee table next to the worn photo album and sits next to me. Grabbing the album in front of her, she flips a few pages then points to a picture. I move closer to her and look at a faded Polaroid of her and Freddy Adams, standing in front of the Amvets. Mom has big fluffy hair, parted in the middle, and wings for bangs. She is wearing a pair of shorts that hit her about mid-thigh and a Steve Miller Band T-shirt. Freddy has one arm around her, his hand on her waist, and the other is clutching a beer can. They both have big smiles on their faces. Freddy's dark, curly hair and dimples remind me that he's the spitting image of his son Roland.

A dozen other people are milling around in the background of the picture. Some are familiar, but I can't put names on them. My dad isn't in the crowd. "Where's Tenesy?"

"He was taking the picture. This was the last night we saw Freddy. It was my birthday, and we had moved the party outside. There were so many people at the Amvets that night. It was hot, and we decided to get some air." She points to a picture of Freddy and Tenesy. They're wearing dark glasses and business hats, and their arms are crossed in front of their chests. "They thought they were the Blues Brothers. Oh, they were funny. And here." She points to another photo, but I stop her.

"Tell me about him."

She keeps flipping through the album and stops on one page. She's staring at a picture of Freddy sitting at a picnic table with two little boys. One is blond and wearing the dark sunglasses from the other picture. The other has dark hair. His hands are spread wide, and his mouth is open as though he's telling a story. Clay and Roland. They're all laughing.

"Everybody loved him. He was funny, smart, and not afraid of anything. Well, that's not true. He was afraid of one thing—your father—but they were the best of friends. They got in a big fight in high school, but instead of hating each other, they realized they were a force together and became buds. Rudy was with them. He followed Freddy around like a pup, taking the leftovers. He never had the looks or the personality to get the girls like Freddy did, but Rudy would snag one every once in a while. He was a nice enough guy, but dumb, real dumb." She laughed. "Hard to believe he's now the sheriff of Cherokee County."

No shit.

"Where was Freddy's wife in all this?" I see several pictures of him and the boys, but I don't see anyone who might be Donna Sue Adams.

"She didn't come out with us. She did when they were dating, but once she had kids, she didn't party any more. Stayed home, cooked, and cleaned. Tried to get Freddy to stay home with her, but he was a free spirit. He loved her, though, in his own way. He used to say, 'There are women to marry and women to party with, rarely are they the same.' I, of course, was an exception to that rule." She smiles as if that is something to be proud of.

I don't know how I got to be so responsible. It certainly didn't come from my parents. I can't imagine leaving Grace at home and going out with other women. Maybe I just got a good one, I don't know, but it sure seems that cheating must be a lot of work.

"Sounds like a great guy," I say sarcastically. Reminds me of his youngest son, Roland. I wonder if womanizing is something passed down in the genes. I flip the album back to the first picture she showed me of her and Freddy standing outside the Amvets. "What happened the last night anybody saw him?"

"We were at the Amvets, and we were coming and going as usual. Freddy was hanging out with Vera Shatner, Cass's mother. He thought the world of that nutty broad. They would drink with us, go outside for a while, then come back in, like everyone else. It was a revolving door out there. It'd get so hot inside, and of course we'd go outside to smoke a joint once in a while."

It's kind of hard listening to your mother talk about pot-smoking and getting liquored up as if that's what the average person does on a Saturday night. After growing up around it, I shouldn't think it's a big deal. But it is. It's against the law.

"Freddy took Vera home and then went home early, and Tenesy and I eventually got drunk and came home. That's about it." She leans forward and takes a drink from her coffee then sets it back on the saucer.

"Where was Rudy? I thought he was always around too." Hell, I know he always was. He slept on our couch so often that I thought he was an uncle until I was seven.

Mom leans back on the couch, crossing one leg over the other. "I don't know. I was drunk. I didn't have any reason to babysit Freddy or Rudy that night."

I pick up the album. "I'll bring it back. I want to make some copies for Clay."

"How is Clay taking it?"

"He went to visit the kid today, but I don't know if he plans to go see his dad or not. It's a lot to take in." I stand, but she grabs my arm so hard that I almost drop the photo album and pulls me back onto the couch.

"Oh no, he can't do that." Her voice shakes, which is unusual because she is usually pretty cool headed.

"Mom, what the…"

She pushes a stray hair behind her ear and clears her throat. "Freddy's been gone so long, and things are fine for Clay. He doesn't need to talk to him. Freddy might say something that Clay doesn't want to hear."

He already knows his dad was an ass, so what more could there be? "Like what?"

She shakes her head. "There's so much, and it's in the past. It needs to stay there."

"Clay's a grown man, Mom. He can handle whatever secrets Freddy has."

She taps her hand on the photo album. "Kids always think they can handle their parents' secrets at any age. That is, until they hear them."

Chapter 12

Lola

"I talked to the sheriff's office today, and there won't be a problem for Cass. A bit surprising that the sheriff was so quick to drop it, but sometimes once they know a first-rate attorney is involved, they lose their ability to bully, and back off." Richard is standing in his bathroom with the door open, and I can see him in the mirror, putting on deodorant. He's wearing nothing but his Speedo underwear, and his thin, loose skin looks pasty white against the deep red of his bikini. He's showered, brushed his teeth, and is now applying deodorant. I feel my toes curl up. I know what deodorant means.

The first time I saw Richard in his underwear, I almost laughed. I thought it was the male equivalent of lingerie, worn to entice me into sex. Not that seeing his wrinkled, withered body in tight undies would turn anyone on. But I didn't laugh, and it's good that I didn't. He says they are the only underwear he finds comfortable. He claims they hug his crotch tightly, which makes him feel as if he's constantly getting a mini hand job, even when he's wearing his thousand-dollar suits in court. He says they make him feel manly.

"I'm worried about Clay," I say. Grams called this evening and spilled everything. I'm a bit anxious about Cass, my baby sister, being pregnant at thirty-seven. But that's more exciting than concerning. Clay's problem, on the other hand, must feel overwhelming. And he's a man, which means he won't get over it easily.

"He's a man. People leave, and we get over it," Richard says, as though reading my thoughts. Here we go again. He's thinking about Esther, his first wife. Esther left him over twenty years ago. Once the kids were raised and she was left alone with him, she up and left. They had tried to enjoy life, or so he says, and were traveling across the country, something they'd always wanted to do. Somewhere in western Nebraska, while Richard was busy gawking at a Stonehenge replica made of cars, she disappeared. She got in a truck with some good buddy and was gone.

He got divorce papers in the mail from somewhere in upstate New Hampshire and paid dearly for their twenty-plus years of marriage. Esther's now living with a bartender in a cabin in the woods, spending her days painting or shoeing horses.

Despite his casual dismissal when I bring her up, I know Richard can't forget her. I've seen a picture of the bartender, and I'm quite sure he would look better in the Speedo. But I would never say that to Richard. He is a wonderful man. He's very good to me. But this isn't about him and Esther. A spouse leaving is a bit different than your father leaving you. I know from experience.

"Well, it's a lot to take in," I say. "And although his dad left, now he's come back after so long." I've gotten past the fact that my father deserted Cass and me, and I've moved on with my life. But if he were to suddenly reappear, it would disrupt all that I've hidden over the years, and that isn't a pot I want stirred. I'm sure Clay has some stored-up emotions as well. I wonder what Richard would do if Esther showed up on our doorstep.

I finish filing my nails and put the emery board on the bedside table. Richard shuts off the light in his bathroom and walks toward the bed. I consider rolling over and claiming I have a headache or pretending to sleep, but my mental calendar says it's been two weeks. I know from past experience that two weeks is the brink of how long you can effectively hold off a man without him wanting to stray. Well, with my first two husbands, it was more like two days, but with Richard, it's two weeks. He is almost eighty, after all, and although he won't admit it, an active libido went about the same time his hairline did.

Richard stands next to my side of the bed, as if he's waiting for an invitation. I take a slow breath and give him one. "Come to bed, Richard. Tomorrow is a long day."

He smiles and wiggles his eyebrows. I hate that, but I smile back. It's not that I don't love him. I do. I have an unlimited credit card and a beautiful house in one of the most enviable Springfield neighborhoods. I have a cook and a housekeeper. I have pretty much anything I want. All I have to do in return is look pretty, smile for his friends, not get drunk in public, and have sex with him once every two weeks. But that's the part I don't particularly care for—sex—in general.

Grams asked me about my sex life today, and I cringed a bit. *Don't remind me*, I thought. Besides, who talks about sex with their grandmother? She said my colors were off the last time I saw her and that would explain it. She's making me a special tea that she says will help. I promised I would drink it, but I don't see the point. Richard is happy, and I'm fine.

"I'm going to release the monster," he says in a deep voice as he pulls his Speedo to his ankles and slides out of them. He stands with his legs spread, balled fists resting on his hips, like some naked, aged superhero ready to save the world. I giggle. *You're not going to save the world with that, Superman.*

My first lover was ten years my senior, and he knew how to rock my world. Sex was amazing, always different, and he lived by the rule that "Lola comes first." I was twenty, and I thought I had discovered the secret of life: orgasms. It didn't take long before I realized that men who took their time were worse about using sex as a weapon than women were. He could control me with it. I took his abuse. I took his infidelity. I took it all as long as Lola came first. I thought it was love, but when I got pregnant, I soon learned how alone I truly was.

After breaking away from that, I tried to find another man who wasn't as mean but just as horny. Most, though, were only interested in pleasing themselves. I'm not sure some of them even realized women were supposed to have orgasms. Finding some satisfaction became a useless attempt, so I changed my perspective.

Now, I see sex as the equivalent of cleaning toilets. It's a dirty job, but I don't have to do it very often, and it doesn't take too long. When it's done, it's done. I wash my hands and know I can sit comfortably for the next interval in between cleanings. I don't actually clean toilets anymore. I have a housekeeper for that. Why can't Richard be more of an ass and have sex with the staff?

"Well, come save me, Hulk." I hate it, but I do remember enough from my younger days to know how to get it over with quickly. And I use that knowledge. I have a mindful of dirty words at my disposal, which I practice in the bathtub, where Lola still comes first. I know which way to move, what to say, and when to grab that bony ass and push him to the breaking point. I lie there and count strokes. My record is eight. He makes it to thirty-four.

"Sorry," he gasps. "Damn, you have to be quiet. You know I can't hold it when you talk like that."

"It's okay, honey. Really." And it is. The day he takes his last thrust, I'll have ten million and a lake house. The rest will go to his two daughters, which is fine. I'll be fine. I try to calculate in my head. Those few minutes were worth about three hundred thousand a stroke. Not bad at all. I give Richard a full minute to settle in bed and catch his breath before returning to the conversation I wanted to have.

"And of course, there's Cass," I say. "I called today and got her an appointment with Dr. Button and Dr. Gross. Grams is bringing her up tomorrow."

"Cass, pregnant. Now, that's a bigger shock than the missing dad, isn't it?" He puts an arm around me and pulls me close. I don't mind that part.

"I'm going to go back with them after the appointment tomorrow. Grams said Cass is acting funny, and with the Clay thing and the baby thing, Grams might need some help with her for a few days." I've gotten to know a lot more about Cass since she killed her husband. She does pretty well when her life is uncomplicated, which it has been for the past few months with Clay. But when things get to a point where she doesn't know what to do, she reacts in odd ways. Last time, she killed her husband. I don't want her to kill anyone else.

"Of course. Do whatever you can." Richard cares for my sister in some strange way. They are night and day, and she makes fun of him every chance she gets, but there's something about her that makes him smile. Maybe it's paternal, I don't know. But I'm very glad he has no qualms about me running off to Deacon for a few days when I feel she needs me.

"I'm going to take a bath." I lean over and kiss his cheek, then roll back and get up. I bend over to grab his discarded Speedo, and he slaps my ass. I throw him his drawers, glancing at my nails to make sure I didn't crack one.

"I hope she's okay," he says.

I presume he's talking about my sister, but I know in my heart that it's Esther he's worried about.

I grab clean pajamas from my bureau, and over my shoulder, I whisper, "I'm sure she's fine."

I sit naked on my vanity stool while I wait for the water to fill the bath, then I turn on the whirlpool jets. I have enough of my Himalayan bath salts to last a year, and I generously fill the steeping ball with the fragrant mixture and place it in the water. As the bathroom fills with the scent of rosemary and peony, I feel my muscles begin to relax even before I get into the water. I hadn't realized I was so tense.

As I lie back in the hot tub, my thoughts go to Cass. I know her life with Roland was hell, and no one noticed. I do feel bad about that. I hate thinking that she was being abused, physically and emotionally, and didn't reach out to Grams, me, or anyone.

Although she always said Roland was her soul mate, she never talked about what that meant to her. A woman can claim she's in love because she thinks she's being loved. I know that from experience. But with Clay, things are a lot different. He is definitely not Roland. He's kind and compassionate and seems to truly love my sister.

I scrub my body, paying particular attention to the areas that Richard dirtied. In my own way, I guess I loved all the men I had in my younger days too. I didn't kill any of them, but that doesn't mean I never wanted to.

I know about being pregnant too. Grams said Cass was acting funny and that she didn't want to tell anyone about the pregnancy. I know what that means and what she's feeling. I can't let her think she's alone. I had my chance, and I blew it, but I won't let her do the same. I was lucky—I found Richard, who gives me things I would have never had otherwise. But he can't give me a baby. And what happens when he is gone?

I stand and dry myself with one of the thick towels neatly stacked beside my bath. After putting on my silk pajamas, I crawl into bed next to Richard and listen to him snore. "Please don't die yet," I whisper. *I need you.*

Chapter 13

Benny

It's six a.m., and Grace is already making breakfast. I hadn't expected her to be up so early. I thought maybe I could sneak out without her hearing me, but not a chance. After talking to Rudy and my mom, I need to know the real Freddy Adams story. I guess *need* isn't the right word; I *want* to know. So I called down to the prison and got my name on the visitation list to see Tenesy. It's been a while since I saw my dad, and I'm sure he needs to call me some new names. Knowing how Rudy and Tenesy behaved when they were younger, though, I can't say I have any high expectations that Freddy was the pride of the community.

Grace tried to talk me out of going to Tenesy about it. "It's none of your business, Benny." She's right, of course. Normally, I would listen to her, but Clay deserves to know.

"Are you going to mention to Clay if your father tells you anything?" She raised one eyebrow. She might also be able to read my mind.

"Maybe. Maybe not. I guess it depends on what Tenesy says." My father might know something that could help Clay work his way through his personal drama. If so, then hell yes, I'm going to spill it to him. But if the information is bad, it could make things worse.

"You are needlessly putting yourself in a bad situation," Grace said. "If Tenesy reveals something bad, and you don't share it with Clay, fine. But things always seem to come out, and if—or should I say 'when'—Clay finds out, he'll know that you knew and didn't say anything."

"But I can't decide until I know what it is I'm trying to decide about," I had said. "So I'm going."

Now, I hope she isn't up early just to give me grief about it again. At least she's making breakfast.

I grab a cup of coffee and sit at the dining room table. Grace sets a plate of bacon and eggs in front of me and walks toward the bedroom. "Eat up and change clothes. Wear street clothes. We need to be out of here in the next thirty minutes to get there for visiting hours."

"We?" I hadn't planned on Grace joining me for a trip to the prison. "Damn it, Grace, I don't need an escort."

"And I don't want to sit in this house all day on my day off. It will be fun. Besides, you haven't been to the prison in three years. I wouldn't want you to get lost."

"It hasn't been three years."

"Yes, it has. Eat. I'm getting ready."

She put on her makeup, a pair of jeans, and a sweater that was a little too low cut for a men's prison. Then we left Deacon before sunup, sneaking out by way of the old highway.

I wait until we're thirty minutes down the road then call the hospital to check on Britt. He's still a banged-up mess, so no big change. Dennis is still there and so is the mother. I make a few other calls then sit back and listen to Grace maim "Rhiannon," "Gold Dust Woman," and "Landslide." There's a Fleetwood Mac marathon on the radio. I guess it could be worse.

Hominy, Oklahoma sits forty-five minutes northwest of Tulsa, out in the sticks. Dick Conner Correctional Facility is ten minutes outside of Hominy, which puts it somewhere in the twigs. There isn't much else out here other than a small casino, one road, grass, and the large white buildings that make up the two prisons: medium security and minimum. After showing our identification at the gate, Grace pulls the Tahoe into a numbered parking space in the lot for medium security, right under a sign that warns "VISITORS: LOCK YOUR VEHICLE!" Well, no shit.

An armed guard stands in a metal shack, monitoring the parking lot. Six other guards, all carrying rifles, patrol the top of the fifty-foot block wall that surrounds the prison.

"I hate this," I say. Being at a prison is bad enough, but having to come here to see my own dad makes me ill.

"Oh, stop," Grace says. "It's your dad, and it's about time you came to visit." She takes a lipstick out of her purse and readjusts the rearview mirror.

"I didn't put your name on the list," I admit.

She nods. "I'm going over to the casino. You two need to be alone. And besides, it smells like ass in there." She smacks her lips together and puts the lipstick back in her purse, waiting for me to get out. I take a deep breath, unbuckle my seat belt, and open the door. Grace reaches for my arm as I pull my leg out. "Wait. Leave everything in the truck except your driver's license." She reaches in her purse and pulls out a Ziploc bag full of quarters. "And take these."

I don't even ask. I empty my pockets, pull my ID out of my billfold, and tuck it into my pocket. Then I wedge the wallet into the glove box and take the bag of quarters.

"And mention that you're a cop," she says. "To the guard at the desk, at least. They all want to be cops." Grace gives me a little wave and pulls the Tahoe out of the lot before I can get to the first concrete building.

A large sign with red letters reads, "Visitors, stop here first!" I shake my head. *Damn.*

"I'm—" I start to say.

"Prisoner's name." The guard sitting behind a gray steel desk doesn't even look up when I enter. He's young and skinny and reminds me of Jimmy Ray. His name tag reads Sergeant Deal. Another guard, a female, circles me like a vulture over a wounded rabbit.

"Cloud. Tenesy Cloud. The prisoner," I say, shifting from one foot to the other.

Deal traces his finger down the sheet of paper in front of him and stops on Cloud. "ID."

He examines my driver's license then looks at me. He scratches something on his pad and puts my license in the top drawer of his desk. The female cop starts patting me down without saying anything. I flinch when she touches my groin area, too close for comfort. She pulls the Ziploc of quarters out of my pocket, inspects it, then gives it back to me. By the time she gives the kid behind the desk the thumbs up, I feel as if I'm the one who has done something wrong.

"Have you ever been here before… Ruben?" Deal asks.

It has been a while since anyone called me by my given name. Nobody even knows it except my momma and Grace… and Tenesy. "It's Ben," I say.

Then, remembering what Grace said about mentioning that I'm a lawman, I add, "Chief Cloud. I'm a cop."

Sergeant Deal looks up when I say that and smiles as if I offered to blow him. He stands up and sticks his hand out. "Tim Deal. It's a pleasure. Chief?"

"Deacon, Kansas. Chief of police." I straighten up to my full height. I recognize a suck-up when I see one, but I'm out of my element, and I could damn well use a friend.

Deal points at a sign on the wall. "Visitors are expected to know the rules." But he rattles them off to me anyway. "You are allowed one hug when you first walk in and one when you leave. Holding hands is okay, but no other touching allowed. You sit in the blue chairs, and the prisoner is to stay on the other side of the table in the orange chairs. You may use the vending machine and the restroom if needed." He leads me to a door in the back, opens it for me, and points me to a building fifteen feet away. "Go through there, through the metal detector, and the guards will take you to the visitation room. Any questions?"

I shake my head and start off on the path to building B. *Deal.* I tuck that name in the back of my mind. You never know when a kid like that might come in handy.

Another guard checks me through the metal detector. "You are allowed one hug when—"

"Yeah, I already heard that." I don't intend to hug anyone, especially not Tenesy. Hell, I can't remember when I've ever hugged the man. The last time I remember him even touching me was when I was sixteen, and punching me in the face for being late for dinner doesn't count as a fatherly hug.

The visitation room is made up of glass on three sides and one long white wall. A soda machine, a snack machine, two bathrooms, and a small area with kids' toys are all along the wall. The place is packed tighter than a home-rolled Lucky. Men in khaki jumpsuits sit in orange chairs, and women, men, and kids sit in blue chairs. A little girl, who couldn't be more than three, is running around the room, carrying a dirty rag doll with one eye missing. A guard stands against one of the glass walls, and another sits in a chair next to the soda machine. I nod to them both and walk to an empty table at the edge of the room. A young black woman sits at the table next to me. She's pregnant, sitting at a table with a rough-looking dude in a gray jumpsuit. I sit in a chair, a blue chair, and wait. Grace was right. It smells like ass.

It's been eight years since Tenesy's court hearing, in which he was found guilty as charged with first-degree robbery. The judge wouldn't have given him thirteen years if it had been his first time, but the law was already familiar with him. And the fact that he punched a police officer while he was being arrested didn't help much, even if it was Rudy Drown.

I hate to say I was glad to see him go, but I was. I wasn't chief then, but I was on the force. It was bad enough that I had a loser for a dad, much less a criminal. Sure, he did most of his business across the state line, but lines never meant much to Tenesy. My mom cried. Some women don't realize they are better off with no man than with one who isn't any good. But she cried. And that made me hate him even more.

One of the glass doors opens, and a skinny old man in a gray jumpsuit shuffles through. The little girl runs to him and lifts up her doll. He points to me. "See that big fella over there? He likes dolls." He walks slowly toward my table, talking loudly. "You do still play with dolls, right, Ruben?"

The guard standing against the glass is smiling, and the tough-looking guy at the table next to me stares me down. The old man sits across from me in an orange chair and lifts one side of his upper lip in a sneer I recognize. *Oh damn, Tenesy got old.*

"You look like shit," I say. Tenesy was always a big man, not tall, but wide. His dark-skinned body was always muscular, and he always had a long dark braid down his back. The man across from me is thin, almost bald, and his skin is as dingy as his jumpsuit.

"Well, fuck you too." He puts his hands on the table, and I watch the left one shake. His fingers move together as though he's counting money.

"What's wrong with your hand?" I ask.

He puts the other one on top of it, trying to make it stop, but it's shaking too. He reminds me of one of the druggies I busted last year.

He shrugs. "Sawbones says I got some kind of palsy. Fine by me if it'll get me out of this shithole."

"You're being released?" Now, I know Grace keeps in touch with Tenesy, and I'm already pissed that she didn't tell me how bad he looks. Maybe she didn't because she thought I might take some pleasure in it, which I probably would have. But if he's getting out, she damn sure should have let me know.

"Nah, transferring me to Lexington. Country club living." His right eye twitches, and if I didn't know better, I would think he's winking at me. "Prison ain't what it used to be."

The little girl sits on the white tiled floor next to the black man's chair. He doesn't seem to notice; he's focused more on her momma's cleavage. The two guards look as if they're more bored than I am.

I figure the chitchat is over; it's time to get down to business. "Freddy Adams. Ring any bells?"

Tenesy leans back in his chair. "Yeah. Is he dead?"

"Not yet, but getting there. Bad liver."

Tenesy nods. "Well, you can't blame that one on me, so what the hell are you doin' here?" He doesn't care one way or the other.

"I wanted to know what kind of a guy he was."

He sneers at me again, like a palsied Elvis. "Bullshit. You drove all the way down here for this?"

"I don't expect you to understand. But Clay Adams is a friend of mine, and he's going to have it hard with this, so if I know anything that is going to help him—"

He tries to laugh but starts coughing instead. "So you're being nosy. Figures. It ain't none of your business."

I knew this was going to be a mistake. But I also know if I sit still and take some of his abuse, he'll talk just to keep me around. It's a power thing with Tenesy, but over the years, I've figured it out. I know how to manipulate too.

"Have you let your mom know about Freddy yet?" he asks. It's easy for me to think of Freddy, Rudy, and Tenesy running around Deacon when they were younger, being asses. It's harder for me to remember that my mom was right there too, mixed up with them.

"Yeah, I talked to her last night." I thought about telling him that Rudy beat me to it, but I don't need him going off before I get to hear the whole story.

"You shouldn't have said anything until he was dead. Her and that bleeding-heart shit. She's liable to get on a plane and go hold his damn hand."

I shrug. I'm not promising anything, and he knows it.

He spies the bag of quarters in my hand. "Fine. I ain't got nothin' else to do." He scrunches his lips together and stares at the ceiling. "Freddy was an okay guy. The women loved him, and he took advantage of that. He could outdrink me, which wasn't easy, and he told everyone dirty jokes. He had some doozies."

Tenesy and I have a different measure of what makes a man. "That's an okay guy?"

"He was also good to Donna Sue and them boys. Too good, if you ask me." He points a crooked finger at me, and I resist the urge to grab it and twist.

"Good to them? He cheated on his wife and then abandoned the whole family. He hasn't tried to contact them for thirty-five years." I make a fist on the table and look him in the eye.

"Bullshit. Donna Sue damn sure knew where he was." I stare at his face as he says it. I've been a cop long enough to know how to watch someone's eyes. If they move up and to the left, it means a person is thinking. If they move up and to the right, it usually means he's lying. Tenesy flinches but keeps his eyes straight. "He didn't abandon them. She made him leave."

"Well, if he was sleeping with every girl in town—"

"No." He twitches again and leans in close, a little too close. I can smell his cheap soap and cigarettes. "*He* caught *her*. She rode his ass for years about partying too much, and then he comes home and catches her in bed with another man. *His* bed. Donna Sue wasn't no angel; I don't care what she tried to play out. She tried to get me to do her a few times, but I had the pick of the litter." I see the flicker of a grin and know he's trying to make me mad, another one of his sick games. But I refuse to let that happen.

"She filed a missing person report," I say. It doesn't make sense, and I know that Tenesy is full of crap half the time. I'm hoping this is one of those times.

"Her boyfriend told her she could collect his life insurance after he was gone for seven years. If no one found him, that is. He came back after he'd been gone for a week, and she said she was in love and he needed to move on. Then she filed the report. That ain't true about the life insurance, by the way, but she didn't know no better."

"So he just left? Left his kids, never to contact them again?" Sounds like a fine man to me.

"He wrote them letters. Tried to call, but Donna Sue wouldn't let him talk to them. He finally quit tryin'."

I've questioned a lot of criminals. The professional ones, like Tenesy, don't often give you anything without dancing with you first. I don't know why Tenesy would come right out and spill this, but I'm curious enough to take the bait. "How do you know all this?"

He crosses his arms over his chest. "I know all this 'cause Freddy told me. We kept in touch up until about two years ago. Then he must have got sick and didn't want to talk no more."

"Wait." I stop, realizing what he's saying. "There's an open missing person case on him. You knew where he was, and you didn't say anything?" I'm talking very low, not wanting anyone else to hear but not knowing why that matters.

Tenesy shrugs. "Hell, it wasn't my job to help the law. Missing person, my ass." A thin line of spittle leaks out of the corner of his mouth.

I feel sick to my stomach. I had been expecting Tenesy to tell me about Freddy in his younger days. I didn't think he would know any of the stuff that happened after he left. "He had kids that didn't know. Damn, Tenesy, you really are a sorry ass."

"Hell if they didn't know where he was," Tenesy fires back. "He came back to Deacon about thirteen years ago. The oldest one was in the army, but that younger one, Rolly, he was married to one of them Shatner girls. Freddy couldn't help but tell him how stupid that was. His kid shut him down. Told him to get lost or he'd kill him." The tone of his voice gives me a chill, not to mention the idea that he might, for once in his life, be telling the truth.

I let out a slow breath. Roland knew, and he never told Clay. He never said a word when Britt showed up. "Why would Freddy care who Roland married? He wasn't around."

Tenesy sneers at me again. "You know, you got a lot of questions. Seems you being nosy ain't gettin' shit for me." Tenesy's eyes are small, as though he's trying to shoot fire at me.

I feel sweat on my forehead, but I'll be damned if I let him see me wipe it away. I wave the bag of quarters in front of him, and his gaze goes toward the vending machine that is chock-full of chocolate, chips, and Twizzlers, which I know he loves.

"Vera Shatner was Freddy's side candy. He hit that more than Hank Aaron hit home runs. Can't say I blame him. She was a looker, even if she was flakier than a biscuit."

"That don't make no sense," I argue. "The fact that he slept with Cass's mom back in the day doesn't give him a reason to go back to Deacon after all those years. And how did he even know Roland and Cass had gotten married?"

"I told him," Tenesy says. "He wanted me to go school that boy of his so he'd dump that Shatner girl, but it wasn't my problem, so fuck that."

"I still don't get it. He didn't even know Cass. Hell, he didn't even know Roland, and LA is a long way to—"

He starts laughing, kind of a half-snicker, and I know he's going to call me a dumbass again. Damn, it's hard to believe he's my blood. Then I get it. "Oh shit." Had Roland been married to his half sister? My stomach turned over. "No."

He leans back in his chair, crosses his arms over his chest, and smiles. "You ain't as dumb as you look, Ruben."

I push my chair back and stand up. "We're done here." I'm not whispering, but my voice comes out a bit louder than I intend. The guards don't seem to notice, but the pregnant woman next to us gives us a sideways glance.

"Good. I need my peanut butter balls anyway." He stands up and holds out a hand—for the bag of quarters, I assume. I pitch the whole bag underhand toward the little girl, who's now standing in front of the soda machine with her one-eyed doll under her arm. Tenesy flips me a crooked finger and starts heading for the door. Then he walks back until he's close to me, so close I think he might try to hug me. I watch him sneer for what I hope will be the last time.

"Speaking of sorry asses, how's my buddy Rudy doing these days?" he asks.

Now I'm pissed. I'm not falling for his bullshit again. "This ain't about Rudy."

His head shakes as he tries to focus on my eyes. "No? Who do you think it was that Donna Sue was sleepin' with? The one who talked her into filing that missing person report?"

My feet are suddenly so heavy, they feel like they've become part of the linoleum floor. Tenesy is one of those guys who likes to hold out on a story and throw one last punch, just to see your reaction. I should have seen the blow coming, but I didn't.

Rudy Drown was the boyfriend Freddy caught his wife with. No wonder Rudy wants Britt to get the hell out of town and doesn't want Clay to talk to his dad. He's afraid Freddy will spill the beans, and once he does, Rudy will get thrown in the pot. He knew Donna Sue filed a false missing person report, even talked her into it. That's a scandal bigger than Texas.

"I thought you was leavin'?" Tenesy is laughing again, but I don't care. It's all a game to him, and he doesn't give two sheets that real people are the pawns.

"And Rudy knew about Vera Shatner too?" I ask. Rudy was caught up in something illegal. Roland, and now Clay, were possibly sleeping with their own half sister. If Rudy knew about that, too, and never said anything… Well, that makes him not only a crook, but an asshole.

Tenesy motions to the guard to let him back in and leaves without answering my question. But he doesn't have to. Of course Rudy knew.

Chapter 14

Cass

"You can't say anything, Grams. Not yet."

"But, honey, he needs to know," she says.

After Clay left for work this morning, I dragged myself out of bed, threw on the same clothes I wore yesterday, and went to Grams's house. I need to check on my truck today, and I need to figure out what to do about this baby growing in my belly. I know Grams is worried that if I don't tell Clay soon, I might do something stupid. But maybe what I'm considering isn't so stupid.

"I tried to talk to him last night, but he's got other things on his mind." And I've been thinking, which can be dangerous. I've always wanted a baby. Roland and I tried for years. He said I must have some problem, so we gave up. I guess Roland was wrong. But I'm not as sure about going through with this now. I'll be forty in a few years, and Clay is already there. I'm not worried about him, though. I'm worried about us. I'm worried about me.

Grams is looking at me hard. Maybe she knows what's going on in my mind but doesn't want to say it. "I talked to Lola yesterday. She made you two appointments for today. Your head doctor can tell you whether your medicine is going to interfere with anything. And she knows a baby doctor too. We'll make sure you're healthy."

I can't believe she told Lola. Yes, I guess I can. I don't want to go to either appointment, but I know she's right. I do need to know those things. But it's not only the healthy part I'm worried about. Clay and I are about perfect together. He does his thing, and I do mine, and we seem to click together. I don't want that to end because a baby is thrown into the mix. Maybe I'm already a tad bit jealous of the attention he'll be giving it instead of me. That's silly. It's a baby. And I love babies. And this would be Clay's baby and mine. I would be the momma and… and that's where the other problem comes to mind.

My momma couldn't take being a parent and killed herself, leaving Lola and me with Grams. And I am documented crazy. What if I can't handle it either?

"Okay," I say. Maybe these are things I should be talking to Dr. Button about, anyway. At least if I agree to go, it will keep Grams from blabbing about it to Clay. She's already blabbed it to Lola. I trust my sister to keep her mouth shut, but it isn't about trust. The problem with secrets is that the more people who know one, the easier it is for it to get out. Grams knows. Angus knows. And now we've thrown Lola into the mix.

"She'll keep it quiet," Grams says. "And she's so excited!"

I swear, I'm carrying this thing, and I'm the only one who isn't "so excited" about it. I'm supposed to be the one who is nuts, but so far, I think I'm the only levelheaded one in the bunch. It's a baby, one everyone else will want to play with once it's here. But in the meantime, I'm the one who has to carry it for nine months. And when it comes, I'm the one who will be taking care of it day and night.

I wish I hadn't said anything to Grams about it until I knew for sure what I was going to do. Yes, I always wanted a baby, but now that I might actually have one, I'm not so sure about anything. I don't like decisions, I don't like problems, and I hate to disappoint Grams. I want to say, "Don't get too excited. I haven't decided between the pillars yet."

"Let's get moving," Grams says. "I'll drive in case you need to rest."

So first, I have to be in the pink-mobile all day. Second, since Grams is driving, the forty-five minute trip to Springfield could take a few hours. She hands me a plastic bag that has a jar of pickles and a banana in it. "In case you need a snack. Salty or sweet. Both healthy."

I follow her to the car and crawl in the back. "I'm tired," I say, which isn't exactly a lie. I am a little tired, but most of all, I don't want to talk about babies right now. I fall asleep before we pass Joplin, still holding a bag of Skittles left over from Halloween that I threw in my purse when Grams wasn't looking.

Call Me Daddy

Grams dropped me off at my shrink's and went to pick up Lola. Dr. Button and I had a long talk, mostly about me having a baby inside of me and a little about my mother, Vera. He knows her story and told me that I was a much stronger woman than she was. Well, I haven't hanged myself in a closet like she did, at least not yet. And I was stronger than the wire hanger she tried to use on me before I was born. But that doesn't keep me from thinking that the nut doesn't fall too far from the tree. He gave me a prescription for a different medication that wouldn't interfere with the pregnancy. He also told me I should tell Clay but that in the end, it was my choice. He did urge me to consider my options before I made any decisions.

Grams and Lola aren't due back for another thirty minutes, and I know our next stop is to see another doctor, a baby doctor that Lola knows. While I wait, I decide to do just what Dr. Button suggested: consider my options.

I've walked by this place a few dozen times; it's in the same office building as Dr. Button's office. From the outside and from the sign, it resembles any other medical office—a door with the number 231 and the name Eden Women's Health Clinic printed in block letters. I would never have known it was an abortion place if it wasn't for the protestors standing outside every Friday. Maybe if they didn't stand there advertising, people wouldn't even know.

Prenatal Care, Vasectomy, HIV Testing, Birth Control, Menopause, In-Clinic Abortion. There are rows of pamphlets in the small office, and I can't decide if I want to be here or not.

"Can I help you, ma'am?" A young woman in scrubs stares at me from behind a window of glass. She isn't smiling, but she's not necessarily frowning, either.

"No, I got it." I grab one of the brochures randomly and sit in a brown padded chair. *Genital Warts*. Great. Sounds like wonderful reading material, especially if you've been having sex with toads.

Four women, two of whom might be teenagers, sit in other brown chairs, also pretending to read pamphlets and magazines while listening to the piped-in radio station playing "I Shot the Sheriff." The woman behind the counter calls a name, and a woman dressed in a pink sweat suit with *Princess* stitched across the butt bounces through the door and follows her to the back. I start reading about genital warts.

If you asked me a month ago, I would have said that never in a million years would I consider having an abortion. My momma tried that once, and it didn't work. She ended up in a mental institution and came out with me. But it's like anything else—I say I won't do something, but then I find myself in a situation with all these decisions to make, and things are different. I'm thirty-seven. I take medication to keep me from being crazy. And I've never even had a puppy.

"Ma'am, you need to sign in." The nurse behind the desk seems overly concerned with me sitting in one of her uncomfortable brown chairs. I doubt she would believe I was here to have my warts checked. I walk to the counter and pick up the pen next to the sign-in sheet. *Name.* I scribble, "Cass Adams." *Reason for visit.* "I don't know." I put the pen down and go back to my pamphlet.

The nurse calls another name, Hailey something, and one of the teenage girls stands up. Her face is red, and she holds her stomach as she walks slowly toward the back. The other two women don't say a word, so I figure Hailey is alone. It sucks to be alone. I try to focus on my pamphlets to take my mind off of other things. After deciding that genital warts doesn't look like much fun, I start on *HIV*. It's not much fun, either.

Halfway through *Vasectomies*, the nurse calls my name. I pass Princess on my way to the back. She is standing at the counter with a pink sack, smiling at another nurse and talking about prenatal vitamins. My nurse directs me to a room with a sign on the door that reads, "Counseling." I let out a quiet laugh. I hope it's not a hallway that leads straight to Dr. Button's office. I sit in a red leather chair, a step up from the waiting room chairs, and wait. Pictures of trees and flowers adorn the wall. They seem out of place, but I guess covering the walls with pictures of genital warts and penises might be tacky.

I've never been much for lying to people, never saw much use in it. But I have learned that you can leave things out and not make them so mad at you. I don't care much about getting people riled up, but there are a few I do care about—Grams, Lola, and Clay. I called Clay before we left this morning to tell him I was going to Springfield, but I omitted the "visiting doctors" part, so it wasn't a lie. Grams and Lola already know about the baby, though, which could prove to be a bad thing.

A tall woman wearing a white coat and her hair tied up in a bun walks in and sits behind the desk. She nods to me and tries to smile, but it's fake.

Call Me Daddy

She folds her hands on top of the desk. "Ms. Adams? I'm Sally. What can we do for you today?"

I've never been much for counselors or therapists. They're so nosey. They ask a bunch of questions about me, then try to figure out what's wrong based on my favorite color or whether I put my toilet paper on the roller with sheets coming over the top or under the bottom. I like rainbows, and my toilet paper sits on the counter. Analyze that. And what's wrong with me now doesn't need much figuring out. What I'm going to do about it is a different story.

"I'm pregnant, and I want to know about abortions." There, I said it.

She's taking notes instead of looking at me. I hate that. "Do you know how far along you are?"

"No. Does it matter?"

"Yes, it does." Sally points to the brochures sticking out of my purse. "There are a lot of options if you don't want the baby. An abortion should be your last. Have you read about abortions?"

I shrug. "No. Just genital warts. I don't have those."

Sally nods. "Well, we can talk about all of your options, but you need to be examined first."

"Options? Either I have it or I don't, right?"

"Well, yes, but there is also adoption and—" There's a knock at the door, and Sally looks pissed. "Come in," she yells.

A nurse opens the door. "Ms. Adams, there's someone here who wants to talk to you. She's a bit upset, so maybe you should come." The nurse is wringing her hands and turning back toward the hall. I can hear Lola yelling my name.

I get up and look at Sally. "Sorry, that's my sister. She's not as crazy as I am, but she's close." I walk toward the waiting room, and Lola is standing there in designer jeans and a cashmere sweater. Her face is as red as a rare T-bone. "What are you doing here?" I ask.

"Stopping you from doing something stupid." She grabs my arm and pulls me toward the door. The two women in the waiting room are peeking over their magazines, watching but not watching. "What the hell are you looking at?" Lola says to them. They go back to their magazines.

Lola doesn't lose it very often, so I let her drag me out the door, past the picketers, to Grams's pink Cadillac. I know I'm about to get a lecture, so I get in and wait. She gets in the backseat with me and tells Grams she needs to talk to me for a minute alone. Grams doesn't even question Lola—she would me. Instead, she mumbles something about needing some morning air and gets out of the car. Lola's face is red, and if I didn't know better, I would think she was about to cry. "What are you doing, Cass?"

Lola and I haven't ever been close, but we've never been distant, either. She's older than me by five years, and when we were young, she was more of a momma to me than a sister, even more so after our mother killed herself. But as we got older, we had different friends, and we enjoyed different things. I liked to hang out with Roland and Maryanne. Lola partied with everyone.

"How did you know where I was?" Grams has the sight, and she says I do, too, but Lola has never shown any sign of it or any interest.

"You weren't in Dr. Button's office, and I know you better than you think I do." One of the picketers is standing right in front of our car, waving a sign at us that says, "BABY KILLERS." I flip him the finger.

"I was asking them questions. That's all." I know I couldn't talk to Grams about this, but I figured if anyone could understand, Lola would. She has never had kids, and I kind of think she would have wanted to, but she spent most of her life as a bum magnet, and none of those guys were daddy-worthy. Now that she's married to someone who makes her happy, she's too wrapped up in herself to have a kid, and Richard's too old anyway.

"No. That's how it starts. You ask questions, and then…" She looks away from me, and her voice cracks.

Oh no. I realize Lola has done this before.

"Lola. I…" I'm not good at being the kind of friend who listens, but she is my sister. The truth is that I don't know what to say to her. I guess being straightforward is the way to go. "You had one, didn't you?"

She takes a deep breath and lets it out slowly. "Yeah. Years and years ago."

I let that sink in. "It seems so easy," I finally say.

"It's not easy. First, they try to talk you out of it, give you a list of places you can get support if you need it, and encourage you to talk to your family. That was hard enough, having to make the decision. The procedure itself? That was easy, all right. You go in pregnant; you come out not. Takes about an hour. Simple. Problem solved, and no one knows any different."

I know she's not trying to, but she's making it sound pretty good at this point. I could just go on with my life, and no one would ever know. Problem solved. "So…"

"If I had had the baby, she would be twenty years old now. Imagine, me with an adult daughter."

I can't imagine. "It was a girl?" I don't know what else to say.

She shrugs. "I don't know, but I tell myself it was a girl." She turns to me, and I see she's crying. "You see, I'm not making any excuses. I made the choice, and at the time, it seemed like the right one. And maybe it was, but"—she stops and clears her throat—"but I think about it a lot. I see someone with a baby and think that could have been me. I see someone proud of their kid's stupid win at the spelling bee and think that could have been me. She could have been all the things I wasn't, and I didn't give her a chance."

"She could have been a nutcase too. It runs in the family."

She puts a hand on mine, and I let her. "Is that what you're worried about?"

"Well, yeah. And I'm worried about me too. What if I drop it? Or forget to feed it? Or teach it stupid stuff?"

"You'll have help, Cass. Plenty of help. And all moms teach their kids stupid stuff, but they also teach them good stuff." I can feel her hand shaking, and I feel sorry for her.

"Our mom didn't teach us anything good," I say.

"She taught us to be different than her. I was stupid. I had an abortion anyway, and I pay for it every day. I don't want that to happen to you."

Grams is coming back toward us, and I don't want to leave her out there too long. She stops to talk to one of the picketers. "But I'm not you, Lola."

"If you can't handle it, I'll take her. I'll raise her. I'll adopt her if you want me to. Please, don't even consider this, Cass."

The teenage girl, Hailey, is walking out. She's moving slowly and crying. Several protesters start waving their signs in her face and yelling at her. Lola and I both grab our door handles at the same time. When we get to her, Grams already has her arms around Hailey and is weaving her way through the crowd while picketers scream names at them both.

I get between Grams and one of the people with a sign, blocking his way. "Get away from them, asshole." He's a foot taller and has at least one hundred pounds on me, but I'm not afraid. I've been known to take down men his size.

He starts to say something, but I hiss at him, and he turns away. "That's right," I say. "I am busting with crazy, and I'm not afraid to use it."

Lola has gotten Grams and Hailey to the car, and I jog over without looking back.

Grams pushes Hailey's hair back from her face. "Are you alone, honey?"

The girl points toward a beat-up black Kia in the parking lot. "My boyfriend. He's over there. I need to get to the car." She starts to walk toward it then doubles over and pukes.

Lola hustles to the black Kia and pulls a skinny young guy from the car. "You are supposed to be helping her. Get your ass over there and take some responsibility!" she shouts. I haven't seen Lola this mad in years.

"Lady, I don't know who you are, but…" The kid isn't too happy about Lola dragging him through the parking lot right through the maze of angry picketers.

"I'm one woman who can make your life miserable, so don't try to screw with me. Take care of your girlfriend. At least try to be a man."

I'm leaning against the car with my arms crossed over my chest. Lola doesn't need my mouth; she's got this.

"Come on, Hailey." He takes her arm and turns to walk away. "At least this shit is over with."

Hailey doesn't move. "I didn't do it," she whispers.

"What?" The boyfriend drops her arm. "I thought we decided. Dammit, Hailey, I don't need this shit." He walks away, toward the black car, and leaves Hailey standing with us. The picketers are watching, and I get the feeling they are going to swarm us like bees at any second.

Lola is hot. "You're a loser," she yells at the guy. Then she turns to Grams and me. "Wait here." She puts her arm around the girl and walks her straight through the crowd and into Dr. Button's office.

"What's she doing?" I ask.

Lola is a take-charge kind of person, but she doesn't usually butt into someone else's business who isn't family. That, she does a lot. But for some reason, she's running on high emotion today. I guess that's partly my fault.

Grams smiles. "Being Lola."

A few other people show up with signs, but their signs say things like "RIGHT TO CHOOSE" and "SAVE THE CLINIC." At least Grams and I are no longer getting any attention. I watch, waiting for the two groups to start brawling in the parking lot, but all they do is stand and yell at each other.

After a few minutes, I get tired of watching them and turn back to Grams. "Those people need to get jobs."

The crowd divides when Lola walks back through alone. I guess they realized they don't want to mess with her. I crawl into the back of Grams's Cadillac, and Lola gets in the driver's seat. Grams puts on her seatbelt in the front and looks straight ahead. "Where's the girl?" she asks.

"I called her a cab, gave her the money for it, and told her to wait in Dr. Button's office until it gets here." Lola backs the big Caddy out and glances at me briefly as she turns around to check traffic. "You have a doctor's appointment with the ob-gyn in one hour."

I nod. I guess I'm going to do this Lola's way.

Chapter 15

Clay

I HAVE A MORNING ROUTINE. I get up at six and tend to my worms. I'm in the shower by seven, which gives me an hour to lie back down with Cassie before I get up, make breakfast, and go to work. I like schedules. They keep me grounded. But this morning, I'm up at five after a night of restless sleep and a bad dream. So I start on the worms early. But my day is already upset. I can't get the dream out of my mind.

In it, I'm a kid, and I'm searching for my pup. Roland is laughing at me, and my momma is telling me the pup is gone. But I keep looking. I see other kids with their dogs, and I check each one, but none are my pup. I'm crying, and I want my dog back. But he's gone, and there's nothing I can do.

Cassie mentioning that she never had a dog as a kid might have seemed like an odd thing to say considering our conversation last night, but I know what she was talking about. I never had a dog, either, or a cat, or a rabbit. The closest thing to a pet I ever had were the squirrels that used to live in the trees behind my mom's trailer. When I was little, I would watch them run up and down, but when I tried to get close, they always ran off. It didn't keep me from naming a few and saying they were mine, though.

We couldn't afford a dog. It was all Momma could do to keep us fed, and a dog was another mouth. A pet wasn't a necessity, but eating was.

That's what happens when a kid like Cassie or me is thrown into a situation in which getting through life takes priority. Cassie's dad left, her mom killed herself, and Babe and Jack Shatner tried to raise her and Lola without any major problems. But both of those girls had problems. I can picture Babe saying, "Honey, we can't handle a dog." That's another way of saying, "we got enough to handle without a pet around." With my momma, the line was "we can't afford one."

But dogs and cats are good for kids. For both Cassie and I, a pet might have made a big difference. A dog isn't a replacement for a dad, but it's something to hold and play with and share your secrets with without being judged. But neither of us had that opportunity.

It's chilly out this morning, but after I have the worms situated for the day, I sit on the picnic table and look out toward the back of our lot. After Cassie dug Roland up from his grave on the Hill and gave him a proper funeral, we had him cremated and buried his ashes out there, right next to my momma. Although I can't see their graves in the low morning light, I know they're there. Some people are permanent. Others aren't.

I pull out my phone and call the hospital to check on Britt. The nurse at the desk puts me on hold, then Dennis is on the phone. "I didn't mean for her to wake you up," I say.

"I wasn't sleeping. Hospital chairs aren't very comfortable." His voice is low, and I can hear how tired he is. "He's been awake some, though. Hard to talk with a mouth full of gauze, and they're keeping him sedated for the pain. But they said he'll most likely move to a regular room today, which is great news."

I'm trying to care. I do care—I mean, he got hit by a truck... Cassie's truck. If he dies, she could be in a can of worms. And Britt is a man, so I should care because he's a human being. And I guess I should care because he's my half brother. But the problem is, I'm trying not to hate him too. "Dennis, do you know if Britt had any dogs growing up?"

He doesn't say anything. I'm sure that comes off as an odd question, especially when I should be concerned with how badly the kid is going to be messed up after all this. I immediately feel bad for asking. *Not this guy's fault.* "Never mind," I say. "You should get back to him."

"It's fine. Stef is with him right now. She's planning on leaving this afternoon, once he gets moved out of ICU."

Britt's mother. Freddy Adams's wife. I close my eyes and try not to picture them, but no matter how hard I try, I see them standing next to a red Camaro, my dad's arm around a pretty blonde, and a red-haired boy at his feet.

"Well, keep me posted." It's all I can think to say.

"Cats," Dennis says as I'm about to hang up.

"What?"

"He had cats as a kid. Loves them. We have a Savannah—Balou. It's damn near a bobcat, which I think is a little weird, but she's Britt's buddy. In fact, he's worried about her more than himself right now."

"Balou?"

"He likes old Westerns."

Me too.

"I'm going to go get some coffee and then relieve Stef. We'd sure like to see you if—"

"I got work today, but I'll try." I am trying. I think.

"Now that the weather's getting cooler, I suggest you use some of the crawlers if you're going out," I say to Norm Dinger later that day. Although I work for Mr. Logston, I never pass up a chance to push some of my homegrown worms on a customer that I know fishes the river.

"I'll take your word for it," Norm says. "You haven't steered me wrong yet."

I pack up a few cups of worms and put them in a Logston's logoed bag. Norm stares at me a little too long, and I realize he knows. *Damn.* I look around the store and realize the other customers keep glancing my way then turning their heads when I look straight at them. Everyone knows. *Damn. Damn.* I put my palms flat on the counter and let out a slow breath. This is Deacon, Kansas. I should have known something like this wouldn't keep quiet for long. "How'd you find out, Norm?"

I've known Norm and Wendie Dinger my entire life. They went to the same church we did growing up. Wendie was my Sunday school teacher when I was in fifth grade, and I remember having a boyhood crush on her. Norm never was the partying type, but like everyone else in this town, he knew Freddy. He nods and lowers his voice to a half whisper. "Wendie found out at her church group. I guess one of the ladies has a daughter at the hospital and—" I hold my hand up, signaling him to stop.

"I'm sorry." Norm takes off through the plumbing fixtures aisle.

I watch him go then see Pet Harper walking toward me. He's carrying a bundle of brown fur in his arms. I take a deep breath. He sets the dog on the counter when he gets to me, and it immediately pees. Pet doesn't seem to notice.

I scratch behind the dog's ear. "There you go. He's a cute thing, ain't he?" He wags his tail and looks up at me with big brown eyes. "What kind is he?" He has short brown fur, and his front paws are white. The little black dot between his eyes would probably make him cross-eyed if he tried to look at it. His ears and tail are bushy.

"The free kind," Pet says. "Heinz 57. A bit of everything in him, I guess. But his momma and his daddy neither one were very big, so I s'pose he ain't gonna be too big, either."

I'd seen Pet at the 7-Eleven on my way to work this morning. He'd gotten off a night shift at the mop factory and was heading home. I know if there's anything I need, I can ask Pet. All I had to do was mention a pup, and Pet knew someone with a litter old enough to start finding homes.

I reach under the counter and grab some throwaway rags and disinfectant to clean the counter with. Then I pick the pup up and check him over thoroughly. His tail is still wagging, and his mouth is open as though he's smiling at me. I smile back.

"He looks healthy." I pull him close, and he licks me.

"Had his first shots and everything. He's even been fixed already," Pet says. The pup barks. Yeah, I'd bark, too, if someone was walking around announcing to everyone that I'd had my balls cut off.

"I'm happy to pay for him, Pet."

"Nah, he was free. You owe me one."

Actually, I owe him several, as does everyone else in town.

"Say, I heard about your dad and that kid that got hit. That's some tough shit there, Clay." Leave it to Pet to not beat around the bush. And if he knows about my dad, then his brother Daze knows. That means that by the end of the day, everyone in the four states will know too.

I shrug. "Yeah, well, nothing a pup won't cure."

Logston sees the pup, walks over, and holds his hands out for the little guy. I give him the dog, and Logston holds the thing right up to his face and starts talking to him as if he's a little kid. There's something about a puppy that brings the boy out in every man. "Oh, he's a keeper, Clay. You sure about this?"

Mr. Logston has been about the best boss anyone could ask for. He knows the story with Cassie and me, and although he probably regards her as crazy like everyone else does, he seems to go along with me and not judge.

I take a deep breath. "A big step for us, but yeah, Cassie had a fine idea here."

Logston nods and talks to the pup again. "Well then, why don't you and I go pick out a nice toy to take home?" He walks toward the pet aisle with the dog in his arms.

"Oh, I almost forgot." Pet digs in his shirt pocket and pulls out a cheap cigar. He's taken a Sharpie and scratched across the wrapper, "It's a Dog!"

I can't help but grin. "Thanks, Pet."

"No problem. And say, if you need me to watch him when you go see your dad, I'm happy to."

"I'm not going anywhere."

Logston returns, waving a red-stuffed worm in front of the dog's face. "Look here, he's like his daddy." He sets the dog on the counter with the toy, and the pup lays his muzzle on it as though it's his best friend.

Yep. Just like his daddy.

Mr. Logston scratches the top of the pup's head in between his ears, and the dog closes his eyes and lifts his head up as if asking for more. "Why don't you put your apron up and take this guy home? I'll close tonight."

It's not like me to leave early unless there is an emergency, and getting a dog doesn't really seem like one. But I know Logston is trying to give me a chance to skip out before anyone else starts talking about Freddy Adams, and I do appreciate it. I thank him, put my apron under the counter, and close out my drawer.

When I get in my truck, the pup whines when I put him down on the seat next to me. I pick him up and let him nuzzle my neck as I drive home one-handed. I figured that once he was inside the house, his curiosity would make him explore, but he wags his tail and follows me right to the kitchen.

The black cat clock lets out a screeching meow, which causes the pup to growl. "It's a stupid clock, buddy." I hold him up to the clock. Its eyes and tail are moving back and forth, keeping time to the minute. The puppy paws at the tail and growls at it again.

I hear Cassie pulling up out front and want to hide the pup from her so I can surprise her. She has been in Springfield all day, and I'm sure she's tired, but she's going to like this. We need it. We both need it. I hear her slam the door on the Cadillac, and I set the dog in the kitchen sink, putting one finger up to my lips to shush him. I turn around with my back to him, hiding the sink as Cassie walks in the front door.

"I brought you some of Grams's blueberry cobbler." She holds out a small casserole dish as she walks through the living room.

The pup is pawing at the back of my shirt, and I'm trying not to smile. "I got you something too," I say. She stops in the doorway to the kitchen, cocks her head, and gives me that odd little look. "It's in the sink here."

"The sink? I sure hope it isn't dirty dishes." She sets the cobbler on the counter and takes the aluminum foil off the top. She opens the cabinet and starts to get a bowl.

I stop her. "Don't you want to see your present?"

"Don't you want some cobbler?" she asks. I can tell she has something on her mind, but I have a feeling she's going to show me that smile again any minute. I pull her close.

"Cobbler can wait." I turn around with her in my arms, and there, peeking over the top of the sink, is the pup. His ears are up, and his tail is keeping a beat on the stainless steel.

"It's a puppy," she says. That's it.

"You said you never had one, and, well, I figured it was about time you did."

She stands and stares at him. He starts whining, tired of being in the cold sink.

"Go ahead," I tell her. "Pick him up."

She looks at me then back to the dog. She reaches for him, and he gives a little growl, which backs her up.

"Oh, stop it," I say to him as I reach into the sink and grab him. "This is your momma." He licks my chin. I hold him out to Cassie, and this time, he looks at her with the same cocked head she has for him.

"Clay, I didn't mean… I don't know."

I put him against her chest, and she puts both hands on his scruff. He's wiggling around and trying to look at me. "Hold on to him. He needs to meet you."

She's reluctant but finally grabs him around the belly with both hands and holds him out in front of her. He gives a soft bark. "See, he says hello," I tell her.

She smiles a little. "Hello." He barks again.

She pulls him close, like a baby doll, and turns around and around with him. I'm not sure I've ever seen her so happy, and that makes me happy too. She holds him out again to look at him, right over the counter, and he pees. Cassie drops him, right in the cobbler.

Her chin quivers, and she runs out of the room.

"Cassie, it's okay. He's all right," I call after her. But I hear our bedroom door shut.

I pick him up. He's covered with blueberry syrup and is trying to lick it off his whiskers. "Well, aren't you a mess," I say. I put him in the sink again and try to wash off the cobbler. His white feet are stained purple. I dry him off as much as I can and set him on the floor with his worm toy.

When I walk into the bedroom, Cassie is lying on the bed, staring at the ceiling. I lie down next to her and take her hand. "He's okay. It ain't a big deal, Cassie."

"I didn't mean I wanted a puppy. I never had one, that's all."

I take a deep breath. "I guess we could give him back." I don't want to. I already love the little guy. But if he's going to be here, Cassie has to love him too.

"It's not that I don't like him. I do. But…"

"But what?" I need to know how she's thinking, and sometimes with Cassie, that is really hard.

"What if I hurt him? I mean, on accident? Hell, two minutes with him, and I already dropped him."

I put my arm around her and pull her close. "Here's the thing about a dog. As long as you love him, he forgives you for the accidents. Shoot, he thought that was a big game. He loved the cobbler."

She doesn't say anything.

"Cassie, you're not going to hurt him." I hear the pup whimpering by the side of the bed. I look down and see that he's dragged his worm in with him. I pick up him and his toy and set him on the bed in between us. He leaves me with the worm, walks over to Cassie, and licks her ear. "See? He wants more cobbler."

She tries to move so he can't get to her ear, and he starts a tug-of-war with her hair. She starts giggling.

I wrestle him from her hair and put him on her chest. He lays his head down and gives her those sad brown eyes. She reaches out and rubs the soft fur on his back.

"Okay, I'll try," she says. "But no more cobbler for you. That was for Clay."

I rub behind his ears. "That's okay. I like your cobbler better than Babe's anyway."

Chapter 16

Cass

I took Dog out back this morning to let him get acquainted with our land. I don't know where he was living before, but I doubt he ever went outside. The weather was a little cool; the wind blew the leaves around, and the puppy chased them all in circles. He likes the orange ones the best. I do too.

When we got back to the house, he passed out on the kitchen floor with his legs still hanging out the door. I have to remember that he's a puppy and gets worn out kind of fast. I pulled his feet inside, lay down on the cold tile next to him, and fell asleep. I've been getting pretty sleepy myself lately. Oh yeah, I have that baby in me. I guess that would do it.

Now I'm awake, lying here and watching the dog sleep. Every once in a while, his front paws move as though he's running. I can't help but giggle. Then I remember, and I quit laughing.

Yesterday, after Lola busted me out of the abortion clinic, she took me to another doctor about the baby—a real doctor, not like the one we have in Deacon. Her office was as big as Archie's Discount Liquor and a lot cleaner. Lola came in with me, and Grams sat in the waiting area and read magazines.

Dr. Gross asked a bunch of questions, made me pee in a cup, and weighed me in. I didn't say much. I let Lola do the talking. She's an expert at that. Then Dr. Gross made me take off my pants, put me on a table, and wedged my feet into stirrups so I was spread wider than a turkey getting stuffed.

"Is it a boy or a girl?" I asked.

"Oh, we don't know yet." Dr. Gross was feeling inside me, and it hurt.

"Well, as far up in me as you are, I'd think you could see a tiny penis if there was one." She laughed. I was glad someone was having fun.

Now, Dog opens his eyes then jumps up, ready to go again. I take him out back and try to get him to pee. "Pee, Dog." He wags his tail and gives me a low bark. So I make pee sounds, thinking he might get it. "Ssssss." He growls as if he thinks I might have swallowed a snake.

I get on the ground on all fours and lift one leg. He cocks his head and looks at me as though I'm stupid. Then he jumps up at me, grabs a mouthful of my hair, and starts a game of tug-of-war.

"Maybe potty training is more of a job for Clay," I say. At the sound of Clay's name, Dog stops tugging and starts running in circles. I feel like that sometimes too.

After Dr. Gross defiled me, we went into a different room and she asked more questions, this time about Clay, me, and our health histories. I didn't know a lot of the answers, but Grams was with us for that. She knew a lot about me, but we were clueless about Clay. Then Dr. Gross asked if there was any mental illness on either side. All three of us sat there and said nothing.

"Well?" she asked.

"Yeah, there's a lot of crazy stuff," I said. "Is the baby going to be crazy too?" I had wanted to ask that question, but I didn't know there was a way to find out beforehand. Maybe this appointment wasn't a bad idea after all.

"Some mental illnesses have a genetic component, and I want to make sure we have as much information as possible."

"Yes, there is a history of mental illness," Lola said. "Our mother had, uh, problems, and Cass is being treated for some things as well."

"What types of problems?" the doctor asked me.

"I see dead people. Sometimes." I figured there wasn't much reason to lie. "But Doc Button said it was okay to have a kid, so I guess it is."

"Dr. Button?" she asked.

"Oh, my shrink. I saw him this morning." I dug in my purse and pulled out the prescription he'd given me. "He said as long as I take this instead of my other pills, it'll be fine."

She took the prescription and wrote a bunch of stuff on her pad. "Okay. Anything else I need to know?"

I thought about telling her I wasn't sure yet whether or not I wanted to have a baby, but I didn't want to upset Grams or Lola again. So I didn't say anything.

Now, I sit on the ground and cross my legs. Dog immediately jumps in the middle. He stands on his hind legs, tail wagging, and puts his paws high up on my chest. His tongue is out, and he is staring at me. His front paws are still purple from being dropped in the blueberry cobbler, but I figure that will fade away in another day or two.

I swear I can see the love in those big brown eyes, and I realize I'm smiling. I've done a lot of that this morning. Clay was right; all I had to do was give it a chance. Clay usually is right. "I sure hope he feels that same way about a baby as he does about you." Dog licks my chin. I lick him back. Clay will be fine. I sure hope I feel the same way about a baby as I do about Dog.

After the doctor's questions, we went to another room where someone put a bunch of jelly on my stomach and said it was so she could see the baby. She pointed to a screen, but all I could see was a blob in a spotlight. It reminded me of what a peanut must look like in its shell. Except this peanut had a head. Lola and Grams both started crying.

"What's wrong?" I asked. "Is there something wrong with it?"

"No, the baby looks fine," the woman with the jelly said. "We're going to call it twelve weeks, which puts your due date at April 15th." I kept staring at the screen. *Peanut*.

"You're making me nervous," I said to Grams and Lola. They were hugging each other and smiling, but there were so many tears between them that I was afraid I would slip on the floor when I got up.

"I'm sorry, honey. I can't believe it. A baby!" Grams pulled a tissue out of her purse and blew her nose. "Can you tell if it's a boy or a girl yet?" she whispered.

I didn't take my eyes from the screen, and neither did the woman with the jelly rod on my belly. "No, it's not in a position to see. If you want to know, we can do another scan in a few months. We should be able to tell by then."

Dog's ears perk up, and he puts his paws on my leg, looking behind me. He starts barking, and I turn to see what has his attention. I see Mama Adams by the tree line, wearing her flowered housedress and picking flowers.

"You see her too?" I ask. Dog glances at me and turns back to Mama's ghost. He's still barking.

"Don't bother," I say. "She won't talk to me. I doubt she's going to talk to you, either." Maybe if I tell her I'm pregnant, it might catch her attention, or maybe not.

I stand up, wipe the dirt off my butt, and walk toward the house. Dog follows me. As soon as we walk in the back door, he squats on the kitchen floor and pees.

I sigh. "Well, close, I guess."

After I spent hours with Dr. Gross, she deemed me healthy enough to have Peanut and gave me some information about a test she wants to run in a few weeks. She wants to stick a needle in my belly and make sure Peanut doesn't have any problems. Lola said I should definitely do it, but she isn't the one getting needles stuck in her belly. I tucked the papers in my purse and hightailed it out the door. Being pregnant isn't easy, and I'm only at the beginning.

I watch Mama picking the flowers. Dog stands on his hind legs, leaning on the door and looking through the screen. He's watching too.

I scratch behind his ears. "Why don't we go out to the Hill, and you can meet Old Man Booker? And maybe Roland will show up." Dog growls when I say Roland's name.

"Yeah, I have pretty much that same reaction. Tell you what, let's go meet your Grams and your Aunt Lola first. Maybe they'll have some more cobbler for you." Dog wags his tail so hard, his entire butt moves. I pick him up and kiss him right on the nose. He licks mine back. Maybe having a baby won't be so bad after all.

Chapter 17

Clay

Dog got up with me this morning to check on the worms, which made me happy. He might as well start learning now that we are a worm family, and tending to the herd is how we start the day. He walked outside with me, sniffed around, and found a spot to relieve himself.

"Good boy," I said. His tail wagged as he followed me, watching my every move.

It was cool outside, but that doesn't necessarily mean much for Kansas. We could be swimming by noon or smothered in three feet of snow.

When I came into the bedroom after my shower, Dog was curled up with Cassie in bed. I was extra quiet so as not to wake either one. Seeing them together, one would think they have been friends forever.

As I left, I thought about how Cassie and Dog are the closest thing I've had to a real family in thirty-five years. When I was little, it was my dad, my mom, Roland, and me. But that didn't last long. After that, Momma was working most of the time, Rudy Drown came by to check on us, and Roland was, well, Roland.

In the army, I had a wife for a short while, but that didn't work out too well, either. Then, of course, I adopted Shaylene, but she never lived with me, so she was more of a part-time daughter. I'm talking about a real family, one that lives together in one house, helps with the worms, and curls up together in bed in the morning. Cassie and Dog—they're my real family.

On my way to work, I remembered that I had told Dennis I would try to go to the hospital last night. I had every intention of calling him to say I couldn't make it, but I forgot. *Damn.* I'll make sure I go to the hospital today. I'm sure the busybodies will be out in force, and the last thing I want to do is try to work and answer questions about Freddy Adams, especially when it's none of anyone's business. I'll ask Mr. Logston if he can spare me again this afternoon so I can go visit Britt, my half brother, my family.

The morning crowd buzzed like flies on a watermelon. After three hours of dodging questions from townsfolk about the mystery of my missing father, I hung up my apron and hightailed it out of work. Mr. Logston was more than happy to send me home, even if it was a Saturday afternoon.

I stopped to check on Cassie's truck. Lucky Dean had finished cleaning it up and was sitting in his office, watching college football. "Radiator was the worst of it, and the front fender damage. There ain't nothing like these old Fords. You can run over a guy and keep going."

"She'll sure be glad to get it back." I went over the job he'd done, and as usual, I couldn't find anything to complain about. Not that I thought I would. Lucky has been the town tow man and mechanic for forty years. He's an honest man and a hard worker. Not only does he know everyone in town, but he knows their trucks too.

"Yeah, I bet. Driving that titty-pink Caddy don't seem much her style." We go back to his office so I can settle the deductible. There are pictures on the walls of half-dressed women draped over race cars, and the office smells as much like motor oil as the shop does.

Lucky goes behind the counter and grabs a pile of paperwork. "Sorry to hear about your dad." He flips through the papers then pulls out my tally.

"Yeah, thanks." When the first few people that week had said, "Sorry to hear about your dad," I was quick to tell them that I wasn't. But I've figured out over the past few days that the best way to cut conversations short about Freddy Adams is to politely thank the inquirer and not go into the whole story. It has worked pretty well, but Lucky takes my response as an invitation.

"I still remember that red Camaro he used to drive. A '79 Berlinetta. That was a cherry ride back in the day. And your dad was proud of that car. Shoot, I remember one night out at the VFW, Roy Harper tried to get him to race it up Nineteenth Street. Your dad said there ain't no way he was going to risk hurting that car. Personally, I think he knew that Chevy didn't have the speed to beat Roy's Dodge."

I snorted. Freddy Adams wouldn't do anything to hurt his car, but he damn sure didn't feel the same way about his family.

Lucky lays the bill on the counter, and I pull the checkbook out of my back pocket. He keeps talking. "He sure was a funny guy. Had more jokes than the Pope has sermons." I'm starting to sweat. I write the check and hand it to Lucky without saying a word.

"When you talk to him, say hello for me and the wife, will ya?" He writes *paid* across the ticket and gives me my copy with the keys.

I leave the keys on the counter and walk toward the door. "I'll have Cassie come pick it up this afternoon." I get outside and stop to wipe my forehead. Damn, I'm tired of hearing about what a great guy Freddy Adams was.

I turn my truck toward Joplin and give Cassie a call to let her know the truck is ready. At least I can count on her not to mention Freddy Adams. She says she's taking Dog over to Babe's house to meet Lola. I forgot my sister-in-law is in town for a few days and that I need to stop and visit her too. I promise Cassie I'll come by this afternoon after I go visit Britt, and I suggest that maybe we should plan on a big Sunday meal tomorrow.

"I'll mention it to her," Cassie says, "but you know Lola—we'll end up doing whatever she wants us to do."

I never knew Lola Shatner well growing up. She was Cassie's big sister and a few years older than me, but she was a wild thing in high school. I was never much into the party life. What I knew of her was that she was an okay gal. She wasn't considered crazy like her sister, but she dated guys who weren't worth their weight in mud. Some women are like that; I've never understood why they're attracted to bums.

After a few failed marriages, Lola married a rich old lawyer, Richard Warner, and moved to Springfield. Everyone thought she was a gold digger, and maybe she was. But I've come to know them both the past few months, and they seem to get along pretty well. Who am I to say an odd relationship won't work since I live with the woman who killed my brother?

Lola and Cassie are night and day. They don't even resemble each other if you put them side by side. Lola is tall and blond with brown eyes, and Cassie is small, not even five foot, with hair the color of sand and eyes as green as a tree in summer. Cassie doesn't care much about anyone outside of her circle, whereas Lola can be a bleeding heart. She takes care of herself and hers first, but she seems to have plenty left if a stray needs a handout. She talks as if she's been to school, but I know she hasn't. Maybe hanging out at the country club for the past ten years taught her all those big words. And Lola definitely likes to have things her way.

I've figured out that brothers and sisters aren't always that much alike. Pet and Daze Harper are definitely from the same mold, but most siblings I know are as different as Cassie and Lola. Not many similarities, but they find a way to get along, or at least be there for each other when the chips are down. Roland and I were certainly opposites—he was an ass, and I try not to be. But we didn't like each other at all.

I'm still not totally sure why Roland hated me so much. I tried for years to keep the peace, but he couldn't bend. Cassie says deep down he was jealous of me, but I don't see how that could be. I felt more like he resented me for trying to step up when we were kids and be the man of the house after Freddy left. He didn't appreciate me acting like his daddy instead of his brother. Yeah, I'm blaming that one on Freddy too.

I sure wish it had been different, though. I've had to make my family as I got older, but blood is different. At least that's what most people say. And maybe that's another reason I keep checking on Britt Chandler. So far, all the blood I share has proven to be bad, but maybe the kid got a good vein like me. I texted Dennis to say I was on the way, and he messaged back that Britt was awake and excited to meet me.

The hospital is hopping today. Saturday must be the day everyone comes to visit. After cruising the parking lot for a good ten minutes, I find a spot toward the back and squeeze my truck in between two foreign-mades. I grab my hat off the seat next to me and take a deep breath before getting out of the truck. Time to see what kind of man Freddy made out of this one.

For someone who's damn near been broken in two, Britt Chandler is in pretty good spirits. His leg is still elevated with a trapeze, and his arm is in a cast. He can't move around a lot, but between him and Dennis, they've figured out a way to sit him up using pillows as props, and he's typing one-handed on his laptop. I knock lightly. Britt shuts the laptop when he sees me standing in the open doorframe of his room. "I'm done."

Dennis introduces us as though he's the hostess at a party, and Britt sticks out his good hand to me. I take it. "It's nice to meet you," he says. "I hope you're not going to try to kill me too." His lips are purple and swollen, he's missing some teeth, and his words come out slurred. But even with his face a mess, I can tell he's smiling.

"I figure if Roland and Cassie couldn't kill you, it's a waste of my time to try," I joke. I take a chair next to him, one a little more comfortable than the ones in the ICU.

Dennis laughs. "See, I told you he was okay. You picked the wrong one to try to talk to."

"Why *did* you go find Roland instead of me?" I figure he knows I have a lot of questions, so I might as well jump right in. I want to know about him, but I need to find out if he's on the level. If so, then we'll have plenty of time to get to that.

"Luck of the draw, I guess. I knew where you both worked, and the first time I came, I got here at night. I didn't expect his reaction. The other night, I went back because I'm hardheaded." He's looking me up and down, and it makes me a little nervous. But then I realize I did the same with him a few days ago when I was here, so I let him look.

I take a breath and figure I'll lay everything out for him. "You know your dad left us when we were kids. Little kids. Took off and never turned back. We had no idea where he was, nothing. So I don't know what kind of reaction he expected from Roland, or me for that matter, but I guess my opinion is the same as Roland's was. I don't care to see the man."

Britt tries to lick his lips, and Dennis gives him a drink out of a Styrofoam cup with a straw. He struggles to swallow it and tries to clear his throat. "He said Roland knew. He said he talked to him about thirteen years ago, and it didn't go very well. I thought you knew."

My face is hot, and I talk through gritted teeth. "He's lying." But I'm not entirely sure. Roland was an ass, but would he not have told me if he talked to Freddy? I don't know which one I hate more, father or brother.

Britt looks at Dennis then back to me. "I'm sorry," he says.

"You ain't got nothing to be sorry about. Roland was a loser, a lot like his dad, I guess. Hell, the only thing he got from our mom was heart trouble."

"Oh damn. Dennis, tell the nurse to get my meds. She's always late.

Sorry, that reminded me. My dear mother blessed me with her diabetes. Shame they can't only share the positive traits."

Wouldn't that be nice?

Dennis leaves us alone to chase down a nurse, and I squirm on my chair. Britt seems like a nice kid, but he knows things I've only wondered about my entire life.

"Clay, do you want to know about our dad?" he asks, as though reading my mind.

I don't know what to say. Now that I'm in a position to find out about Freddy Adams, I'm not sure I want to know. Britt seems to understand my reluctance. It's clear that he's trying very hard not to push, and I appreciate that.

"He's not 'our' dad," I say. "He's your dad. He quit being mine when he chose to leave. I can't get over that, Britt. I've tried to let it go, but I can't. I see you, a young guy who's been to college and had a happy childhood, and that could have been me. But it wasn't. It isn't. I'm not a man who holds a lot of hate, but I honestly don't know what I'd say or do if I ever saw your dad. I'm sorry."

He nods. "It wasn't all wonderful. My childhood. He had a lot of expectations I couldn't live up to. Being an only child made it even more difficult. So in a way, I get it. But he's still my blood, and I can't help but try to save his life."

"Save it? I thought he was dying."

"He is. He drank for so many years, he basically destroyed his liver. He was on the transplant list for a while, but they have guidelines, and it's been difficult for him to follow the rules. He's been sober for two months now, but that isn't long enough to get back on the list, and he won't make it much longer without a liver." It's hard to discern his expressions with all the bandages on his face and his mouth swelled up, but his voice cracks, so I know he's sad.

"Well, there isn't much you can do." I don't know much about livers and transplants and such, but I do know if you haven't got one that works, you're pretty much screwed.

Dennis returns and assures Britt that the nurse is on her way with his medications. He sits in a chair in the corner, as if he is trying to be invisible and allow us to continue our conversation.

"No, there isn't much I can do. Or my mom. We both have diabetes, and we're not good matches otherwise, so giving him a part of our liver won't work. He needs a compatible donor."

Compatible donor. His words hit me like a wrecking ball. "Are you saying that's why you came to find me and Roland? To see if we're willing to give up our livers to save Freddy Adams?"

"Not your entire liver," Britt says. "Only a piece. It will regenerate. In a few months, you'd have the whole thing back again as if nothing ever happened. I know it's asking a lot, but—"

I stand up. I want to say I can't believe what I'm hearing, but I should have known there was more to this kid than meets the eye. After all, he is the spawn of Freddy Adams.

Dennis stands too, as if he's ready to intervene if I try to choke Britt, which does cross my mind. "Clay, it's just a question. You may not even be a match. It's a long shot, and it's understandable if you say no."

I run my hand through my hair. "No." I pick up my hat. I'm done.

Britt reaches toward me. "Don't leave, Clay. I understand. But I had to ask."

"Why? Why did you have to ask? He killed himself, and from what I've heard, he hasn't been so great to you, either. So why not let God take what's his? Damn, Britt, I thought..." *I thought we might have become friends.*

"You're right. I shouldn't care so much." Britt looks down at his swollen knuckles. "It's not my fault and not my responsibility. But I do care. Because he's my dad. And as bad as he is, my mom loves him. And I'd do anything for her."

That hits a spot with me, because I do understand the connection between a mother and son. *But damn.*

"And it's not the only reason I came. I want to get to know you." He tries to scoot up in the bed with his one free arm but falls back on the pillows. "For all the bad that's happened, maybe there's something good that can come from it."

I'm not the kind of guy who lets my emotions show much, but in the past few days, it seems as if I can't quite keep them in check, and I don't care to let everyone see what I'm feeling. I'm mad, and I'm resentful, but I'm also trying to find a way that this can all be okay. For some reason, I think of Cassie. I really want to be with her right now, not standing in this room, fighting back my anger with what little bit of hope I have left in me for "something good."

I nod and mumble something about getting some air. Outside the hospital, I realize I have no intention of going back in. I head straight for the back of the parking lot, not knowing if I'm just walking to my truck or walking away.

Chapter 18
Lola

Waking up in the bedroom that Cass and I shared as kids is a lot more stressful than I thought it would be. I've been in the room several times since I arrived at Grams's, and I thought I was used to it, but waking up after dreams of shopping trips and babies to the sight of the yellowed white walls and pine furniture of my childhood causes me to take a sudden breath. I can't move for a few seconds, and I can feel my heart race.

The furniture is arranged how it has been forever: double bed against the wall with a window at the head, one bedside table next to it, a dresser and chest of drawers next to each other at the foot. It's not a very large room. It seems to have too much furniture in it, and I have to stand to the side of the dresser to open the drawers. And it gets worse—I roll over and find myself staring at the open closet. I squeeze my eyes tightly shut to make the vision of my mother go away.

I didn't see her after she hanged herself. I had fallen asleep on the couch that night, and someone had put a blanket over me and left me to sleep there. Since my mother, Cass, and I all shared a room, one of us usually slept on the couch. It was my turn that night. I woke up to the sound of Grams screaming for my Grandpa Jack. When I got up to see what was the fuss, he was already in the bedroom. Grams was leading Cass out and shut the door. Cass had found her hanging in the closet with a belt around her neck.

I didn't see it, but I can picture it in my mind. I open my eyes slowly. The closet is empty. I swing my feet to the side of the bed and feel claustrophobic in this room. I stumble to the bathroom in my pajamas to wash my face.

Call Me Daddy

My mother was never there for us anyway. What I can remember of her, she was usually out partying, and when she was home, she was either very loud and happy or very sad and quiet. We never knew which person we would get. I remember playing outside with Cass and always making sure I went in the house before her so I would know which Vera was there. If I laughed, Cass would laugh. If I was quiet, she would be quiet.

I hardly remember our father at all. All I remember about him was that he had blond hair that always looked dirty. He lived with us on occasion, and on those nights, I would sleep in the living room. It was the best. Grandpa Jack would help me make a tent out of kitchen chairs and blankets, and I would play like I was camping. Sometimes, my tent would be a castle, and I would sit in it, eating apples and waiting for my prince to come. He never came. Maybe the apples were poisoned.

But it never lasted long. After a few nights, my mother and father would get into a fight, and he would be gone. Then one night, my mother was gone. She stayed gone for a while. When she came back, she had Cass. My father left shortly after. I felt as though she traded Cass for my daddy, but that was okay with me. Cass was my baby doll.

I get my Yves Saint Laurent Forever Youth out of my overnight bag and begin my morning routine. First, I wash my face with the cleansing foam, then I apply the facial serum and the additional eye serum. I know they're expensive, but they're the only products I've found that work well for me. And price is not an issue. I married well.

Growing up, we didn't talk much about my mother. I was eight when she killed herself, and I knew what she had done. I asked a lot of questions, but I was a teenager before I asked Grams to tell me the whole story. She was reluctant, but I guess she thought I was old enough to hear it by then. She told me about my mother having mental problems and that she tried to give herself an abortion. She ended up in a mental hospital, which is where she gave birth to Cass. It was enough. I never asked again. We never talked about it.

I was twenty when I got pregnant. The father, Nicholas Dixon, was a jerk, and I told myself that was the reason I had an abortion. Nick was not father material. I had lived without a dad, and I didn't want a baby that had to do the same. Yes, that's what I told myself. But as we all do in our lives, I lied to myself because I couldn't accept the truth. Now that I'm older, I understand. It wasn't Nick that I was afraid would screw up. It was me. My mom had problems, and what if I did too? What if I had a kid, then all I wanted to do was hang myself in a closet?

When I saw Cass at the women's clinic, all of those memories came flooding back, memories I've tried to tuck away. I know how Cass is feeling because I had the same fears. But I won't let her make the same mistakes I did.

"Oh finally, you're up." Grams's voice startles me, and I drop my skin tone perfector in the sink, losing half the bottle in the basin. Money literally goes down the drain. I'm glad I have plenty of both—the makeup and the money.

"I've got something I want to talk to you about before Cass gets here," Grams says. "It's important."

I finish my face and pad into the kitchen. The scent of cinnamon fills the air, and I know Grams has made enough cobbler, pastries, and breads to feed a small country. I shut my eyes and inhale deeply. My cook is good, but my kitchen never smells like this. I sit at the small dinette that has been in the kitchen for too many years. A worn yellow file folder with a rubber band around it sits on the table. "What's this?"

Grams sits next to me and taps the file. "It's everything I have about your mother. After trying to answer that doctor's questions… Well, I should have given this to you years ago." She drops her shoulders and looks down at the table.

"It's all right, Grams. I never thought much about it. I guess I should have, but…" I put my hand on top of hers. "You did a good job with us." I mean that.

She pulls a hankie from her apron and wipes her face. "I don't want Cass to see any more than she has to. She's not you."

No, she isn't. We know she has issues, and Dr. Gross asked about those yesterday. We know nothing about our father and not much more about our mother. Now we have a baby coming, and she deserves every chance we can give her. I will spend every dime of Richard's money if I have to, but some things, money can't buy.

I stand up, put my arms around Grams, and hold her tight. "It's the right thing, Grams. I know it's hard since we tucked her away so many years ago, but now we need to know."

A tear falls on my arm. "Tucked her away?" Grams whispers. "Oh no, honey. I don't talk about her because I don't want you girls to have to carry the same guilt I do. But Vera was my daughter. She's with me every day."

I take the rubber band from the chart and slowly open it. A stack of pictures lies on top, secured with another rubber band. A Polaroid of my mother, standing in a field and wearing a pink bikini, is right on top. One hand is pulling at her bikini bottom, while the other rests on her knee. Her hair is long, blond, and thick. I vaguely remember what she looked like, but seeing her through the eyes of an adult is different. She was beautiful. "Whoa. What is she doing in a field?"

Grams takes the picture from me and smiles. "Nancy Sinatra."

"Who?"

She cocks her head and continues to gaze at the picture. "That's a pose from one of her albums. When she first heard that song about the go-go boots, she loved Nancy from then on. Your grandpa said she was a ringer, and once I bought her a pair of boots, she wore them with everything." Grams flips through the pictures and finds another one of my mother posing. She was wearing a short, white, sleeveless dress and white boots with a small heel. Heavy eyeliner encircles her almond-shaped eyes, and there's a soft pink shine on her pouty lips.

I Google Nancy Sinatra on my laptop and pull up several images from the late sixties and early seventies. Other than the fact that my mother had blue eyes and Nancy had dark eyes, there certainly was a resemblance, an almost eerie resemblance.

"She used to walk around the house in those boots, even with her pajamas on, singing that song," Grams says. "She said the boots made her feel pretty, but she didn't need no boots for that."

I continue to flip through the images of Nancy Sinatra on my laptop. I find a black-and-white photo of her with flowers in her hair, several of her in a white dress with white boots, one of her in the pink bikini, then one picture of her against a black background with a black top, black hat, and blond hair. "The woman on the wall," I say.

Grams peeks over at the computer at the picture. "Oh yes. *Movin' with Nancy* was the album that cover came from. That poster hung there until the edges curled. It was her pride and joy."

The front door opens, and we hear Cass talking to someone. Grams grabs the folder and throws it and the pictures on top of the refrigerator before Cass makes it to the kitchen. A little brown dog runs into the kitchen first and squats on the linoleum.

"Sorry, he's trying to learn." Cass grabs a paper towel and cleans up the mess then picks up the dog and puts him right in my face. "Dog, meet your Aunt Lola." He looks at me for a second then squirms out of her arms and runs straight to Grams.

"Oh, he's adorable." Grams picks him up, and he licks her face. She doesn't seem to mind at all.

"A dog, Cass?" My sister, who can barely take care of herself and is about to have a baby, goes and gets a dog.

She shrugs. "Clay got him for me. Consider him practice. You know, for Peanut."

"You told Clay you were pregnant, and he got you a dog to practice on?"

"Not really." She grabs two bowls from the cupboard and fills them both with cobbler from the refrigerator.

"Which part, 'not really'?"

She puts one bowl on the table and the other on the floor. The dog wiggles his way free from Grams and runs straight to the bowl. "The telling-Clay-I'm-pregnant part."

I shake my head. When I told Cass and Grams I was coming back to Deacon with them, they assured me there was no reason to. Cass said that other than an occasional barfing spell, she felt fine, and Grams could handle that. But the real reason I came was to get Cass to accept this pregnancy and be excited about it. The first step in doing that is for Clay to get on board. I know he'll be thrilled, and I'm not quite sure why Cass is so reluctant to tell him.

Maybe she needs our support, and if that's the case, Grams and I would both be happy to be there for her. "Do you want us to be with you when you do?"

She finishes her cobbler and drops the spoon in the bowl. "No. Tonight. Promise. Last night, he brought Dog home, and we were busy. Today, he's at work, and he called me to say he was going to visit that kid in the hospital this afternoon. Clay has a lot on his mind right now. I don't want to add to it."

"How is the kid? Britt? Is that his name?" I'm sure Grams is genuinely concerned, but I think she's trying to change the subject. Maybe she's seeing something I don't, or maybe she is trying to baby Cass as she always has.

Cass shrugs. "He ain't dead."

"You know, maybe he would have some information on Clay's dad's health history that might be useful," I say. "You and Clay, neither one, know much about your parents' health, and it would be helpful to have for the baby."

"Yeah, I'll get Clay to ask once I tell him about the baby. And I believe he got Dog for himself more than me. To keep his mind off of the other stuff."

"You do need some information, though. Maybe I could go talk to Britt." I can't say I'm not curious, and besides, I don't care two hoots about Clay's dad.

"Dr. Gross said sticking that needle in my belly will give us the important stuff." Cass is at the refrigerator again. She grabs the milk, pours herself a glass, then pours some in the dog's bowl.

"Not everything, and besides, that's weeks away. It'd be nice to have a history," I point out.

There's another knock at the door, and Grams is up and heading toward the living room. I hear Maryanne Spencer's voice and roll my eyes. I don't know why Cass has let that woman back into her life. I sure as hell wouldn't have after she went and had a kid with Roland. But Cass accepts her, so I'll be nice. I'm not sure about the connection between these two, but maybe Maryanne can be helpful in getting Cass on board with the baby.

"What's new?" Maryanne is dressed in tight jeans and a top that is cut so low, her boobs are about to spill over the top. She sees me, and her smile disappears briefly before it's replaced by an obviously fake one. "Oh, Lola. I didn't know you were here."

"Cass is pregnant," I blurt out. There. The more people who know, the harder it will be for her to keep it from Clay.

"Oh. That's... great!" She turns to Cass. "I know you didn't want any kids, but it'll be great."

"What makes you assume I didn't want any?" Cass stares at her. "I always wanted a baby. But I guess Roland only had one in him."

Nice dig, Cass.

"Oh no, I mean... he said you..." She sits down at the table with us and shakes her head. "Never mind. It's so exciting. Clay must be thrilled."

The dog is scratching at Cass's leg, and she picks him up. He lays his nose on her shoulder. "He doesn't know yet, so don't say anything. I'll tell him tonight after he gets home. Jeez, it's just a baby."

"Tonight, Cass, and at least find out his blood type," I urge. "Remember, the doctor said she wanted to know that soon." Bit by bit, I'm going to get this information.

She nods. "I'll get it, don't worry. Maryanne, take me to get my truck. Clay said it's done, and I'm ready to be driving it again instead of Grams's pink-mobile. And I need to go home and take a nap."

"Oh. Sure." She stands up and seems anxious to leave. "Nice seeing you again, Lola." She gives Grams a hug and immediately heads for the door.

"You want us to come over tonight?" Cass asks me.

"Let's do dinner tomorrow. Grams and I have a project we're working on."

"I hope it isn't baby stuff."

"It's not." Well, it kind of is, I guess.

After Maryanne and Cass leave, Grams pulls the folder back down from the top of the refrigerator. She grabs the stack of pictures again and starts looking through them. I start on the stack of papers in the folder. I find medical bills, doctors' statements, and discharge papers from the hospitals she frequented. After ten minutes, I put all the papers back in the folder. "I can't do this."

Grams is still engrossed in the pictures. "It's okay, honey. I know it's hard. Let's forget about it and focus on the good."

"I mean, I don't understand this crap." If the papers talked about plastic surgeries and liposuction, I would understand, but all the mental stuff is Greek to me.

Grams sighs. "I know someone who can read it all, and I believe we can trust her."

I hate letting anyone in on our family's dirty secrets, but hell, who am I kidding—I want to know. She was my mother.

"Grace Cloud," Grams says. "She works on a psych ward at the hospital. Nice girl. Smart, too. She'll help us."

I lean back in my chair and cross my arms over my chest. Grace is a nice girl, smart. And she's also Benny Cloud's wife.

Chapter 19

Benny

DON'T LET A LAWMAN TELL you he keeps everything about his job from his wife. It ain't true. In fact, if he's a smart one, he has to tell her a few things, even things he probably shouldn't. Otherwise, she would let him out of the house for his eight-hour shift and expect him to be home for the other sixteen hours of the day. That isn't how it works. Sometimes, the job requires more.

Granted, the whole Freddy Adams mess doesn't have much to do with my work, but I still gave Grace the rundown of everything I knew up to this point. Maybe most guys wouldn't have told the wife everything, but most guys don't have a wife as wise as Grace. I'm one of the lucky ones.

"Benny, this is serious. And Roland knew? Oh, I wish you'd have kept your mind on your own business," she scolds.

I kind of knew that would come, and I had my spiel ready. "Yeah, well, I didn't, and now I don't know what to do. I mean, it's all no more than a rumor, and I'm sure there's more to it than what Tenesy says. And I still need to talk to my mom again. She didn't tell me all that. Or about Rudy." Which makes me think she's hiding something else too.

I also wouldn't mind hearing Rudy's take, but I don't say that to Grace. Rudy was sleeping with Freddy's wife, Donna Sue, which means he was a real jerk. He even convinced her to file a missing person report, which makes him a criminal by my standards. If that's all true, I could leak it around the election and get one up on him. But then all this will come out, and Clay will get caught in the crossfire. I want to win, but I don't know if I want to throw Clay in the fire to do it. There's also the fact that Tenesy is full of crap more than not, so it's possible that none of what he said is true.

Before I even consider sacrificing Clay for my election, I need to know if Tenesy's story holds water.

Grace crosses her arms over her chest. "Well, you're a grown man. I can only suggest what you should do. But be careful. You might find out some things you don't want to know."

"I already have found out things I don't want to know. Jeez, Roland may have been married to his sister? And now Clay's married to her too? That's an episode of Jerry Springer waiting to happen."

Rudy must have known. Why else would he want Britt to get out of town so fast? Oh yeah, the problem of Clay's momma and him would make him not want Britt around. *Damn.* I wish I didn't know.

"*Half* sister. They never had any kids, so at least it's not all bad. I guess. I swear, Benny…" The phone rings, and Grace gets up to answer it. It's three o'clock in the afternoon, and she's still in her pajamas. That's what happens when you have a wife who works the night shift. I hear her in the kitchen, speaking in a muffled voice, then I hear her say, "We'll be over in an hour." *Great.*

She passes me from the kitchen on her way to the bedroom. "You better start figuring out how much of your recently found knowledge you're willing to share."

I follow her. She's taking a pair of jeans and a sweatshirt out of the closet. "Why? Who was that?"

"Babe Shatner. Her and Lola have been digging, too, and they have some questions they want to ask me about medical stuff."

Terrific. Lola is in town. This day keeps getting worse.

"What does that have to do with me?" I could call Jimmy and have him radio me with an emergency. No, Grace would see right through that.

"They told me I should bring you along, and I think that's a great idea."

Of course she does.

Grace already knows a little bit about Vera Shatner, at least the bits that came out while Cass was in jail last summer. She knows about Vera's attempt to abort Cass and about her stay in the mental hospital and about Vera's suicide. But she's never heard all the stories about Vera before or in between either of those episodes. Neither have I, for that matter, other than what I've learned in the past few days.

My wife is basically the best person I know. She does her thing and doesn't worry much about what others do. She minds her own business and doesn't care to have others in hers. But even Grace can't resist digging into Vera Shatner's past. Maybe she wants to be helpful, or maybe she's as nosy as me. I'm pretty sure it's that last one. She's been a nurse for almost twenty years. Normally, when someone asks for her opinion, she gives them a vague answer and tells them they should talk to their doctor. But not now. No, Babe Shatner calls, and she's getting dressed and heading across Deacon at lightning speed. She's nosy all the way.

Walking into Babe Shatner's house always makes me nervous. It's been painted four different colors for several years. She says it's to keep the bad spirits out, but there sure seems to be a lot of them hanging around. It smells like a bakery and old dust. Grace accepts a hug from Babe, and I hope she doesn't try the same with me. Lola walks out from the bathroom, and Grace spends a minute fawning over her, complimenting her long blond hair, asking about her fake nails, and other general woman bullshit. Lola smiles, and if I didn't know her, I would say it was genuine.

"Hello, Benny," Lola says without looking my way. Then she leads us both to the kitchen. *Fine.* Grace can read about Vera Shatner while I eat some baked goods.

Lola was always a pretty girl, and now that she has money, she's an even prettier woman. Her complexion, which was spotty in her twenties, is now perfectly smooth in her forties. Her teeth are straight and white. Everything about her shines. And she smells like money.

We sit at the kitchen table with Lola, while Babe dishes up something fresh from the oven. Maybe this wasn't a bad idea after all. She sets a bowl of peach cobbler in front of me that still has steam coming off of it. I take a bite and taste heaven.

"These are some of my mother's papers," Lola says. "Basically, I want to know if any of her problems are genetic. I know it's a lot of crap, and I hate to get anyone else involved in it, but we need to know." She pushes a faded file folder toward Grace, who immediately digs in.

Grace holds up a picture first. "This is your mother? Oh, she certainly was beautiful. You look a lot like her, you know." She passes the picture to me. Damn, I had no idea. Vera Shatner reminds me of one of those girls in an old Frankie Avalon movie.

"Spitting image. Except for the eyes." Vera's were the lightest blue, and

Lola's are as dark as chocolate. I take another bite of cobbler as Babe sets a glass of milk in front of me. This is definitely worth the trip.

"Cass and I don't know much about her medical history, and we know nothing about our father."

Grace is reading papers, and I don't know if she's paying attention to Lola or not, but she answers. "So far, any of your mother's problems that are hereditary, you would have noticed by now. I know your sister has some issues, but they're pretty much under control now, right?"

Lola looks at Babe, and she nods. I spoon up another helping of cobbler.

Lola clears her throat. "Cass is pregnant."

I drop my spoon in my lap, and a glob of cobbler lands squarely in my crotch. All three women turn to me, and Grace gives me the stink eye. *Pregnant. Oh shit.*

"She hasn't told Clay yet, and I'm guessing it's because she's worried about this, so we want to know. I'm trusting you won't say anything." Babe drops a wet rag in my lap, and I try to clean my crotch. "That means you too, Benny."

"Of course," Grace says, continuing to read the papers in the folder. She glances at most of them briefly, but she reads a few with her forehead all scrunched up, so I know she's really considering something. I don't know how she can be so calm. Cass and Clay might be brother and sister, and she is *pregnant*.

Lola sits with her perfectly manicured hands folded on the table, watching Grace read. Babe Shatner is flipping through pictures, smiling at each one. I try to refocus on the rest of my cobbler, but I seem to have lost my appetite.

Grace puts the papers back in the folder and sits back in her chair. "Vera was bipolar. They called it manic-depressive disorder back then, but it's bipolar. Basically, that means she would be very energetic and overstimulated, even very happy, and then she would be very, very depressed."

"Yes. The highs weren't so bad, but the low times… It would break my heart." Babe Shatner is usually a pretty upbeat gal, but she's sort of sad and gloomy today. "Lola wasn't an easy birth. Vera got real sick. Something was wrong with her blood. After she had Lola, it was the worst. I bottle-fed her because all Vera did was lie in her bed. She took her medicine, but it didn't seem to help. Once she got healthy, she swore she'd never get pregnant again. But she did."

Grace flips back through the papers, seemingly searching for something, but continues to talk. "Probably postpartum depression. It's much more common in bipolar women, and yes, I can imagine it was rough for all of you. I'm very sorry." Babe nods and fingers the stack of pictures in front of her. Grace finds the paper she's looking for. "Her blood type was O negative. Do you know your blood type, Lola?"

Lola hasn't said much since Grace started in, which is unusual for Lola. "Uh, yes. B positive. That's pretty common, though, isn't it?"

"Yes, definitely. But a positive baby with a negative mother can make the mother sick, especially if the doctors don't know. Usually not with the first one, but it does happen."

"Dr. Kenney was her doctor," Babe says. I roll my eyes. That quack has been around forever. Considering the mess he made with my medicine for all those years, I wouldn't be surprised if he got his medical degree from a mail-order magazine.

"That must have been why Dr. Gross wanted to know Clay's blood type," Lola says. "She said Cass is negative. A negative."

"A lot of things are important to know when you're pregnant," I blurt out. Grace kicks me under the table, and I try not to flinch.

"What about the other stuff? Is it genetic? I mean, Cass has some problems, but nothing like that. And the baby…" Lola seems concerned about Cass's baby. She has no idea.

"There is a lot of research that says it is genetic. But there is also a lot that says people more frequently exhibit mental illness if they have the genes *and* have had a stressful childhood. So it's possible the baby might have some medical problems, but if the child has a loving and supportive family, and they know how to identify problems early, well, it should be fine," Grace says soothingly. *Not likely*, I think.

"We didn't know much about it," Babe says in a small voice. Grace reaches across the table for her hand.

"Okay. So now we know, and we can tell the doctor and watch out for it," Lola says. "I'm sorry, Grams, but we needed to know."

I get up from the table and put my bowl in the sink. I can't take much more of this. They are all so concerned about the baby. I am too, but for a different reason. Damn, I want to say something, but Grace shakes her head.

She was right. I should have kept my nose out of this.

I hear someone at the front door. Lola shuffles the papers back into her file and puts it on top of the refrigerator. Babe sticks the stack of pictures in her apron pocket. Damn, I can't stand the mouth on Cass, but the only thing worse would be if it were Clay. And here he comes. Just my luck.

He looks at Grace and me as if we are peas in ice cream. I don't even know how to explain why we're here. Babe saves us.

"Oh, Clay! I was going to read Grace's cards." Clay's face is red, and he keeps clenching and unclenching his fists. "What's wrong?" Babe asks.

"I came from the hospital. Now I know what Britt came here for."

Oh shit. "Grace, maybe we should read the cards another day," I say.

She nods and pushes her chair back, but Clay stops her. "No. You're a nurse, and I need to know a few things. If you have a few minutes."

Grace pushes her chair back up to the table. I have a bad feeling about this.

"Where's Cassie?" Clay asks.

"She went home to take a nap," Babe says.

"Good. I don't want her to hear this, anyway."

I'm not sure I want to hear it, either.

Chapter 20

Clay

AFTER LEAVING THE HOSPITAL, ALL I want is a handful of worms. I may not be the smartest guy in the world, but I know that most people—hell, all people—have certain things they put before others, including certain people. For some reason, Britt holds Freddy Adams high on his list, to the point that he would go track down his abandoned children in an effort to get a liver to save the sorry drunk.

In a way, I understand. I guess if it were Cassie or Shaylene, I would do the same. But I still don't like being the guy who's asked to give up a chunk of liver, and I have no intention of saving Freddy's life. What did he ever do to save mine?

Driving back to Deacon, I try to let it go and focus on my life as it is. Britt has a few more days before he's discharged; then he can go back to Dallas or go wait by his daddy's deathbed, but I'm not going to be there. Maybe somewhere down the line, Britt will understand, but if not, I'll write it off as a few days of my life that are best forgotten. I've had a couple of those, and adding more shouldn't be a big deal.

Instead of going home, I drive to Babe's house. The pink Caddy is here, but Cassie's truck isn't. I sure hope she went to pick it up today. If not, I'll take her now, and we'll start getting our life back on track. Benny Cloud's car is in front of the house. I hope nothing is wrong.

Grace is sitting at the table, and Babe says she's been reading her cards. I don't see any cards on the table, so I figure they have been talking about other things and don't want me to know. I don't want to know. However, Grace is a nurse. She'll understand the whole liver thing, and I want to get it off my chest. And I would rather not talk to Cassie about it right now.

She's been acting funny, and I don't want to upset her. She holds a lot in, and I'm sure the entire Britt thing has been weighing on her pretty heavily.

Grace is happy to talk to me. Babe and Lola don't move from the table, which is fine. Whether they are curious or concerned doesn't matter much to me, as long as they don't tell Cassie about it. Benny stands by the sink, and it's hard not to notice his crotch is wet. Again, I don't care to know.

"Apparently, Freddy Adams needs a liver, but he's too much of a drunk to get one the usual way. He wants mine." I lay things out right out of the chute, and it feels good to say it.

Benny lets out a deep breath. "That's it?"

I turn on him. "That's quite a bit, Benny. If your dad wanted your liver, would you give it to him?"

"Well, I don't... I never thought about that." He looks at Grace for help, but it's Lola who says what's on my mind.

"Well, you kind of need yours, don't you?"

"It would be a portion of your liver if he needs a transplant," Grace says calmly. I don't know how Benny got such a levelheaded woman. That's just another mystery of the universe. "It's the only organ in your body that regenerates, so your piece would grow back, and the piece he gets would grow large enough to take care of him. Are you a match?"

"I don't know, and I don't care. He hasn't bothered all these years to contact me, and now that he's dying, he wants me to try to save him. And how could I be a match if Britt isn't?"

"Well, not all kids are matches, and it doesn't even have to be a kid. There are a lot of things that go into it, but the health of the donor is important, as well as blood type. But there are other matches that make it more likely the liver would take, so a relative is usually the best bet for a close match." Grace seems to know quite a bit about it, so even though I have no intention of giving it to him, I'm happy she at least explains why Britt can't.

"Do you know your blood type, Clay?" Lola seems to have found a reason to be interested.

"A positive, according to the U.S. Army." That seems to satisfy Lola, even though I have no idea why.

"What about your dad?" Grace asks. "Did Britt say?"

"No, but it doesn't matter. That man has done nothing for me. Why should I do anything for him?" I hate being hateful. I want this to go away.

Babe pulls a stack of pictures out of her apron pocket and flips through them. She stops on one and lays it in front of me. I recognize Freddy Adams. He has dark, curly hair like Roland's, dark eyes, and those big dimples. He looks to be the same age as the picture I have of him standing by the red Camaro. He's at a bar with no shirt on, and a blond woman in a pink bikini is standing next to him, a little too close. "He wasn't all bad," Babe says.

"That's not my mother," I say, staring at the blond woman. It makes me even angrier. Was this the woman he ran away with?

"No, that's my Vera," Babe says gently. "They were friends. Good friends. In fact, it's safe to say that Freddy was the only person she ever called a friend." She points to another man in the background, who is smaller and shirtless. "There's Tenesy." Benny comes up behind me and looks over my shoulder. "This was taken at the Amvets. It was *Beach Blanket Bingo* night, and everyone dressed in bathing suits." She's off somewhere in her mind, and she smiles. "Those were great times. Pauline took pictures of everything. She gave me this one after Vera…"

I can't remember ever seeing a picture of Cassie's mother, but I have to say, if I'd seen the picture without the explanation, I would have thought it was Lola. The hair is bigger, the makeup darker, but it definitely looks like Lola. "She was gorgeous."

"A blessing for some, a curse for Vera. She had a lot of problems, and men often tried to take advantage of that." Babe lays a hand on my arm. "Your dad made sure that never happened when he was around. He took care of her. The minute she walked into the Amvets, he'd take her under his wing, and everyone knew better than to mess with her. Tenesy, even Rudy Drown, helped keep her safe. She was a grown woman and liked to go out, and Jack and I couldn't always be with her. We were thankful."

Lola scooted her chair closer to see the picture. "Where was my father?"

"Who knows? Riley was as flighty as a bat. I never knew what she saw in that man, and I doubt she loved him much. It's hard to explain. Sometimes you get stuck with someone that you really don't love, but you stick it out. Or you run away."

Her words hit me hard, and I think they did Lola too. Both of our fathers weren't much for sticking it out.

"But I'm glad Riley left," Babe continues. "Oh, I know, Lola and Cass didn't have a daddy around, but sometimes having one around, depending on the man, can be worse. I have a feeling that if Riley had stayed put, the girls' lives would have been a lot different. A lot worse."

"I don't mean to be disrespectful, Grams, but what do you mean when you say Freddy 'took care of her'?" Lola asks. "I mean, she liked to party, and so did Freddy, right?" Lola is dancing around the question I have: Were my dad and Cassie's mom involved in some way? I guess it doesn't matter, but still, my momma was somewhere in the picture, sitting at home.

Babe taps a finger slowly against her temple. "One night, Pauline called us from the Amvets and said we needed to get there quick. Vera was in trouble. Riley was already gone by then. We had the girls. Cass was just a baby, and Jack wasn't feeling well. So he stayed with the girls, and I went to get Vera. When I got there, Percy was there. He was still chief of police then, and there was a crowd outside, circled around Daryl Greggs. He'd been beat up pretty bad. Looked like he'd been trampled by a herd of mad cows.

"Roy Harper saw me and couldn't wait to blab to me about what had happened. He said Daryl was sitting with Vera at the bar and talked her into going outside with him. He tried to get too friendly with her in the parking lot, and Freddy pulled up and saw what was going on. Daryl told him it was none of his business, but Freddy made it his business. Tenesy had to pull him off, or Freddy might have killed him. It was bad. Then Vera and Freddy got in his car and left, and I guess Pauline called Percy."

"I don't…" Vera was a grown woman, so I'm not sure my dad beating up Daryl Greggs when she was getting friendly with him *was* any of his business. Unless…

"No, you don't understand. Vera was my daughter, and I loved her very much. When she was a girl, we'd go to the fields, and she'd sing to me while I gathered wildflowers. She had the voice of an angel, sang in the adult choir at church when she was eight, and everyone felt His presence when she shared that gift." Babe's chin quivers, and she tries to smile. "Then she got older, but I can't say she grew up. She had the mind of a twelve-year-old. She couldn't always make the right decisions. Your dad was kind to her, never made fun of her, although a lot of people did, and never tried to take advantage of her. That night, after Percy and Pauline got Daryl all bandaged up, I told Daryl if he tried to make trouble, we'd make sure Vera filed charges against him for attempted rape. Mrs. Greggs would not have taken too kindly to that. I went back home, and Vera was sitting with Jack and the kids, watching TV as if nothing had happened. Freddy had brought her home. It wasn't the first time. Or the last."

I shake my head. "I'm sorry, Babe. I know it must have been hard. But I don't see what that has to do with me giving him a liver. I'm glad he was nice to Cassie's mom, real glad, but he wasn't nice to me."

Babe's forehead scrunches like a wet dishrag. "You know why I've lived so long? Because I try to find the good in people. Oh, I know a lot of people in this town say things about me. They say things about Cass, and they used to say them about Vera, but I let that go. I find the good in them. It keeps hate from growing in my heart. Hate is poison. It will kill you if you take in too much."

My hand is shaking, and Babe puts hers on top of mine. "I know your dad did wrong. We don't know what went on between him and your mother. We only know things didn't work out for them. Not keeping in touch with you boys was bad. But for every bad thing he did, there is at least one good thing about him. And you're only hurting your own heart by holding on to the hate."

"He never called. He never once tried." I feel my eyes getting wet, and the last thing I want to do is start crying in front of Benny and Grace, and Lola for that matter.

"He made a mistake. And then another. And then another. Sometimes we get so deep into our own mistakes that we can't dig ourselves out, even if we want to. I don't know. All I'm saying is, revenge and hate are not in you. You're a better man than your dad or your brother ever was. Don't become them. Be the better man."

Grace stands up from the table. "We should go." She squeezes Lola's shoulder and gives Babe a hug.

"If you need anything, Clay..." Benny says then follows Grace out the door.

I wipe my face and don't look at Babe or Lola. "Right now, I need Cassie."

Chapter 21

Cass

I HAD A DREAM THAT IT was my wedding day. Not my real wedding day, when Roland and I went to the courthouse then across the state line to Laverne's Marriage Parlor to say "I do," but a different wedding day. I dreamed of a church wedding with white lilies and blue carnations. The entire town was there, and they were happy. I was wearing a long blue Cinderella gown, and Roland was standing at the front, smiling so wide that his dimples looked as if they would choke him. He was dressed in jeans and a pressed plaid shirt. When he took my hand, I felt a peck on my cheek. When I turned, it was Clay giving me away. It should have been the other way around.

Dog is asleep next to me. His mouth is open, and he's panting. He swipes at something imaginary with his paw every now and then and makes a little yelp. He's dreaming, too, and I don't want to interrupt. I roll over slowly and face the clock. It's almost four. Clay will be home in an hour. I'm not ready yet.

I'm worried about being a mom; I can't lie about that. But Lola and Grams will be a lot of help. Hell, they'll take the baby if I want them to. And I know Clay will be wonderful with it. He's wonderful in every way. I'm worried about the kid being goofy like me, but I think of what Lola said when we left Dr. Gross's yesterday—if we know to watch for it, we'll know what to do. So I think that can be okay too. The real problem, what I can't say to anyone, is Roland.

I know he wasn't the greatest husband, especially at the end. If he had been, I wouldn't have killed him. But that doesn't mean I didn't love him. I just couldn't live with him anymore, so when I saw the opportunity, I took it. It's on my mind a lot, and I've decided that if I had the chance to do it all over again, I would do things the same way. My brain wasn't right, and that was his fault. Roland didn't get me the medical help I really needed, and I couldn't change that. I wish I could, but I couldn't. But that doesn't mean I didn't love him. And in a way, I still do.

Of course I love Clay. He's everything that Roland should have been. But Roland is still with me—his clock in the kitchen, the truck, and of course, the Hill. If I could make him go away forever, then I could focus my love on one man: Clay. But I can't make him go. Or maybe I'm not ready to let him go.

Dog lets out a wide yawn. He stands up quickly on the bed, falls back over, then stands up again. I scratch his ears then swing my feet off the side of the bed and sit. I've learned in the past week that if I get up too quickly, I feel as though I might fall over too. I look at the clock. Four minutes later than the last time I looked. I'm still not ready to tell Clay.

I'm sure I need to talk to Dr. Button about this, and maybe I should go back with Lola in a few days to do that. I haven't found a way to shock him yet, so I'm sure spilling the fact that I still have feelings for my dead husband, and his alive brother, won't come as much of a surprise. I've seen him enough to know he'll say I have to get rid of one, and that choice is kind of obvious.

"I should have given him to Maryanne when he was alive," I say to Dog. That reminds me of the way she reacted when I said I was pregnant. She had said she was happy for me, but on the way to pick up my truck, she acted strange, almost as if she didn't believe something wonderful was happening to me instead of her.

"Are you sure you're having a baby?" she had asked. She gave me that twisted-face look a mother gives a child when she knows the kid is lying.

"Of course I'm sure. I'm not that stupid."

She kept her eyes on the road. "It's... unexpected. Roland said you never wanted any kids, and I believed him." She believed a lot of things my husband told her. And if they were talking about me, apparently he told her a lot.

"Why the hell were you and my husband talking about me having babies?" Maryanne and I have made some kind of peace with the whole she-loved-my-husband-and-had-a-baby-with-him thing, but it still burns me when it comes up. It's one of those things that I've learned to forgive, but I would just as soon forget.

She shifted on her seat as she pulled in to Lucky's and cleared her throat. "Well… it's… nothing. It came up in conversation once, and—it's nothing."

I knew better, but I didn't care to hear any more about her and Roland. I knew I had to tell Clay tonight about this baby, and the more I can push Roland out of my mind before I do that, the better.

The clock says two more minutes have passed. This is ridiculous. I can't sit here and watch the clock and wait for Clay to walk in. And I can't *not* tell him again. I get up and grab a jacket, leaving Dog in the bed, and decide to go for a ride. If I go to Grams's, it will be all about babies. If I go to Maryanne's, it'll be all about her. If I drive around and talk to myself, it'll be about Roland and Clay. I want someone to take my mind off of this stuff.

I crawl in the truck and start it up. It's chilly out, so I put on the heat. When the air blows, I can smell Roland. It's as if he's been hiding in there all summer and couldn't wait for me to turn on the heat. I have a box of Shatner's candles on the floorboard, so I turn the heat on low and try to remember if there is anyplace I need to deliver to. Then, driving into town, it hits me. *Little people.* According to Grams, they're magical, and I happen to know one.

A Little Bit of Ink has been located on Military, right between Murphy's and the Westco store, for about ten years now. I've never been in a tattoo shop and honestly never thought I would have a need to go in one. I don't want to walk in without a reason to be there, and I figure Angus was nice enough to me the other day that I could give him one of Shatner's candles.

A bell rings when I open the front door, and I stand in the entrance. Pictures of tattoos cover the walls, and a big glass case at the front holds different kinds of jewelry. The place smells like aftershave.

"Well, hello, strangah." Angus is walking toward me, wiping his hands on a rag. He has that great big smile that doesn't seem to go away.

Clay told me everything he knew about Angus. He's from some small town in Massachusetts, which is why he talks so funny. They must have classes in school to teach them how to not use an R right, but it is kind of fun to listen to him. One day, he showed up here on his motorcycle, bought the building on Military, and opened a tattoo shop. I guess he enjoys sticking people with needles. I'm okay with that.

I point to his outfit. "Why are you wearing that?" He's still wearing the mini-Benny costume he had on the other day.

"I'm on call. Auxiliary police, remember? Benny kind of requires that I at least wear the uniform."

"Benny's an asshole," I say.

"Well, he's also my boss."

I give him the candle in my hand. It's cinnamon, which is supposed to be for cleansing, and to me, it smells the best. "Here. That's for not being an asshole."

He seems happy about the candle. "You didn't have to bring me a gift." He sets it on the counter, pulls some matches out from the cash drawer, and lights it. "It does smell sweet, though. Thank you."

"Are you tattooing someone?" The shop is divided into cubicle areas, kind of like an office.

"No, just cleaning up. Why, do you want one?" He smiles again. I like his smile.

"Hell no. Roland had one, and I never could figure out why he would do that. Why he'd want to look at the same picture every day on the back of his hand."

"The symbol for Earth." He points to a picture on the wall. The drawing of a circle with a cross in the middle looks like the tattoo Roland had. "I did that one."

"That's what it meant?" I never asked. But it seems appropriate now. I wish I had known that when I buried him. I walk over to a small couch, and Angus follows. He doesn't seem to be in a hurry for me to leave.

"Tell me about dwarfs and midgets." Clay thought it would be rude if I asked, but I'm curious. And Angus doesn't seem to mind.

"Well, midgets—and by the way, they prefer to be called little people—are proportionately small. Every body part is smaller than average. Dwarfs are different. Everything on a dwarf grows normally except for their long bones. Basically, the bones in their arms and legs."

"Everything else is normal?" I'm not about to ask him to drop his pants, but the thought did cross my mind.

I'm pretty sure he knows what I'm thinking. "Yes, everything."

"What about elves? And gnomes?"

"Well, those aren't real."

"Leprechauns?"

He shakes his head.

"So you're from Massasusas? Massachusas? Massa…"

"Massachusetts." He gives me a wink. "That's why I say Chiner instead of Chin-ah." He has to force the A sound out. Hell, I can't pronounce his home state, so who am I to make fun?

"Now my turn." He sits next to me, and his brown eyes look right into mine. "How did Clay take the news?"

I shift on the couch and stare at the wall, where there are pictures of tiny black stars, astrological signs, and a smiley face. I hear a radio playing very low somewhere, and I recognize the Turnpike Troubadours. I hadn't pictured Angus as a lover of country music. "I'm telling him tonight. I guess. I'd rather not talk about it."

"Is there a reason why you're putting it off? You don't have to share with me, but you can, you know."

I focus on the wall again and see a black cat, numbers, and Bugs Bunny. I want to spill everything. Without Doc Button right here, it's tempting to drown Angus with my thoughts. For some reason, I think he would understand, but I'm still not comfortable spilling all my secrets to someone I don't know very well. I let out a long sigh. I don't know if I want to or not.

"Angus, you know I'm crazy, right? I mean, diagnosed and everything. If I don't take my meds right, well, let's not talk about that." I don't know if this is the best way to start or not, but I want to make sure he knows who he's dealing with.

He nods. "I know your history. But to be honest, I suspect we're all a bit nutty in our own way. Some of us are peanuts, some almonds, ya know?"

I want to correct him because technically, peanuts aren't really nuts, but I kind of want to be his friend, and I don't think calling him an idiot is the way to do it. So instead, I decide to go with the truth, or most of it.

"Roland and I were married for a long time."

"We all make mistakes."

"What? No." I'm starting to wonder if this was such a great idea. Angus may be nice, and he doesn't mind that I'm crazy, but even the logic seems crazy to me.

I rub between my eyebrows. I'm getting a thinking line like Grams. "We were happy, for the most part, and didn't have problems until the end. I know they were big problems, but I'm not sure that takes away all the good stuff. And now I'm pregnant, and it's Clay's baby, and it doesn't seem fair."

"You do love Clay, right?"

"Oh yes. But is it weird if I still love Roland some too?" There, I said it.

"I see. It hasn't been very long. And you still have some sense of loyalty toward him, or maybe even a bit of guilt about being pregnant without him being the father?"

I lower my head and nod. "Yeah. Maybe love isn't actually what I have. I mean, I hate him at times, but I still have something. We were together since we were teenagers, and he was okay then."

Angus starts to put his hand on my knee then pulls back. "It's normal. After someone dies, a lot of people have those feelings, and it's healthy, in a way, to remember the good things about someone instead of the bad."

"And Clay is perfect, but I thought that about his brother once too. What if Clay turns out to be the same, and I have a baby with him?"

"Everything I've heard and seen about Clay Adams leads me to believe that he is quite different than his brother. You know, you seem like the kind of woman who would want a baby."

"Oh, I always wanted a baby. It didn't work out that way."

"Well, you shouldn't feel guilty. Clay is a worthy man, and he's able to give you a baby, something his brother wasn't willing to do."

"It wasn't that he wasn't willing. We tried. A lot. All the way up until two years ago. I couldn't get pregnant. I went to doctors, I had tests. Roland said it was all the pills I was taking, but I couldn't *not* take them. He must have been right, too, because now that I'm not on them, bam, I get pregnant."

Angus's smile is suddenly replaced by a look of disbelief. "What?" His mouth gapes open. "I… Cass…"

"What? You can't believe we tried so much? Roland loved to try, believe me."

He holds up a hand to stop me. I guess he doesn't want details. "Cass, I can't believe… He had you going to doctors? Wow. I can't even…"

I thought Angus was pretty smart, but maybe he doesn't understand how this whole pregnancy thing works. "He knew I wanted a baby, and I wasn't getting pregnant, so it made sense to find out what was wrong. They didn't figure it out, though."

Angus looks angry. "No, I'm sure they didn't. Cass, I want to be friends with you, and therefore, I want to be honest with you. But I don't want to hurt you, and if I tell you something, I'm afraid—"

"What? Tell me." I hate to think this magical little person has the secret to getting pregnant when all the doctors I saw were clueless. It figures.

He takes a deep breath and lets it out slowly. "Roland had a vasectomy. At least, he claimed he did. He certainly knew a lot about it, so I didn't doubt him."

"What? How would you know?"

"Rocky, the doorman at Tina's, was talking about getting one, and Roland volunteered a wealth of information. Several of the bouncers were there, and he basically told us the entire procedure, from start to finish."

I shake my head. "No. He must have read about it somewhere."

"He said he'd had it done years ago. In his early twenties. I specifically remember that because he told Rocky it was so long ago that maybe they do it differently now."

I double over, my stomach rolling. If I could dig him up, I would kill him again.

Angus's hand is on my back. "Are you okay?"

"I'm going to puke."

He jumps off the couch and runs toward the back. My head is spinning like a bobblehead doll, and if I stand up, I know I'll fall down. When Angus comes back, he has a small plastic trash can that he puts at my feet and a wet towel that he lays on the back of my neck.

I start to cry, not from the pain, but I feel something coming up from my insides other than vomit.

"Maybe I should try to get ahold of Clay. Or your grandmother."

"No. I need to—" I lose my lunch in the wastebasket. It all makes sense now. That's why I couldn't get pregnant all those years. Roland couldn't do it. And he knew it.

I stand and turn toward the door. "I need to go."

"Are you okay? I'm so sorry," Angus says.

Everything is spinning, and I stumble. I feel him grab me around the waist, and I fall into his arms and feel my eyes tear up. I've never been much for crying. I know a lot of people cry when a tree falls, but not me. I guess Peanut has something to do with it, as well as the new medication Doc Button put me on. Either way, I don't care to do it, and the tears don't last long.

I know Roland was an ass, but he was *my* ass, and I always thought he loved me at least as much as I loved him. Sure, he did some bad things and said some bad things to me, although I can't be the easiest person to live with. But he knew how much I wanted a baby, and he made sure that would never happen. He lied to me about it and convinced me that it was my fault I couldn't have any kids.

"He kept it a secret," I say at last. At least, he kept it a secret to me, but obviously not to any dick at Fat Tina's.

"Maybe there was a medical reason for it." I know Angus is trying to make it not so bad, but he knows better. It is bad. It's horrible.

I glance at him as I swipe a hand across my face. "He had a kid, you know. He didn't claim her, but he did have one."

"Yes, I know."

Hell, everyone in town knows now. That was a secret for eighteen years, so why should I find it hard to believe he could keep a vasectomy from me? Only Maryanne, Roland, and Clay knew about the kid. Surely Clay didn't know about this. But Maryanne...

I'm off the couch, and I can feel the fire in my face. "I gotta go."

"Wait, don't go away angry. You might—"

"Do something crazy? Don't worry, I can't kill him again." Although I sure wish I could.

I get in the truck, and the Roland smell from the heater hits me the minute I turn the ignition. "Damn you," I scream and turn off the heat. I would rather freeze than have him around me again. Angus watches me from the doorway. I don't even wave as I pull out into traffic and head down Military.

Maryanne lives in her mother's house, the same one she grew up in on East Avenue. When we were kids, her dad worked at the dynamite plant across the state line, and her mother worked at the C&S Restaurant as a waitress. They were the kind of family that went their separate ways during the day and met up every night at the dinner table. I was at her house so much growing up that once in a while, I used to pretend they were my family too. I loved Grams and Grandpa Jack, but it always felt as though there were ghosts at our house. Nothing bad happened at Maryanne's.

Her parents died in an accident right after she came back from college. It was hard on her, but she was at least happy they died together. She said they would have wanted it that way. I guess sometimes when people die, it helps the living to think fancy things like that. I kind of think they would have preferred to stick around and see their grandchild grow up. Maryanne moved into their house with Shaylene, and she's been there ever since. Of course, she didn't ever make it the nice family home that her parents did, but she entertained my husband a lot, so maybe that counts.

I knock on her door and get no answer. I know she's here. It's late afternoon and way too early for her to go out slutting, so where else would she be? I knock again, harder. "I know you're home."

She opens the door, wearing a bathrobe. Her hair is wrapped in a towel. "I was in the shower. Jeez, you don't have to break it down." She walks back toward her bathroom, and I follow without closing the door. She stands in front of the mirror, takes the towel off her head, and starts brushing her hair.

"Roland had a vasectomy," I say.

She spins around and looks at me. "What? How do you know that?" I never was much for spotting a liar, otherwise I would have been on to Roland years ago. But I do know when someone is trying to avoid saying something, and Maryanne is as nervous as a pig at a barbeque.

"Angus told me. And you knew, didn't you?" I put my hands on my waist to keep myself from wrapping them around her neck.

"The little guy? Why are you so fascinated with him? Honestly, I don't—"

"Don't change the subject. This morning, you said Roland told you I didn't want any kids. Now, why would my husband tell you that?"

"Cass—"

"And on the way to pick up my truck, you were acting weird. You couldn't believe I was pregnant. I thought you were just jealous, but it's because you knew."

"It wasn't my place—"

"Neither was sleeping with my husband, but that didn't stop you."

At this, she quits brushing her hair. "I thought we were beyond that. I can only say I'm sorry so many times."

"I don't want your sorry. But you knew he had a vasectomy. And you never said anything. In all those years."

"We didn't talk for fifteen years! And he said you knew."

"Well, I didn't know. I spent all those years trying to get pregnant, and he was more than happy to do his part. And all that time, he had been cut."

She looks down at the hairbrush in her hands. "He had it done when Shaylene was in kindergarten," she says softly. "I remember because he came over right after, and Shaylene was throwing a ball in the house and hit him right between the legs."

At least Shaylene had my back. "That was thirteen *years* ago. That son of a bitch." I bang my fist on her bathroom wall until my knuckles hurt.

"Cass, calm down. It's over now. You're pregnant, and there's nothing you can do about Roland. He's dead."

"Oh, there is definitely something I can do. I'm through with him. Forever."

"Well, he's dead, so I'd hope so."

Maryanne doesn't know I still talk to him. Otherwise, I'm afraid she would want me to give him messages.

"Yeah, he's dead. Thirteen years too late."

Chapter 22

Clay

THE BLACK CAT CLOCK LETS out a screeching meow. It's six o'clock. Dog is asleep on the linoleum floor, and Cassie is nowhere in the house. I know she's not at Babe's, so I call her phone and get her voice mail. Wherever she went, I am a bit surprised she didn't take Dog with her. She's starting to warm up to the pup, and I'm happy about that.

"Come on, fella." I don't know when Cassie took him outside last, so I scratch behind his ears to wake him. His left foot moves like it's scratching, and he slowly wakes up. His tail wags as he stands up, yawns, and pisses on the floor.

I know I'm supposed to get mad and spank him or something, but he's a baby, and I don't have the heart. Instead, I give him a stern look. "You know better." He sits on his haunches and hangs his head. Maybe I can guilt him into going outside. I doubt it.

Maybe it's a good thing Cassie isn't here right now. On the way home, all I wanted was to hold her in my arms, take in the smell of her hair, and talk about anything other than Freddy Adams. *My father.* But I'm still shaking, and I feel empty inside. She would notice, and I don't care to put my troubles on her mind. My job is to take part of her load, not for her to take mine.

I grab a paper towel and clean up Dog's mess, then I go out to check on the worms. Dog follows, jumping and tugging at my pant leg. He wants to play, but I still have work to do. Well, it's not really work, more what I call my relaxation time.

Thinking about Cassie makes me smile. Sure, I've been in love with her since we were teenagers, but nobody ever knew that, except that stupid brother of mine. But now that we are living together, I swear, I love her more than ever. She has her odd moments, but hell, I play with worms, so I guess I can't be talking. I know she loves me too.

I'm sad for Babe. I know it must have been hard for her. It's difficult to love someone who not everyone understands, and it has to be even harder if it's your daughter. You appreciate those who seem to get it. I'm glad my dad was nice to Vera Shatner. But if he was her only friend, then he left her too. I'm not sure Babe sees it that way, but I do.

And she may be right about my mother. I loved her with all my heart, and I saw her struggle, but she didn't really act as if she missed my dad. She was more mad at him for what he'd done. We all hate to admit that our mothers weren't saints, but she was a woman, and that alone made her hard to figure out. Kids don't always know what their parents' relationship is like. Even if they get a glimpse, they don't really understand it, not even as adults. Women don't really talk about their marriages. Maybe they do with a girlfriend or a sister, neither of which my mother ever had, but definitely not their son. Maybe her heart problems arose from what Grams said—it was filled with hate and couldn't take any more. I don't know.

I reach in the bin and grab a handful of reds. They are moving more than the wigglers, it seems, and they're fighting to get to the top of the pile. I make a ball out of them and squeeze gently, letting them move through my fingers. At the store, I see people buying those balls full of foamy stuff that they squeeze to release their stress. I say all they need is worms.

Dog is barking at something toward the back of our property line, but there isn't anything there. I hear the phone ring inside, but I know there is no way to put the worms down, wash my hands, and get to it before it stops. I squeeze for a few more minutes and put my reds back in their home. The sky is dark already, I'm hungry, and Cassie might have forgotten about dinner again.

Dog is growling and barking, right at the spot where the path leads to Momma and Roland's graves. I walk back and look around but don't see anything. I pick him up and head back toward the house, setting him down long enough to wash up. As I get back in the kitchen, the phone rings again. I answer it, hoping it's Cassie.

"Clay? Is Cass there?" It's Maryanne, and she sounds out of breath. It's not like her to go running at night.

"No. You all right?" Maryanne and I have an odd relationship. We share a daughter that my worthless brother fathered, but one I raised. If it weren't for Shaylene and Cassie, I would have nothing to do with Maryanne. I try not to be so hard on her; she has been making some changes. But still, she's as loose as old skin, and most of the time, her only concern is about getting a feel. I'm proud to say I have never touched that.

"She's not at Babe's. She's not anywhere." I realize she's not out of breath from running. She's worried.

I feel my heart jump. "What's wrong, Maryanne?" Something might have happened to Cassie. I don't know if I could take that.

"She was here, and she was upset, and then… and she got in the truck and left. I tried to talk to her. I tried to get her to stay, but…" Maryanne is trying very hard not to tell me something, and I am not in the mood for her games.

"What the hell is going on, Maryanne?"

"Clay, I can't—just find her," she says and hangs up.

I slam the phone on its cradle, making Dog yelp. I pick him up with one hand and dig the keys out of my pocket with the other.

If Cassie is upset and isn't at Babe's or Maryanne's, there's only one other place she would go—the Hill. God, I hate that place.

Sometimes, Cassie goes into a different world. It's a place where only she can see or hear things, and nothing else matters much. It's one of the reasons people have called her names for so many years; it doesn't seem to be a place she usually enjoys being.

In this place, she believes that some things and some people are never-ending. They're like bad memories that never leave you. With Cassie, the memories are alive—walking, talking, and even arguing with her. I imagine she was in that place when she buried Roland. And as I drive up Booker Hill, I figure that is where she is now.

She doesn't seem to notice when I pull up into the dirt drive. My headlights are on, and I can see her on top of the hill, waving her arms as if she is having an argument with the air. There is a shovel on the ground next to her, and every once in a while, she picks it up and swings it at nothing.

Call Me Daddy

I park, turn off my headlights, and wait. Whatever she is arguing with, I figure she needs to get it out, and I'm fine to wait.

Roland used to pump her full of drugs when she started acting like this, trying to fix her. I guess in his own way, he loved her and wanted her better.

I crack the window so I can hear her. A cold breeze sneaks through the open window; winter is coming fast. She isn't wearing a jacket.

"You lied to me!" I hear her scream, and right then, I know she is talking to Roland. That doesn't surprise me. He is her bad memory that will never leave. "All those years, we tried, I tried, and you sent *me* to have tests done, like it was all my fault. And all the time, you *knew!*" She pauses as if she's waiting for an answer then continues as if she got one. Dog has his front paws on the dashboard, watching. His tail isn't wagging.

"One was enough? You selfish bastard. *I* never got one." She picks up the shovel and swipes the air hard. "If I could kill you again…" Yep, definitely Roland.

"Well, I *am* going to do it. I can take care of it. And guess what? I'm glad it's Clay's and not yours."

"Glad what's mine?" I ask Dog. He whimpers then looks back toward Cassie.

"Stop! That's not true! He does love me." I can hear her voice cracking. Dog lets out a low growl. I figure I should interrupt before she starts swinging the shovel again. I open my door, and Dog leaps over me, tumbles to the ground nose first, gets up, shakes his entire body, then tears off toward Cassie at a dead run. He's growling and barking at nothing, chasing off some invisible threat.

"Cassie?" I ask as I walk up from behind. She doesn't turn but sits on the ground, crosses her legs, and covers her face with her hands. I walk up slowly and sit beside her, knowing better than to make quick movements when she's like this. I keep one eye on the shovel and the other on her.

She's crying, and that makes my chest feel heavy. "You do love me, right?" she asks.

I hesitate because I want to make sure she's talking to me. "More than anything." I put my arm around her and pull her close. She's shivering. She rests her head on my chest, and the only sounds are Dog's barks, her sniffling, and an occasional *moo* from a nearby herd.

She stands up and wipes her eyes. "I'm pregnant." She turns her face to the sky, a clear black slate dotted with stars. "I'm going to have a baby." She doesn't move and doesn't look at me.

That wasn't the news I expected. I want to laugh out loud, jump up and down, and run in circles like Dog. But I don't. I look up and say a silent *thank you* to whatever lucky star is shining on me. Then I stand, towering over her small frame, and pick her up in my arms. I cradle her, kissing the spots where her tears have wet her face.

"No, Cassie," I say. "*We* are going to have a baby."

Chapter 23

Lola

I'VE NEVER BEEN BOOK SMART, but I am intuitive. After Benny, Grace, and Clay left this afternoon, I got to work. Grams is intuitive, too, but she's gone off in her own world, a world of Doors music and scented candles. She disappeared with the pictures she'd had tucked away for so many years. I thought it best to leave her with her memories.

This afternoon, I noticed something pass between Benny and Grace when she was talking about our blood types. I saw a flicker from Grace when Grams mentioned my mother's eye color. I heard Benny groan when we told them Cass was pregnant.

I'm intuitive, yes, but I'm also resourceful, and I know how to Google for information. What I find confirms my hunch. Basically, for Cass and I to have the blood types we do, our father had to have an AB blood type, and most likely be a negative. AB is the rarest blood type in the world. Then there are the different eye colors. Again, it's possible, but quite rare, that we would end up with the different eye colors we have. More likely, Cass and I have different fathers.

And although Grams believes that Freddy Adams was just a "good friend" of our mother's, he seems to be the best candidate for the other daddy.

I sit back in my chair, taking it all in. If I knew that Cass and Clay were half brother and sister, I would never say anything if she weren't pregnant. They are happy, and I know how hard it is to find someone in this world who makes you feel special, even if it happens to be your half brother. But she's pregnant, and that changes everything.

So I call the one person I can trust: Richard. He doesn't take me lightly and doesn't consider my ideas to be random or harebrained; he listens. I need to know what to do. I tell him everything I've found out and share my suspicions. He isn't shocked. He was an attorney for a lot of years, and I guess after a while, things stopped surprising him. I also tell him about my mother. "Nancy Sinatra," he says. "She was a beauty."

Richard suggests I find out Freddy/Rick Adams's blood type. It won't prove anything, but at least it could rule him out as the daddy. I doubt it will, but he's right—there is no need to jump to conclusions without a basis. He also suggests I talk to Grace as soon as possible. If I figured it out, she certainly has, and she's married to one of the biggest mouths in town.

It's almost nine o'clock, not too late for a visit. The phone rings while I'm putting on my shoes, and I grab the ancient wall phone from its cradle. It's Maryanne. She tells me the entire story of Cass's visit and Roland's vasectomy and says she hasn't heard from my sister since. She's worried. I'm not sure I believe that. I try to call Cass's phone, but she doesn't answer. Clay doesn't answer his phone, either. I grab my coat and the keys to Grams's car.

My first concern, of course, is my sister. When I get to her house, all the lights are off and both trucks are in the driveway, so I'm not too concerned. Clay will take care of her. I call Maryanne back as a courtesy because I am glad she called. Cass may or may not tell me about this tomorrow. I never know with her. If Roland had a vasectomy many, many years ago and kept it a secret, it means one thing: He knew his father might be Cass's father, too, and he never told a soul.

I drive by Benny and Grace's and see a light on. Good. I didn't want to wake them up, though I was fully prepared to. Benny answers in a pair of sweatpants and a Kansas City Chiefs sweatshirt. I see Grace sitting at the kitchen table in nurses' scrubs. She has a scratch pad in front of her with boxes drawn all over it and turns it over when I walk in. There's no need for her to. I was making the same little blood-type squares earlier.

"Lola, I'm surprised to see you. Is everything okay?" Grace cocks her head, and her forehead crinkles. She should start Botox now, before those lines become permanent.

"I don't want to make you late for work, but I need to talk to you and Benny."

He sits down at the table next to Grace. He seems ready and eager to hear what I have to say. I guess inviting him into the conversation will keep him from listening at the door.

I turn over Grace's scratch pad and point to the blood-type boxes. "I figured it out too. I know the implications, and I know what I need to do to find out the truth. What I want is for you to assure me that this is going to stay between us."

I look at Benny, but Grace answers. "Of course. If there's anything I can do to help, I'm happy to." But I keep looking at Benny.

"What? You worried I might say something?" he asks. "Come on, Lola, you know me better than—"

"Exactly. I do know you better than that."

He sighs. "I'm not going to say squat. But…"

"But what, Benny? Don't tell me you've already started talking." Damn, it hasn't even been a few hours. He's like a town crier.

"No. But my parents. And Rudy Drown. They told me that Freddy and Vera were… close. They might have figured it out, too, or at least suspected it." Benny hasn't been talking; he's been asking questions.

I hate having half a story. "And at what point were you going to tell me that?"

"I wasn't. I was going to tell Clay. He needs to know."

"Don't say anything. I'll take care of it. And by the way, while you were out asking your parents about my mother, you didn't come across anything else that might be important, did you?"

He glances over my head, and I turn to see a row of porcelain dolls sitting on a shelf. I'd heard that Benny kept dolls, and here they are. He snaps his fingers, and I turn back to him. "My dad said Roland knew where his dad was. Said Freddy came to talk to him over a decade ago, and Roland told him to go crawl back under a rock."

I gape at him. "But Clay didn't know? Roland didn't tell him?"

"Guess not. According to Tenesy, Freddy told Roland to stay away from Cass. I guess now we know why."

I thought about what Maryanne had said about Roland getting a vasectomy so many years ago. It all makes sense now.

Damn.

Last night, I dreamed about my mother. We were in a small airplane. She was flying, and I was in the back seat. Cass was a child and sat in the front, staring out the window. We were flying over an ocean, and I watched a pirate ship in the distance, which was shooting a cannon at nothing. We were getting closer and closer to the water, and I kept yelling for my mother to go up. When we got so close that the waves crashed against the windows, I reached into the front seat and pulled back on the wheel. I could see land in the distance and steered in that direction. "Mom, fly the plane!" I screamed. I couldn't get control from the backseat. Besides, I was strapped in, and I didn't know what I was doing anyway.

"You have to do it, Lola," she said. I steered blindly, my arms around the driver's seat from the back, and I kept the plane high enough to clear the embankment. We made it to land, but my arms were wrapped around my mom so I couldn't see her. After navigating a winding country road, we finally came to a stop. "At least you tried," my mother said, and then she disappeared, leaving the driver's seat empty. Cass never moved; she kept staring out the window.

I hate having dreams I don't understand, especially ones that are so vivid. I feel as if there's a message I'm supposed to get, but I don't, and that makes it even more frustrating. After only getting a few hours of sleep last night, that's what I'm left with. I couldn't have dreamed about lying on a beach somewhere with a mai tai. No, I dream about being terrified in an airplane, while my mother and Cass sit there and wait for the crash.

"You're up early." Grams is in the kitchen, and when she sees me, she almost drops her mug of coffee. "Oh my." She gets close to me and smiles. "Come on. Your hair is wrong. Nothing a little Aqua Net won't fix." I wasn't sure how she would react to me deciding to adopt my mother's look, but she seems pleased, and that makes me happy.

I follow her to the bathroom and let her emit enough aerosol on my head to knock ten minutes off the life of the ozone. I gag from the taste in my mouth while she fluffs my hair. "There." She cocks her head and smiles. "Spitting image. The makeup looks better with your dark eyes, though."

The doorbell rings. It's only seven thirty, so I figure it must be Grace, who just got off the night shift. She knows what I have planned for the day, and I'm hoping she has thought of a better way for me to get the information I want, preferably one that doesn't involve me parading into some half-dead guy's hospital room and asking questions. Or maybe it's Benny, and he remembered something else he found out when he was poking around in our business. Either way, I don't want Grams to know yet. "I'll get it."

I open the door, and Richard is standing there. He stares long and hard at me, then his face beams like a lighthouse.

"What are you doing here?" I'm surprised to see him; he hadn't mentioned he was coming down. But I'm also very relieved. I may seem independent to others, but Richard and I both know I rely on him for strength... and money.

"You're my wife." He says it as if I should understand what that means, kind of like the airplane dream. In a way, I do. He's willing to let me take the controls, but if I panic, he wants to be there to make sure I don't crash. I kiss him. It's a long, deep kiss, the kind I haven't given up in quite a while.

"Oh, Richard! Come in." Grams assaults him with hugs before he makes it halfway across the living room. They are about the same age, and Grams adores him. She knows he's good to me, and that makes her happy. Richard was also there to help Cass when she got in trouble, and that secured his place in Grams's heart. Mine too.

Grams turns to me with her arm still around him and nods at me. "What do you think?" she asks Richard. "It was her idea, but I helped with the hair." I'm not sure how I feel about being on display as if I'm in costume. It's just a little extra makeup.

He smiles. "All she needs is a pair of boots."

Not a bad idea. I have a feeling things are going to get real deep very soon.

"I've left the car running," Richard says. He's a smart man and knows the longer we stay around Grams this morning, the sooner she will start figuring out that he is here for more than just a visit. He turns to Grams. "My lovely wife needs to sign some papers for me this morning. I'll have her back to you as soon as I can." I hate lying to her, but at least the words didn't come from me.

In his car, I sink into the warm leather seats and try to focus on the all-jazz station Richard fancies. But my mind keeps going back to the little boxes I made last night. I wish I had thought to throw the drawing in my purse for reference, but I think I have it memorized. I know what I don't want to hear.

"Do you want to talk?" Richard asks as we pull out of Deacon. I shake my head, and he doesn't say another word until we are parked in the visitors' lot at the hospital. "You ready?"

After a tornado took down the old hospital a few years ago, the townspeople rebuilt like they were on steroids. The new hospital is a state-of-the-art facility, one I wouldn't expect to find in a Missouri town. Richard and I stand at the front door, looking up. It's the first time we've been here.

"Impressive," he says. Then he smiles at me again. I'm not sure if he's talking about me or the hospital. *Not a good time to get horny, Richard.*

I take a deep breath and grab his hand. "I'm ready." Or I'm as ready as I'll ever be.

My phone rings as we get on the elevator. It's Cass. I let it go to voice mail. I'm not ready to talk to her yet.

Grace had texted me Britt Chandler's name and room number. As we approach, we hear laughter from inside. From the condition I heard he was in, I didn't expect that. But I'm glad this won't be a somber affair, at least at first. I check my nails out of habit; a small chip on my pinkie finger draws my attention. *Damn. Already off to a bad start.*

A tall man, muscular and handsome, stands when we walk into the room. "Can I help you?"

A smaller man is in the bed. His face is bruised and his lips swollen. He's obviously missing some teeth. He has a cast on one leg and a sling on the opposite arm.

I can't seem to move or respond.

"We're looking for a Mr. Chandler." Richard sticks out his hand to the tall man. "Richard Warner, and this is my wife, Lola."

The tall man takes his hand. "Dennis. Are you a lawyer?"

"Yes, I am, but that's not why we're here." He pushes me gently forward.

"I'm Lola." *Your half brother's full brother's widow's sister. Or maybe your half sister's half sister.* This is going to be harder than I thought. I swallow hard.

"What a great name," Britt says from the bed. He and Dennis both start singing, "La La La La Lola…"

Like I haven't heard that before. "Yeah. I'm not sure why my mom named me after a transvestite," I say. They both laugh, which eases the feeling in my stomach a little. "I'm Cass's sister. The woman who hit you."

Britt stares at me for what seems like a full minute. "You look very familiar."

I shrug and grab a chair. "Yeah, I get that a lot. Do you mind?" I point to the chair. He nods, and I sit down. Richard stands behind me. I take a deep breath before I continue. "Cass is pregnant."

Dennis and Britt look at each other. "Well… congratulations?" Britt says as more of a question. It's clear they aren't at all sure why I'm telling them this. *Join the club, boys.*

"I know why you came here," I say. "Your dad needs a liver. Or part of one, I guess." Damn, this is hard. Richard squeezes my shoulder. My phone rings again, but it's an unknown number. I put it back in my purse.

Britt sits up in his bed, and Dennis puts an extra pillow behind him. "Look, I know what you're going to say," Britt says. "I didn't know Clay was about to have a kid. I'm sorry. I don't mean to put any more pressure on him. I know how he feels about our dad, but I had to try. He's not even willing to get tested. Dennis and I have talked about it, and… hey, I had to try. I should have come sooner. Maybe if he had gotten a chance to get to know my dad. I don't know. But maybe at least we can be friends. I—"

"Your dad and my mom were friends." I interrupt his rambling. "Good friends." I look at my pinkie finger. The chip seems to be growing. "And Cass is pregnant." Neither of them says anything. I am hoping they will put two and two together. I can't seem to put it out there myself. Richard squeezes my shoulder again. "I need to know what your dad's blood type is."

"Oh shit," Dennis says under his breath.

Exactly. Oh shit.

"Wow. Yeah, okay," Britt says. "He's B positive."

"Thank God," Richard says from behind me.

"Is that good?" Dennis asks.

"It's great," Richard says. "That means he can't be Cass's dad, which was a concern, but now we can forget about it."

But I don't feel relieved. I try to remember my little boxes from last night with As and Bs and Os. I'm in the backseat of the plane, and the water is getting closer. "Tell me something good about your dad."

"Well, he's real funny. Sarcastic funny, if you know what I mean. He loves those beach blanket movies from the sixties, Elvis movies. He watches them over and over and sings along. Oh gosh, I've seen that one about Elvis at the racetrack a million times."

"*Speedway*," Richard and I both say together.

Britt snaps his fingers on his good hand. "Yes, that's it! Hey, now I know why you look so familiar. Nancy Sinatra." He starts laughing. "My dad has a poster of her hanging in his office at the house. He said he was in love with her once but couldn't have her, which I know is bull, but he stared at that poster all the time."

"My mother." It comes out a whisper.

"Your mother is Nancy Sinatra?" Dennis asks.

"No, no. She looked like me. Or I look like her. And she had a poster too. And—" I stand up and put one hand on my chest. I need to get out of this room; I feel like I can't breathe. "Thank you both. I… Please don't tell Clay."

I turn to leave, and Richard puts an arm around me. I'm grateful because my head is spinning, and I don't want to fall. We get in the hallway, and I lean against the wall.

"Are you okay? It's good. Cass and the baby. It's fine, Lola."

I nod and look at him through my tears. "Richard…"

He wraps his arms around me. "You're shaking, Lola. It's over. Let's go celebrate."

"I can't." I feel tears stream down my face and wipe them on Richard's shirt. "I'm B positive too."

When I was a girl, I used to imagine what my daddy was like. All I remembered about him was his dirty-blond hair. I fantasized about reasons he might have left—strong reasons, valid reasons. He was in the Marines, dispatched overseas, and he would come back a hero. Or he was an astronaut, sent on a long mission to find life on other planets. Or he was on a ship, stranded at sea with Tom Hanks. I guess I wasn't a kid with that last one, but I guess someone never quits fantasizing about a lost father.

In every daydream I had, he was always the blond man. He was out there somewhere, wanting to come home, needing to see his two girls. I never imagined it was anyone else.

"Are you sure about this, Lola?" Richard stands next to me while the nurse gets the needle ready. After we left Britt and Dennis, we went to a waiting room and had a long talk. Then Richard got on the phone. He knows people, people who can get information and pull any string that needs a good tug.

"Yes. I have to know. And this is how I do that."

The needle pierces my skin, and I think about Roland. I hated the man, but in a way, I know why he did what he did with the vasectomy. He loved Cass, and he thought there was a chance they were brother and sister. He found a way to make sure that wasn't an issue, and he never told her. His actions were gross, in a way, but still. *Find the good in everyone*, Grams always says. *It keeps hate from growing in your heart.* Roland's eyes were blue, like his mother's. Freddy Adams's are brown, like mine.

The nurse finishes, puts a cotton ball on my skin, and secures it with tape. "I'll get this sent off right away. You should know something by tomorrow. Depending on how quickly the hospital in California can match it." I nod and roll down my sleeve. My phone rings, but it's an unknown number again, and I don't answer it.

"Now we wait. What next?" Richard asks. It never ceases to amaze me how supportive he is. I guess I haven't done anything too crazy since we've been married, so it shouldn't surprise me. He seems to get why it's important to me, though. And I love him even more for that.

"I tell Grams. Everything." It's going to be a blow to her as well, I know, but she's tough. She'll handle it. And she'll be on my side like Richard. I know that. She always has.

"Okay. Then we wait."

"Yes. Then we wait." I look out the window and imagine a wave crashing against it. I need to get away from the water. Then I'll figure out how to land this plane.

When we get back to Grams's house, she is sitting at the table with a worn deck of tarot cards in front of her. Her blotched face shows that she's been crying, and I already feel bad before I say a word. Richard and I sit down, and I take her hand.

"Tell me," she says.

I clear my throat and try to be as specific as possible about what I've discovered in the past day. "Yesterday, something seemed off to me. Cass and Clay have the same blood type, but mine is different than Cass's.

Freddy and my mom were close. Maryanne called me last night and said that Roland had had a vasectomy many years ago."

She stopped me there, though I was on a roll. "He did what? Now, why would he do that?" I didn't say anything; I waited for her to connect the dots. A second later, she let out a low sigh, and her shoulders slumped. *Yes, Grams. Exactly.*

"So I Googled blood types and went and talked to Grace last night. Then today, I went to see Britt Chandler in the hospital to find out Freddy Adams's blood type. I'm sorry, Grams, but with Cass pregnant, we needed to know."

She's blinking fast, and I know she's holding back tears.

"But it's not Cass. It's me." I look at my hands, folded neatly on the table. "I had my blood drawn in Joplin, and Richard called the hospital in LA where Freddy is. They're doing a type and cross-match. The results won't be in until morning, but I already know. Deep in my heart, I know."

When I'm finished, she collects the cards in front of her and puts them back in their pack. Richard's phone rings, and he walks out to the front porch, leaving Grams and me alone.

"I don't think Vera knew," she says. Of course she knew, or at least she had an idea. But Grams is trying to preserve a memory, and that is okay. She knows better, but sometimes it's easier to tell yourself something other than the truth. "As for Freddy, I don't know."

"Grams, could that be the reason my dad, or Cass's dad, left?" There I am, still considering the blond man.

"Riley? No, I doubt it. He always did his own thing. He came around when it was convenient. They never got married. He was there. Then he wasn't."

I nod. Strangely, I understand it.

Richard walks back in and nods to me. I take a deep breath. "Grams, I'm going to talk to him. Freddy."

I expect her to say it's a bad idea, but she doesn't. "There are things that only he can answer," she says. "But remember, sometimes we think we want to know the truth, but the lie we've told ourselves is often easier." She tries to smile, but it's more like a jagged cut across her face.

"I thought about it, and Richard and I talked about it. I'll be okay."

"I know you will, honey. But be careful what you share with Clay. He has a high vision of his momma, and I hate to see that memory tarnished. Even if it is wrong. Does that make any sense?"

"Yes. I understand. I'll be careful."

Richard's phone rings again. He answers it, but he doesn't go outside. "Hold on," he says. Then he muffles the phone against his chest. "This is it, Lola. I can still hang up." His face shows no indication of what he would do in this situation, and I have to go with my gut.

I reach for the phone. "This is Lola Warner," I say, strong and loud, forcing my voice not to break.

A weak voice on the other end responds. "Well, Lola Warner, I guess you can call me Daddy. Nancy would have enjoyed that."

Nancy. He called her Nancy. And I'll be damned if I call him Daddy. "Nancy? You mean my mother, Vera?"

His voice may be weak, but I can hear the arrogance in it. I intend to control this conversation as much as possible.

"Yeah. Vera." He says her name slowly, emphasizing both syllables: VE-RA.

"Did you know? About me?" I want to get this over with. There is no certainty yet, not unless we want to get a paternity test, but doing the type and cross-match should narrow the possibility quite a bit. Given Freddy's circumstances, the hospital in LA was willing to rush the results.

"I always thought it was the other one. Vera thought that too." He isn't apologetic, more matter-of-fact, as if who your father is doesn't matter much.

"You mean Cass, my younger sister? You knew she married Roland, your son."

"I told him to stay away from her, but he didn't listen. I even flew back to Deacon to let him know that she was probably his sister, but he said he loved her." He draws the word "love" out, making it sound sarcastic.

"He got a vasectomy because of that. He did love her, but he didn't want to have a baby with his sister." I have a metallic taste in my mouth. I don't want to throw up, but I'm fighting the urge.

Freddy Adams laughs. It's a weak, pitiful laugh.

"So you flew into town, told him, and left again? After so many years?" Strange what would seem important to him.

"Well, Roland, my baby boy, didn't care much to talk to me. I didn't want my wife or my kid to know about my trip anyway, so it was pretty easy for me to get on a plane and come back here. I said what I meant to say. But you're the one that had the blood work done, so I'm guessing it wasn't her after all. And a cross-match to boot. That tells me you're thinking about giving dear old Dad a hunk of your liver."

I guess it has been in the back of my mind, but I haven't had time to consider it. Mostly, I wanted to talk to him, but I'm not sure what I want to know. "Tell me about my mother," I say.

He coughs three times and curses between each one, as though it's painful. I take some pleasure in that then shake it off. "You didn't answer my question, Lo-la."

"You didn't ask one." I look at Grams across the table. She is staring at the floor. I don't like Freddy Adams. I don't want him to be my father. I want the dirty-blond dad, the astronaut on a mission, the guy stranded on an island.

He chuckles, and it sounds evil to me. "Are you planning on giving me some liver or not? If so, I'll have plenty to say about Nancy. If not, well, I guess I'm done with this conversation."

"You want to trade memories of my mother for a piece of liver? You're not really in the best bargaining position." I'm trying to remain coolheaded, but I just told this man that I'm his daughter, and he acts like that isn't life changing. I guess for him, it isn't. He hacks and spits loudly on the other end of the phone. "Bargaining position? You're a fancy one, aren't you?" He's not going to say anything about my mother unless I promise something I can't quite do yet. I can tell it's all a game to him, and one that I'm getting tired of playing.

"I won't have the results until tomorrow. Maybe."

Grams looks up at me. She knows what I'm agreeing to, but she doesn't shake or nod. I feel a line of perspiration form across my upper lip, and I resist wiping it away.

"Why don't you call me tomorrow, then? Right now, I got some green Jell-O with my name on it, and I best get to it. Don't want to starve to death, you know?" He hangs up without saying good-bye.

"Well?" Grams asks.

I shake my head. *I don't know. I just don't know, Grams.*

Chapter 24

Benny

GRACE IS SLEEPING OFF HER night shift, and I'm sitting in the living room, watching my Kansas City Chiefs lose again. I've been a fan since I was a kid, but I'm not sure if it's because they are the closest thing we have to a local team or if I enjoy watching them screw up every Sunday. "Run the damn ball!" I scream at the TV. The Chiefs make another pass, and the other team intercepts again. It figures.

I'm dressed in blue jeans and a sweatshirt. At least that's what I call dressed on Sunday. It's my day off unless something happens that requires my attention. That rarely happens, but I stay prepared. Being a small-town chief of police has a lot of privileges, such as the small amount of crime we have to deal with. But the job also has some disadvantages, and always being on call tops that list.

My phone rings. I assume it's one of my men and answer it without looking at the number. "Cloud," I say. The defense is on the field, and the first play out of the hat, they jump sides for a penalty.

It's Rudy Drown, which is not at all who I expected. "I never heard back from you about the Adams problem. I'm going to guess you took care of that situation."

After everything I'd found out the last few days, I thought long and hard last night about what my place is in this mess and what I need to do. The answer is nothing. The Adams family can deal with their own mess. I would still like to talk to my mom, but that's to satisfy my own curiosity and has nothing to do with helping anyone. But here's Rudy calling my phone on my day off, which makes me wonder again if there is even more to this than I thought.

Do I want to know? Hell yes, I do.

"If you mean did I talk to Clay, of course I did. You surely know that by now."

"Is he planning to go to LA to see Freddy?" he asks.

"Says he's not." There's this thing pulling at me that I can't quite put my finger on. Rudy seems a little too concerned about whether or not Clay talks to Freddy. Sure, he's afraid that Clay will find out about Rudy and his momma, but how could that hurt him? As for the false missing person report, that would be Rudy's word against Tenesy's, the sheriff versus a convicted felon. With Donna Sue long dead, no one would be able to confirm it.

I hear him suck air through his teeth. "The Chandler kid is getting out tomorrow, according to the hospital. So I'm assuming he'll go back home, and this will be over."

Damn, I was going to let this go, but the more he talks, the more I want to know. I decide to call him out on it and see what happens. "Rudy, I know about you and Donna Sue Adams. I also know you convinced her to file a missing person report, which is illegal, by the way." I figure it's best to give some and see where it goes.

He laughs. "Well, let's see. I know your momma didn't report all that. So you must have been talking to your dad. How is he? Adjusting to prison life?"

My face feels warm, but I'm not going to let him get to me. "I don't intend to tell Clay Adams none of that. So I figure you owe me the answer to one question." It's on my mind, so it's worth a try.

"I don't owe you shit. But go ahead. I'm curious as hell to hear what you want to know."

"Freddy walked away without much of a fight. Came back a week later and then left for good. I can't imagine it was all that easy, unless Donna Sue had something on him, a card she could play to make him want to stay away from Deacon forever." I'm thinking out loud, but now that I'm saying the words, it's starting to make sense to me, that thing I couldn't quite wrap my head around. A lot of men get caught cheating, but they don't disappear without a trace because of it, not unless they are afraid of something. And from what I've heard about Freddy, he wasn't afraid of much.

"Donna Sue didn't know anything," Rudy says. "Satisfied?"

Not really. If she didn't have anything on him, then maybe her boyfriend did.

"No, I'm not. He had to be afraid of something. But maybe my dad or my mom will know." I don't like loose ends, even if it isn't any of my business.

"Boy, you can't let it be, can you? Let me give you a bit of advice. For your momma's sake, you need to drop this. You understand that?"

My mom? What the hell does she care? She liked Freddy, at least from the way she was mooning over that photo album. So how could she have anything to do with him leaving? Unless... *Oh shit.*

I don't say anything while my mind slowly starts to spark. My stomach drops, and I have that heavy feeling as though I've suddenly heard what I least expected, and now that it's out there, it won't ever go away. Freddy had several women. My mom cared a lot for Freddy. And the only thing I've been able to determine that Freddy might have been afraid of was my dad, Tenesy Cloud. If Freddy was messing with my mom, there's no telling what Tenesy would have done. Leaving behind your life and disappearing is tough, but dying at the hands of Tenesy Cloud might be a bit tougher.

I envision the picture of Freddy with my mom in her Steve Miller Band T-shirt, their arms around each other, smiling for the camera. Then I imagine Rudy, taking up residence with Donna Sue, telling Freddy that if he doesn't go away, Rudy is going to tell Tenesy about him and my mom. That would have been a death sentence for both of them. I think of my mom, who didn't tell me shit, protecting Rudy and also protecting herself. It all makes sense.

"I hear that mind of yours working, Cloud. Maybe you ain't as dumb as I thought."

"I don't believe you." I do believe him, but I don't want it to be true.

"Yes, you do. And you also know that if your dad finds out, he's not going to play too kindly with your momma. Assuming he ever gets out of jail. Is that a risk you're willing to take?"

I hit the end button on my phone without answering him. The game is still on. It's fourth and long with a minute left. The ref throws his flag and says, "Personal foul." I turn off the TV and watch the blank screen.

There's no way to win this game now.

Chapter 25

Clay

It's funny how a person's world can change in an instant. It happened when I was five, that day my momma told me my dad was never coming back. It happened when I was in the army, when I found out the woman I'd married a few months before was found dead in an alley. When Roland died, it took a few days for everything all to take shape, but it changed again. And when I found out I had a half brother, my life felt like a whirlwind. But nothing beat that moment last night when Cassie told me she was pregnant. *Nothing.* My world will never be the same.

It's the middle of the day, and Cassie and I have been lying around, not doing much of anything but letting it all sink in. "Are you feeling okay?" I ask. Cassie is stretched out on her back, looking at the ceiling. I'm on my side with one hand on her stomach. I know it's too early to feel anything, but he's in there—my son or daughter—and I want him to know I'm out here waiting.

"A little queasy. Pissed off more than anything." After we got home last night, Cassie told me about Roland and the vasectomy. I never was a big fan of my brother, but I look at this one differently than Cassie. Sure, in her shoes, it would piss me off, too, but it made me realize how troubled Roland was. Doing something like having a vasectomy and not saying a thing to your wife goes beyond asshole-ishness—it's a mental problem. And he called Cassie crazy.

"Let's forget about that and focus on us. Our family," I say. "I'm excited, Cassie." Dog jumps up on the bed and wiggles in between us. We have a real family, complete with a dog.

"I want to get rid of my truck," she says. "And the land at Booker Hill. Start fresh."

That's not a problem for me. With a baby, she'll need something safer than that old truck she drives, anyway. As for the Hill, I hate that place. "Sounds like a plan." I kiss her forehead and throw the covers off. I have worm tending to do, then I plan to make a nice lunch for my baby momma.

A lot of people have big dreams. I'm not saying I never did, but over the years, my dreams have become somewhat simple: a wife, a child, a home. *A family.* It's something a lot of people take for granted, but I never will. It has taken me to the age of forty to have that within my grasp, and I intend to make the most of it.

I have some reservations, though, and they all relate to Freddy Adams. He had the dream, but it wasn't enough for him, and he walked away. What makes a man do that? How could he not see that he had everything he needed to make him happy right in the palm of his hand?

It snowed a bit this morning, enough to leave a few piles of white here and there. The worms are cozy, still under their tarp with a ceramic heater in place, safe in their cribs. Cassie and I had planned on building a room for them in the spring. *Sorry, guys, that room is going to be taken by another.*

I hear Dog scratching at the back door, and I let him out. He is so excited to run in the snow that he barely squats, instead leaving a stream of yellow as he pads through the white.

My phone rings, so I pull it from my pocket and hit answer. It's Britt.

"I'm being discharged in the morning. We're going to stay the night tomorrow then leave for Dallas." He pauses. "I'm sorry for everything. I want to keep in touch."

I can't help myself. Despite all that has happened, I've taken to the kid. I can't help his dad. I'm sorry for Britt, but he seems to understand. He tried, I said no, and now he seems satisfied to have a half brother that doesn't want to beat him up. I'm glad. My family keeps getting bigger.

"Why don't you and Dennis come for dinner tomorrow night? We'd love to have you." I'll invite everyone for dinner. Lola is still in town, and Grams needs a break from cooking, I'm sure. Britt and Dennis will be a nice addition, and we can all talk about the baby. We won't talk about Freddy Adams, not today and not tomorrow.

"We'd be honored, Clay. Thank you."

The thing is, all those events in life that change you forever? When they happen, they seem strong or overwhelming or even horrible, but after a while, you deal with them and move on. After the week I've had, I don't know that the universe can throw anything else at me that I can't deal with.

No, today is a good day, and it's going to get better. Big things are about to happen in the Adams family. I can feel it.

And I'm ready.

Chapter 26

Cass

WHEN I COOK, THE KITCHEN looks like an episode of *Hoarders*. I pull out everything I need—bowls, pots, pans, food—and put it all together, throwing things in the sink as I go. I'm a decent cook, thanks to Grams, but when it's all done and everyone is full, cleaning up the mess is more of a job than cooking the meal was. Clay, on the other hand, puts on a Grandma apron, moves smoothly from the refrigerator to the stove, and cleans as he goes. It's best when he's in the mood for me to stay out of the way.

When he told me yesterday that he was planning a dinner party tonight, I almost laughed. A dinner party sounds like something Lola would have, where the hired help did the cooking and the cleaning, and all Lola did was eat and drink wine. For us normal folks, I call it early Thanksgiving. But Clay can call it whatever he wants since he's doing all the work.

"I got this." He didn't have to say it twice. He wanted me to take it easy and maybe start coming up with baby names. I don't see what's wrong with Peanut.

Lola's phone has gone to voice mail all day. When I tried to reach Grams, she didn't seem to want to talk, either. I guess everyone needs her space, but I don't like to be left out, so I figure a trip to Grams's while Clay works on dinner is a great idea. It's already four in the afternoon, and dinner isn't until seven.

My truck gets through the snow without many problems. Maybe it's the oversized tires that Roland insisted on putting on it, or maybe it's just a well-made truck. When I drive it, I always pass a lot of cars in the ditch, but I never end up there myself. This afternoon is no exception.

As I turn the corner to Grams's house, the first thing I notice is a Harley sitting out front. Although I've grown kind of fond of Angus in the past week, I'm not sure I'm too happy about him hanging out with my Grams. He's nice, and Grams says he's magical, but who drives a motorcycle in the snow?

They don't hear me when I walk in, but I hear them. They're in the back bedroom, the one I grew up in. The door is shut, and they are both laughing. Grams might be old, but she is a woman, and all women have needs, even Grams, I'm sure. So in a way, I'm hoping she's getting her groove on with Angus, even if they would be the oddest couple in town. I'm afraid to barge in because if they are messing around, well, I won't be able to unsee that. Instead, I stand in the hallway and yell her name.

She opens the door, and I see Angus standing on a chair. No, that didn't make it better. At least he's got his clothes on.

"Cass! I didn't hear you come in."

"Obviously. What are you doing?"

"I am going to paint the back room and get rid of all this furniture. Make it more baby friendly."

Angus jumps off the chair and follows Grams out of the room. "I'm going to do the painting."

"Why?" I ask.

"Because I have something special I want painted on the big wall, and Angus is an artist," Grams says. "What are you doing here?"

"You've been avoiding me all day. So has Lola. I'm wondering why."

The smile on Grams's face disappears for a second, then it's there again. "No one's been avoiding you. We thought you and Clay needed to be alone, that's all."

"Uh-huh." I look at Angus, who shrugs. "Where is Lola?"

"She and Richard ran over to Joplin. They'll be back for dinner." She isn't looking right at me as she walks by me in the hall and heads toward the kitchen.

"How's Clay taking the news?" Angus stands in front of me, smiling that smile of his, but I'm not falling for the diversion.

I follow Grams into the kitchen. "Richard's here? When did that happen?" I don't mind the geezer that Lola married, but she didn't mention he was coming down, and that makes me really wonder what's up.

Grams busies herself at the sink. "Oh, it was a surprise. He came yesterday to check on everybody. They're going back tomorrow. Everything's fine, though."

I know better. I don't believe in happily ever after, and everything has worked out too easily. Clay is happy, and he's having a big family dinner with his new brother, who it seems is okay after all. He's blowing off his dad, and he seems fine with letting him die. Grams and Angus are planning to paint the back bedroom. I'm feeling strong. And Lola and Richard are in Joplin, spending money, I'm sure. We're all getting ready for our big dinner tonight as one big, happy family. Everyone is fine.

But I know what that means.

Everything is far from fine.

Chapter 27
Lola

I HAVE A FRIEND, MORE OF an acquaintance, who found out last year that her husband of thirty years has been cheating on her for the past twenty. It came as a total shock to her, and to most of us who knew them for that matter, but once the secret was out, he couldn't deny it. And he didn't try. It seems that no matter how well a person thinks she knows someone, she doesn't ever really know him—whether it's her husband, her parent, or a man she talks to at the country club each week.

That's understandable, I guess, since we can't ever really know what someone else is thinking. But even more surprising to me is that most of us don't know the one person we spend our entire lives with: ourselves. We can't decide what we want to do with our lives, can't always choose a mate that is good for us, and although we say what we would do in a certain circumstance, we react totally differently when put in that situation.

After talking to Freddy Adams on the phone for what seemed like an eternity, Richard and I drove to Joplin to check in to a hotel. I love staying with Grams, but with Richard here, we need more than a small bed. I got the phone call from the hospital this morning, and the first round of blood tests came back a perfect match. No surprise there. Then Richard and I had a long talk, made some more calls, and now we're back in the car, going to Cass and Clay's for dinner.

If someone had told me a week ago that I would find out my dad was someone other than I thought and that my real dad needed a liver transplant and was basically an ass, I would have said that my reaction would have been to shake it off and go get my nails done. But that's not what I did. I volunteered to fly to California, stay for a two-week recovery, and give half of my liver to a rude, uncaring man who I don't even know.

"We can make it a mini-vacation, stay an extra week and lie on the beach." Richard is going with me. Of course, he wouldn't let me do something like this alone. Not that I need supervision, but he knows I will need emotional support.

"Let's play it by ear. First, I have to get through this dinner and tell everyone what the heck is going on." I hate being the older sibling. Yesterday, it was Cass and me. Today, there are four of us.

"Remember, you can change your mind. There is no contract. You aren't locked in to anything."

"Should I change my mind?"

Richard glances over at me and smiles. "You should do what you feel is right for you. I will be behind you either way." I reach over and pat him on the knee.

We park next to a Mercedes with Texas plates. "I guess the gang's all here," Richard says.

I look in the mirror, reapply my lipstick, and fluff up my hair. Richard watches me with a smile.

I catch his eye. "What?"

"You look sexy with your hair that way. A quickie before this dinner?" *Damn, has it been two weeks already?*

"No, but your enthusiasm is admirable. And I like the hair too. Very retro." *Very Vera.* I put the hair and makeup on this morning as a way to feel a little of what my mother felt. It was an easy way for her to hide, I guess. Maybe she had low self-esteem, and pretending she was Nancy Sinatra was a way for her to feel better about herself. Or maybe she was so far gone that she really thought she was Nancy. It's something I'll never know for sure.

Freddy called her Nancy. I called him today and told him I'd made my decision. I had wanted to give him another chance at being kind, but he didn't want to hear anything that wasn't about his liver or my mother, nothing about his sons or about me. He just wanted to know how soon I would be there to give him a liver. And he said how much he missed Nancy.

"He loved her, you know." It's safe for me to say it in the car with Richard. I imagine that my mother must have felt safe with Freddy, even if he was a jerk. Grams says he wasn't a jerk to her, though. I guess leaving two kids and a wife for Vera Shatner would have been crazy. So it was easier for her to be Nancy, and he could be her prince. All of it was make-believe, and easier to do in costume.

"I'd say you were right." He watches the snow on the windshield, in no hurry to get out of the car. Richard is a patient man, a good man.

"I know you'll be there for me, but Richard, I need to know if you think what I'm planning is crazy. I'm still going to do it, but I need to know."

He puts his arm around me and pulls me close to him. "Absolutely insane. But you've always wanted to take care of everyone, and that's one of the things I love about you. You realize that giving him part of your liver may or may not keep him alive, but it isn't going to save him from himself."

I lean my head against his shoulder. "Maybe it's not him I'm trying to save."

He leans down and kisses my forehead. "I know that too."

Clay opens the front door before we get to the porch. My heart hurts the minute I see him. I doubt the news is going to be much of a shock to Britt; he's already figured out that his dad had more secrets than the federal government. But Clay feels that everything his father did is a reflection on him. It isn't. He is going to be a great father, and I know right now that he is happy and proud. I hate to be the one to change all that.

A fire is burning in the fireplace, and the house smells like cinnamon and Lysol. Richard joins Dennis, who is watching a football game on TV. Britt is sitting at the kitchen table, getting his cards read by Grams. I can hear Cass in the kitchen, slamming plates and dishes.

"I hope you're ready for this," Clay says as he takes my coat and hangs it in the small closet next to the front door. "We made a lot of food."

I smile and turn toward the kitchen to help Cass. "Oh, I'm ready." *I hope you are.*

Dinner is fantastic—not only the food, but also the conversation. We talked about football, babies, law school, and Christmas. No one talked much about "he who won't be mentioned," although he was obviously there, looming in all our minds.

After the plates are cleared and everyone has a piece of spice cake in front of them, I know it's time. I take a deep breath, but Britt speaks before I can open my mouth.

"Everyone, I have some news." His eyes dart around the table as if he's trying to gauge our reactions before he even says anything. Dennis nods.

"My mom called this afternoon. Apparently, someone has stepped forward as a donor. It might be a few weeks, but it's a match so far." The only sound is Cass's fork clinking on the plate as she digs into her spice cake. "I know you all aren't as excited as I am, but—"

"Oh, honey, that is great to hear." Grams gives him a reassuring smile then turns to me. I watch for Clay's reaction. His face is red, and he hasn't moved.

I take another deep breath. "It's me," I hear myself say. "Richard and I leave tomorrow for LA. We'll be gone for at least three weeks, with all the additional testing and the recovery period. I thought you should know."

Cass drops her fork, spice cake coming out of her mouth. "No way. Lola, you've done some dumb shit, but—" Grams nudges her hard, and she shuts up. Clay is staring off somewhere over our heads and doesn't say a word.

"Freddy and my mother were close." I look around at everyone. "Maybe too close, you might say." Richard nods, and I continue. "They were… I'm a perfect match."

Cass's green eyes spark. "You mean…" She stops and looks at Clay, then Britt, then back to me. I nod.

"So I have a sister too?" Britt understands the tension in the room and is trying to hold back his enthusiasm.

"It appears so," I say. "Sorry."

"Oh no. I'm thrilled," he says. "You're leaving tomorrow?"

I glance quickly around the table. "The transplant team said they can do my tests from there as long as my regular doctor signs off, saying I'm basically healthy. My last physical was three months ago, and he faxed them a copy. So several days of testing, then the surgery by Monday."

Grams is wringing her napkin. "That's so fast."

"Well, he is dying," I remind her.

"Wait." Cass puts her hand on Clay's shoulder, but he doesn't move. "Clay and I aren't related though, right?"

"No. Not at all," Richard says. "You are the oddball of the bunch. Or the normal one, depending on how you frame it."

I'm concerned that Clay is still completely quiet. "Clay? Say something, please?" I was afraid he would be angry, and although I haven't seen it for myself, I'm sure he isn't much fun to tangle with when he is. But his silence is even worse.

"Why? Why are you doing it?" His voice is lower than usual.

"I know all the pain he has caused, but in the end, family needs to count for something. I'm sorry, Clay." I don't even know if that is the real reason, but I'm having a hard time explaining it to myself, much less putting it into words for anyone else. I'm not sorry for my decision, but I am sorry that I have hurt Clay.

Clay pounds a fist on the table but still doesn't raise his voice. "He gave up his right to be called 'family' thirty-five years ago. He didn't even claim you, Lola."

"That's not fair. He didn't even know about Lola." I love that Richard tries to stick up for me, but now is not the best time.

"Is that what he told you?" Clay asks. "And you believed that lying piece of shit?"

Now this is more what I expected.

"Clay—" Britt starts to speak, but Clay points a finger at him.

"Don't say a word. I'm trying to keep you separate from him, so don't make that a hard thing to do."

But Britt can't sit there. He has something to say, and I know he's been holding it in. "So letting him die is justice? Payback of some kind? No, it's being *him*. He'll probably laugh about it and relish how similar you are to him. 'My boy,' he'll say. 'Just like his old man.'"

Clay stands up and knocks over his chair. He places both hands on the table. "You think coming here and finding someone to donate a liver to the devil will get you back in his good graces? It won't. He's using you like he has so many others."

Dennis stands at the other end of the table. "You're right. But Britt and Lola deserve to find that out for themselves." He reaches for Britt's good hand. "Come on, we may have worn out our welcome."

Grams is wringing her hands, and her eyes are red. Now I'm pissed. Nobody makes my Grams cry.

"Enough!" And I'm on my feet too. "Look at you. Yelling about something that means nothing. Absolutely nothing. It's a piece of a liver. It will grow back in a few months."

"Yeah, well, I wonder if he'll grow a soul with it." Clay turns to leave.

Cass puts her hand on his arm to stop him. "We all had parents that made mistakes, big mistakes. Some of them weren't their faults. Some of them were because they were stupid kids. Okay, maybe because they were assholes. But guess what? We all turned out okay in spite of them." And that's how to shut up a room: Cass saying something logical. I want to climb across the table and hug her right then.

I feel my eyes starting to get wet, but the last thing I want to do is ruin my makeup, so I suck it up. "I'm putting my foot down. The bullshit stops with our parents. We are much better than that. We are fine, we have each other, and we have a baby coming—one that is going to be loved and taught how important family is. Sure, we're a bit odd, but we're still family."

Grams wipes her face with a napkin.

"Screw Freddy Adams," I say. "I don't care if he lives or dies, but I'm not going to stand around and let him die just because I think it makes up for everything he's done in some way. My mother died and never had to answer for anything. It was too easy for her. Not fair. No, if he dies, it won't be because we didn't show him that we are better than him." And maybe that's the best explanation I can give. I am better than my parents, despite them.

Having said my piece, I sit back down in my chair and look at my lap, leaving Clay and Dennis standing at opposite ends of the table. No one speaks for what seems like several minutes.

"Dinner is over." Clay clears the table then stays in the kitchen while the rest of us say our good-byes.

Cass hugs me and whispers in my ear. "I get it. Don't worry about Clay; he'll be fine." As we walk out the door, my phone rings. It's an unknown number again. I need a diversion from all of this, so I excuse myself.

"Lola Warner." I try to keep my voice steady.

"You said you'd help me. Did you mean it?"

At first, I don't recognize the voice. Then I remember the tall, brown-eyed young girl from the clinic, Hailey.

Chapter 28

Clay

WALKING THROUGH THE AIRPORT IN Los Angeles, I felt a bit of what my worms must experience in their compound. Writhing bodies rubbed together, climbing over and under. An endless flow of people went left then right, turning, twisting, coming together as a unit, yet moving separately through the corridor. I kept expecting a giant hand to grab us and gently squeeze us together like a stress ball. I move with the mass, hoping these people know where they're going. I just keep looking for signs that direct me where to go so I can get the hell out of here. I follow the signs toward "ground transportation" and am led to a transport—more worms packed tightly into a moving container.

The last time I was on a plane was almost twenty years ago in the army, and it wasn't anything like the jet I just got off of. I got the stewardess to move me to a seat that was supposed to have more legroom, but it still wasn't much for a guy my size. I also had to promise to get people off the plane in case of an emergency. If there was an emergency, I figured they would be lining up to get off, so that wasn't much of a promise. I was also informed that the airline workers aren't called "stewardesses" but "flight attendants." I wanted to tell the *flight attendant* to quit calling me "Cowboy" because I wear boots.

I'm here for Lola. I didn't expect Cassie's reaction when I objected to Lola giving my father a piece of her liver. Usually, she's the first person to call someone out on a stupid move, but she was totally supportive of her sister. She said Lola had her own demons to make up for, as if that made any sense at all. It obviously did to Cassie. We had words, not a real argument, but the closest we've come yet. She even called me an ass for thinking only of myself, and that hurt. It also gave me something to consider.

Even though I have no desire to see Freddy, much less help him, I can't make that decision for Lola. She found out her dad is some loser other than the loser she thought he was. And she's my sister, so regardless of the circumstances, I'm going to be there for her, even if I don't agree with her. Oh, I'm still pissed, but I'll be pissed on my own time.

Cassie and Babe dropped me off this morning at the airport in Springfield and said they had some errands to run for Lola and her latest charity case. Cassie didn't go into detail, and I'm glad for that. She and Lola have been closer in the past few months than they've been in their entire lives, and that's important. So if she wants to help Lola with whatever it is she has going on, that's fine with me. I felt bad about leaving her, though, especially when she had a lot on her mind. She said she was fine, but now that I've been flying around in a metal tube most of the day, all I want to do is call her and say hello. I miss her already.

I know most people don't understand the Cassie-and-me thing, but that's all right; we understand it. I've been in love with her since we were teenagers, but she was always Roland's, and I waited all these years for a chance to change that. She changed it when she buried him in their yard. I stepped up and let her know how I felt. The rest, well, it's working out. I knew it would. We are perfect together. She needed someone who would love her and understand that her mind works differently. I needed someone who would keep me grounded but still on my toes. Cassie isn't easy, but that's one of the many things I love about her.

"Hey there, Cowboy, you lost?" A tall, redheaded woman with an LAX badge and a smile brighter than a polished buckle is standing next to me. She's close enough that I can smell her musky perfume. I prefer flowers and fruits.

"Looking for a car rental or a cab or something—anything to get me out of here," I say.

I follow her finger to a line of booths for car rental companies. I'm not excited about driving in a town the size of Los Angeles, so I change my mind and go toward the sign that reads "taxi." I walk right by the ticket counters, and since my return is open ended, it is pretty difficult not to stop right there, get a ticket back to Springfield, and go home. But I don't. I find a cab, give him the address of Cooper Hospice, and ask him to take me to a hotel within walking distance of it. I crawl in the front seat and watch the worms drive by. They're a bit more organized as we weave through the streets of Los Angeles. I am now very glad I'm not driving.

The cabbie drops me off at a Hilton Gardens, which sounds pretty expensive to me, but he says it's not too bad. There's a mall across the street, which he says isn't really a mall because it's not big enough, but it looks pretty big to me. Cooper Hospice is located in a hospital that is two blocks west of the hotel. This sounds perfect, especially since I don't have to do any city driving.

I pay the driver and check in to the hotel. My room is clean and has a big bed, and again, I wish Cassie was with me. I try to call her but get her voice mail, so I leave her a message telling her I made it safely and that I love her. I decide to walk to the non-mall and get something to eat. I also decide I should buy a pair of shoes before I walk down to the hospital and let Lola know I'm here. Right now, I feel like a cowboy boot in a pile full of sandals.

I settle on a pair of Stacy Adams loafers that are half off. They're still forty bucks. Forty dollars seems like a lot for a pair of shoes made by some guy with a girl's name that I might wear to church. But at least they say Adams, so I figure they were made for me. After an overpriced sandwich from some joint that's supposed to be famous for barbeque, I go back to the hotel, change my shoes, and start walking toward the hospital.

For some reason, I expected Cooper Hospice to be some small building with a few rooms where people who are dying can wait it out until it's all over. Maybe I'm used to small-town living and small-town dying. But Cooper Hospice is basically a wing at a hospital that's bigger than all of Deacon. The elevator stops on the fourteenth floor, the floor Freddy Adams is dying on. A short woman with big, round glasses and a tank top that reads *Juicy* gets off, and I glance in the waiting room. *My dad, Freddy Adams, is lying in a bed down this hall, dying.* I'm willing the elevator door to shut, and as it does, I stop it with one of my fancy loafers.

The waiting room is as big as the main hall at the Elks Lodge in Deacon. It has five neat, widely spaced rows of more than a dozen chairs, and everything—the chairs, the curtains, and the wallpaper—is in shades of blue and silver. The colors are surely meant to be comforting in some way, but they make me feel as if I'm getting ready for a Cowboys football game. The room is full of people, adults and children. Some are sitting alone, some are crying, and some are laughing and sharing stories with family. Juicy joins a group of two other women who are talking with a man in a wheelchair. I spot an empty chair behind them and sit.

When my mother died, it was sudden. She had a bad heart, which she apparently gave to Roland. She'd been my rock, my foundation, for many years, and when I found her lying on her living room floor, it shattered my world. I remember calling the ambulance for her and sitting next to her, trying to dab the tea off her flowered housecoat that she had apparently spilled when she fell. I don't know why that was important to me, maybe because I knew how much she liked that housecoat, but more likely because I was in shock, as the paramedics later said. She'd wet herself when she passed, and after they took her away, I scrubbed the already worn carpet of her trailer on my hands and knees. I never got a chance to say good-bye or to let her know how much I loved her.

I listen to Juicy and her family in front of me, laughing and sharing memories. All three of the women call the man "Daddy," and he answers them in a voice that is soft but strong. I know they will all have a chance to say good-bye, as it should be.

I look down the hallway that leads to the patients' rooms. *What do you say to someone who left you like an afterthought so many years ago?* I could ask him why, but no reason he had would give me comfort. I could tell him how it has made me feel, living without a father my entire life, wishing he were dead so I wouldn't have to consider that he just didn't care. But he still wouldn't care. His only concern is his own survival. *But he is my father, my blood.* I walk to the hallway leading to the rooms. Men and women holding IV poles walk the hall; nurses in blue scrubs bounce between rooms. I lean against the wall and focus on my loafers. *He's my blood, but he chose not to be my father. Can I live with myself if I choose not to be his son?*

Another man, thin and balding, is being wheeled toward the waiting room, and my heart beats hard in my chest. They come toward me, and I hold my breath as they pass. *I don't even know what he looks like.* The nurse wheels the man into the waiting room and puts the wheelchair brakes on in front of a younger man, about my age, who has two young boys in tow. They crawl on the older man's lap and hug his neck hard. He hugs them back.

I've seen enough.

My mother deserved this: dying with her family around her, sharing good memories, getting hugs from her sons and grandkids that she'll never know. She didn't deserve to lie in her own urine on the ratty carpet of a run-down trailer. Freddy Adams deserves nothing from me. Nothing.

I get back on the elevator and have to unclench my fists to push the button to Lola's floor. In a way, I guess I do understand why she's doing this. Like Britt, she's grasping at a family that isn't there. We'll never be Juicy's family, sharing the past in a waiting room, not with Freddy in the mix. Lola and Britt have hope. I don't. But I do have them.

My stomach is turning, and I'm not sure if it's from the barbeque, the loafers I'm sporting, the fact that I was just within a few yards of Freddy Adams, or a combination of all of the above. When the doors open to Lola's floor, I step out and see Richard in the hall. I immediately feel a sense of relief.

Richard is in his eighties, at least that's what Cassie says, which makes him forty years older than Lola. Cassie also says Lola loves him for his buckets of money, and he has cement buckets full of that. I don't know if I agree. I've seen Lola reach for his hand when they are walking together, and I've never heard her say a bad thing about him, so maybe she does love him for other reasons. It's none of our business, anyway. They seem happy, so what difference does it make?

Richard smiles and sticks out his hand for me to shake. "Thank you for coming. It's been a rough day for her, and it will mean a lot that you're here. I definitely owe you one."

"Don't let her try to talk me into seeing Freddy, and we'll call it even." Otherwise, I might kill the bastard, and then I would need to call in that favor.

Richard pulls me into the waiting room and sits in a chair. I sit next to him. It's a little strange. I wouldn't really consider Richard and me friends. He was Cassie's lawyer when she killed Roland, and of course, he's Lola's husband, but we don't go fishing together or anything. Maybe we should.

"Clay, she isn't going to tell you this, but I am." *Oh shit, more surprises.* He smiles and shakes his head. "He's a real piece of work."

"You met him?"

"Yes, and I stayed in that room as long as I could stand to, which may have been five minutes. A vile man. Has no remorse, no conscience. Lola tried to tell him that Britt was doing fine, and he said, 'That faggot is dead to me.' That's when I had to leave the room."

I feel my face getting hot.

"I want to say something to you," Richard says. "Not getting tested, not even wanting to meet him—I know these weren't easy choices to make. But don't feel guilty. I know you will because you're a decent man, and I know you're angry, but you need to let that go. I'm afraid that if you'd grown up around him, you wouldn't be the man you are. And that would be a shame."

I've never been much for male bonding, but I think that's what this is. The fact that Richard is in his eighties makes me think of him as a grandfather rather than my brother-in-law. I appreciate his words, but I don't know how to respond.

"So, his loss," Richard says.

"There you are." A young nurse in light-blue scrubs appears in front of us. "The doctor was here to talk to your wife, and she's asking for you. Is this your son? I see the resemblance."

We both start laughing. It feels good to laugh. Richard slaps me on the back. "My brother-in-law. But I sure would be proud if he was."

We both stand, and I stumble a little. "New shoes," I say. But it isn't the shoes. I've never heard those words in my life. I don't care what any man tells you. Having a father who says he's proud, even if he isn't really your father, is a feeling like no other.

I'm feeling strong as I walk down the hallway with Richard by my side. I'm ready to stand with my sister because that's what men do. A few words, a moment, and I am changed. I can do this. And I don't need to worry about Freddy Adams.

When we walk into Lola's room, though, she's packing her suitcase. "What are you doing?" Richard asks.

Lola sits on the bed and covers her face. In an instant, Richard is on his knee next to her. "What's going on?"

She wipes her face. "It's over. We're going home."

"What happened?" I ask. "Did he die?" I guess that wasn't the most tactful way to ask, but damn, I'm new to all this.

"No. Not yet, anyway. The doctor got all my tests back. I can't donate, so it's over."

I would have thought hearing this news would make me feel good, but it doesn't. "I thought you were a perfect match."

She stands up and starts packing again, not looking at Richard or me. "I am. But according to the doctor, I have my own problems to worry about now." She turns around and reaches for Richard's hand but looks at me. "I have cancer."

I grab the rail of her hospital bed. Richard wraps his arms around her and buries his head in her hair. "It's going to be all right," he says.

No. I want to scream it. My mouth is hanging open, but nothing is coming out. I'm holding the bedrail so tightly that it starts shaking. I try to make it stop, but it won't. It won't stop.

Lola clears her throat. "The doctor said they caught it early. A hysterectomy, radiation, and chemo if I need it. I'll be fine. It should be fine. He wanted to do it right away, here, tomorrow morning, but I want my own doctor." She sits on the bed and looks up at Richard. "Can you get us a flight out of here?"

Richard sits next to her. "Of course," he says in a quiet voice. "I'll call Dr. Gross, too, and have her get everything ready. We'll get through this, Lola."

She cups Richard's cheek and turns back to me. "I need to tell Freddy."

I bang the bedrail hard, and one edge of it goes down six inches. I know Freddy Adams didn't give Lola cancer, but since he's surfaced, it's been one heart-ripping event after another. I need to blame someone, and he's the best I have.

"I'll go with you," Richard says, "then I'll get on the phone and get us out of here first thing in the morning."

The blue-and-silver waiting room is empty except for a few people. An older woman watches reruns of *The Six Million Dollar Man* on a wide-screen television that is mounted between two windows. Two guys, maybe in their early twenties, have claimed a corner and are sleeping with their backs to the wall. I'm sitting in the middle of the room with my legs stretched before me when Lola and Richard come back from informing Freddy Adams that he isn't going to be receiving part of Lola's liver after all.

Lola sits next to me. "That's done. You okay?"

I nod. *Fine.*

"Clay, I need to tell you something. Freddy said he did try to keep in touch with you and Roland when you were kids, but your mother wouldn't—"

I cut her off. "He's lying." Freddy Adams has taken no responsibility for his actions, and I will not let that lying son of a bitch find a way to blame my mother. "He lied to Britt. He lied to his current wife. What makes you think he's telling you the truth?"

"Maybe—"

I raise a hand between us, signaling for her to stop. I deserve the memory of one good parent.

We sit there together for five minutes, listening to the TV ramble about the wonders of modern technology as portrayed in the 1970s, then Richard reaches for Lola's hand but speaks to me. "I'm chartering a private jet for in the morning. I'll text you the info. And if you're not there…"

"I'll be there," I say without looking up. Or maybe I won't. I need to think, but I need to be alone to do it.

I stop them before they get on the elevator. "Did you tell him that I'm here?" I knew, up until this last visit to Freddy, that Lola hadn't told him I was in LA. But things have changed.

She looks down the hallway that leads to his room then back to me. "No."

The room is quiet again except for the two guys snoring, the Six Million Dollar Man trying to save the world, and the battle going on inside my own mind. I was pissed when Lola decided to help Freddy Adams, but in a weird way, she was doing it more for herself than for him. Maybe she was doing it for her mother, or she wanted to save a life, or it was some kind of penance, but it wasn't all about Freddy. Whether she realized it or not, she was also doing it for me.

Lola's decision meant I didn't have to choose. I could be angry or resentful, and I wasn't hindering his ability to live by doing so. Now, with Lola's offer off the table, the situation has changed. I will be condemning him to death, in a way, by doing nothing. There is no donor liver coming, and I'm the only living offspring he has left who could possibly be a match. I'm his only shot. It was easy to say no when I was halfway across the country, but now that I'm sitting here, close enough to smell him if I take a good whiff, it has suddenly become more serious, more real.

I could get tested. The possibility exists that I'm not even a candidate; then the weight would be off of me completely. After all, our blood types are different, though I know that isn't necessarily enough to cancel me out.

But if I am a match, then I have another choice, one that I don't want to make. I could save the man who walked away from me, or show him the same courtesy. I know that acting on my hate, anger, and disgust will be a demon I'll have to live with, but I've been living with the one down the hall for a lot of years. I would only be trading one for another.

"He's waiting for you." The nurse's voice startles me. I shoot straight up and damn near pull the arm of the chair off when she speaks. She's speaking to the older woman watching TV. I now notice the woman's clothes are wrinkled, and her hair looks as though it hasn't seen a brush in a few days. She turns off the television and walks toward the nurse. The two guys in the corner have woken up and wander off, mumbling something about finding a cup of coffee and a bathroom. It's quiet now, and I'm alone. I know whatever I do next I will carry with me for the rest of my life. *I'm a strong man, but am I strong enough to walk away?*

If it were my momma lying in a bed down the hall, there would be no question about what I would do. And thinking about her only reminds me of what Lola said. Did my momma really know where Freddy was? If she were here right now, what would she tell me to do? But she isn't here. No one is here but me, and I'm the only one who can make this decision. Regardless of the kind of man I've always tried to be, my hate is real.

I'm a good man. I'm honest, generous, and kind. I'm everything my dad never was. I lean forward, rest my elbows on my knees, and hold my head in my hands. I try to force myself to get up and face this, to get tested and overcome. But I can't do it. I won't do it. And the fact that my decision makes me no better than him is a cross I never thought I would have to bear. Being like Freddy is the one thing I promised myself I would never be. The first tear lands on the toe of my Stacy Adams loafers. I don't try to stop the ones that follow.

Chapter 29
Lola

ONE OF THE PROBLEMS WITH living in the Midwest is the weather; it has a mind of its own. Yesterday, for example, the sun was shining, and it was a cool sixty degrees, with nothing but big, fluffy white clouds in a blue sky. Today, the blue is now gray, the clouds are black, and the temperature dropped twenty degrees overnight. It's Thanksgiving, and I'm stuck in the house, still recovering from my surgery two weeks ago. *Same problems. Different day.*

I pull the picture of my mother, Vera, and my father, Freddy Adams, from the bedside table. She's leaning close to him, and his arm is around her. Both of them have a beer in hand and smiles that would melt Alaska. They loved each other; it's easy to see from the picture. But love isn't always enough. Theirs was definitely one of those cases.

When I talked to Freddy on the phone before going to LA, he wasn't very nice. I thought about dropping everything, but then again, what had I expected? After I decided to go through with it and called him back, the conversation was a bit different. I was surprised by his candor. He tried to be funny, but it came off as pitiful. I told myself he was in pain, and it must hurt to talk. But I do believe he tried. He answered my questions, at least the ones I had about Vera. I didn't tell Clay or Cass. Cass doesn't care, and Clay didn't need any fuel for the fire he's burning anyway. I didn't tell Grams either, but maybe I will someday.

He said that my mother, Nancy as he called her, was much more than a friend. I guess that is pretty obvious since I'm here. He said he tried to leave his wife once so that they could be together, but his wife said she would take the boys, Roland and Clay, and disappear if he did. He couldn't do that, he said. He didn't want out, but he did want Vera Shatner. Donna Sue didn't want to be the woman who was dumped for the craziest chick in town. In a small town, one has to keep face, I guess.

When Freddy caught his wife with another man, he saw that as an excuse to be free. He left, went to Tulsa, and got an apartment. Then he came back for Vera. He didn't explicitly tell me that he wanted her to leave Cass and me with Grams and Grandpa Jack, but I got that idea. But Vera wouldn't go. Score one for Mom, I guess. By then, Donna Sue had already moved on and told him he needed to leave. He wouldn't say who her boyfriend was, but he did say the guy threatened him. He wouldn't go into detail about that, which makes me wonder if the threat wasn't necessarily physical. I can't see Freddy Adams being afraid of a fight, but we all have fears. If you know someone's vulnerability, it's amazing what you can get him to do, even walk away from his family, his life, his kids. He said he tried to keep in touch with the boys, but they never answered his letters. Donna Sue never let him see them or talk to them on the phone. Finally, he gave up. He moved to California, began going by Rick instead of Freddy, and started all over. He never once said he was sorry for any of it.

I understand why Clay didn't want to hear any of this, but it was my responsibility to try to tell him. If what Freddy told me was true, Clay's memories of his mother would be forever changed. And there have been so many lies, who knows what is real or fantasy? Maybe allowing Clay to hold on to the memory of his mother, even if it may not be true, isn't such a bad thing. He's a smart man. I planted the seed, and he can tend it or starve it. It's his choice.

"Mrs. Warner? Your family is back." Contessa stands at my door, still wearing her apron over her black pants and shirt that we call a uniform. She's reliable help and worth the money. The past few weeks, she has been invaluable to me.

I swing my legs over the side of the bed slowly. "Thanks, Contessa. Have a nice Thanksgiving. I'll see you on Monday." She's been here every day since I got home from LA, and although she hasn't complained, I'm sure she wants to be with her own family for the holidays. We can handle dinner. She's been cooking it all morning, and all we have to do is heat it up.

Hailey comes bouncing in right behind her. "You aren't up yet?" She grabs my robe from the chair that sits before my vanity and helps me into it. "Your sister is hilarious, by the way. She asked the ladies at Babies R Us where they keep the babies because she wanted to buy one to go with the one she's got cooking. You should have seen their faces." I've seen that look many times on people's faces.

Hailey is a bright kid. She's not a kid, but a pregnant eighteen-year-old who grew up with the family from Hell. Her father, a Bible-thumping, self-ordained minister, spends his days telling others how they are going to burn for all eternity. Then he goes home to his wife, who has been stoned or drunk for the past ten years. Hailey was left to fend for herself. When she turned up pregnant, they wanted nothing to do with her. It bothers her a lot, but in time, she'll come to see that sometimes, parents can do more damage than good. Family is what you make of it, not necessarily what you were born into.

Richard didn't even balk when I asked if she could move in for a while. He's got a soft spot that few can see. He says I need someone around to mother a bit, but I want to give the girl a chance. It's tough going through a pregnancy alone, and I want to help if I can. Cass says I need someone to save, which might be true. I sure couldn't save Freddy Adams.

Hailey helps me to my vanity so I can put on some makeup and do my hair. I may not feel great, but I'm not going downstairs until I look like a million. Well, maybe a thousand, but more than a ten-dollar bill. She leaves me alone to go help Grams and Cass get dinner on the table.

When I first got to LA, I met my father in person. He was thin, almost bald, and his skin was yellow and pasty. He looked nothing like the picture I have of him and nothing like what I expected. He was also a worse ass than he'd been on the phone. He insulted his wife, said horrible things about Britt, and didn't even acknowledge that Clay existed. He started laughing when Roland's name was brought up. "Wouldn't that have been some shit if he'd have married you instead of your sister?" *It would have been horrible,* I'd thought. *And not funny at all.* I had to remind myself of the positive things Britt had told me about Freddy to keep me in that hospital, and I also reminded myself that the man was crazy. I had no doubt about that.

Since I'd had a fairly extensive physical three months before, the transplant team agreed to have the additional testing, aside from the original type and cross-match, done in LA. They had preferred I have it done locally to save me the trip in case there was a problem, but I'd insisted. What kind of problems could have developed in three months? Well, an aggressive cancer, for one. It was uterine cancer but fairly well contained. After a total hysterectomy, I'm expected to have a complete recovery without any major problems. I hadn't intended to have any kids at my age, but there's still a void knowing that I can't even if I'd wanted to. At least I'm not going to die. And I hear sex will be better.

I decide to do my hair up and put on the heavy makeup. I know it's a little eccentric, but I like the look, and it makes me feel a bit more connected to a mother I never knew. I have a short black dress and a pair of black boots that will be perfect. After all, it's Thanksgiving, so I might as well get dressed for the day.

When I went to tell Freddy that the liver donation was a no-go, he said nothing. He turned to the wall and refused to acknowledge me at all. I guess I was dead to him at that point, just like Britt was. It made it easier to walk away. He died a week later, alone in his room. There was no funeral. He was cremated and now is a pile of ashes in a box somewhere in his wife's house. Britt and Dennis are spending Thanksgiving with his mother. Britt has promised to come for Christmas.

As I zip up my boots, I hear Richard and Clay downstairs. They have become close, which is good for both of them. This morning, Richard took him to the club to teach him how to play golf. Clay says he's going to take Richard fishing when the weather is right. I have to laugh, imagining Richard in waders, with his Speedo underneath, trying to reel in the big one.

After another look in the mirror, I sit back on my bed. My energy is not at all up to par, and I need a break just from the activity of getting dressed. Cass walks in, looks at me in my Nancy Sinatra guise, and laughs. "You are such a dork." She hauls me up and holds my arm to help me downstairs. "Wait until you see all the crap that girl bought this morning. And Grams. Holy smokes. You'd think we were having a litter. Please get better so I don't have to go shopping with them anymore." I start to laugh and hold my stomach so it doesn't hurt too much.

As I walk into the dining room, I have to hold on to the wall for a minute. I watch as my family loads the table with more food. My family. Some of us aren't related at all, some more than once.

Some people grow up in a house that society says is the perfect ideal:

Mom and Dad, 2.5 kids, a dog in the yard, and a plan. Some, like Britt, have to find their family. And others, like most of mine, have had to overcome theirs. But it really isn't about who you grew up with or who donated the DNA; it's about who loves you in the end, who will be there for you when you need them, and who doesn't care if you play with worms or dress as Nancy Sinatra.

For me, taking care of that family is a bit like landing a plane from the backseat. I do my best to make sure everyone is safe, but in the end, some disappear for no reason, while others stare out the window. But at least I try, and that has to be enough.

"Are you okay?" Richard asks as I sit carefully in my chair at the table. Hailey and Grams are talking about baby names, Clay is cutting the turkey, and Cass sneaks a roll off the table and feeds it to the little brown dog at her feet.

"I'm fine," I say. We are all fine.

Chapter 30

Benny

It's the day after Thanksgiving, and the snow is piled up outside. Grace stands at the mirror and finishes putting her hair up in the ponytail she always wears to work. She says it keeps her hair out of her face, but it also makes her look younger. Women are like that, and Grace is no different. That's not true, she's a lot different than most women, but they all have a few similarities they won't admit to, and one of them is that they all want to look younger. Another is that they all want to be right.

"Have you talked to Clay this week?" she asks.

"Yesterday. Saw him at Logston's. He's handling everything fine." *Like a man*, I want to say, but I don't want to get Grace started on her feminist bullshit tonight. I have other things on my mind.

"I talked to your dad today. They're moving him to that medical facility this week. You should go see him more," she says.

As much as I hate to admit it, Tenesy didn't lie to me at all about the Freddy Adams crap, and even though he's still an ass, I have to give him that. He also told me he was always faithful to my mom, and I believe that. That gets him extra man points in my book. It's a shame she didn't do the same for him.

"Maybe I'll send him some peanut butter balls," I say. "He seems to like those." It's a start, and I'm pretty proud of myself for remembering it.

Grace glances at me. "Peanut butter balls?"

I sit on the side of the bed and start putting my boots on. "He said he gets them twice a day. I don't know why they would give him candy, but—"

"He means phenobarbital, which they aren't giving him anymore because his doctor has started him on something different. But he still calls his pills 'peanut butter balls.'" She says it as if it's normal for people to confuse candy and medicine. Not knowing how sick he is makes me feel like shit.

She kisses me before she walks out the door to work. "Don't get in any trouble tonight."

After Grace is gone, I grab my coat and hat and get in the Tahoe. I radio the station to check in with Jimmy, and he tells me that Wilma Jack called in to report some kids out by the Amvets, playing pranks. I head the Tahoe down Nineteenth Street, but when I get there, nobody's around, only a large snowman with a carrot for a penis, standing by the side of the road. *Cute.* I pull in the parking lot and put the carrot in the middle of his head where it belongs then turn toward my mom's trailer. I haven't talked to her much since the entire Freddy Adams thing went down, and I'm not sure I want to yet.

I dodged a bullet on that one. It could have bitten me in the ass, but I guess what it did was make me think more about my own family, my own parents. Tenesy was a jerk—he still is—but he was always there. And my mom… well…

I drive slowly on the gravel portion of her road, navigating the turns carefully so I don't end up in a ditch out here in the dark. As I round the last bend, I see that her trailer is dark. I pull over to the side of the road and turn off my lights, just as I've done every night for the past two weeks.

Maybe I'm wrong, but we all want to believe our mother is perfect; well, not exactly perfect, but the closest one can ever get to it. I guess expecting that is quite a lot, given that everyone makes mistakes and does things in their lives they aren't too proud of. But somehow, it's hard for us to imagine that about our moms.

It's even harder to think my mom might lie to me. Oh sure, as a kid, there's Santa Claus and the Easter Bunny and all that shit, but I never expected her to tell me an outright lie. And I'm not saying she did, but she wasn't completely truthful. She didn't tell me about Donna Sue and Rudy Drown, and she damn sure had to know about it. She also didn't tell me about her and Freddy Adams. She lied to protect herself, and also to protect Rudy. If Tenesy found out about all this and discovered that Rudy knew all along, there would be hell to pay. I kind of think my dad would forgive my mom, but Rudy—never. So I figure that my mom was protecting him more than herself. I couldn't understand why, but I had a feeling. And now, I know.

Her trailer is dark and quiet, peaceful. Her car is in the drive, covered with snow.

And sitting next to it is Rudy's cruiser.

Chapter 31
Clay

I LEARNED VERY QUICKLY THAT ON nights when Cassie says she needs to be alone, the best thing I can do is sit out back with my worms and let her do what she needs to do. Of course, I don't particularly like that she goes out in the middle of the night, but she can take care of herself. As much as I hate to admit it, I need a little time to myself tonight too.

When I was a little boy, my momma told me that we should throw all of our problems out in the yard so the first snow of the year could freeze them and melt them away. The day after Thanksgiving, that snow came, and it was damn near a blizzard. I guess we had a lot that needed covered. A week later, the ground is soft from the melted snow, and I imagine that my backyard is a potter's field, so many problems melting into the ground to be buried forever.

But some things, even an iceberg can't take away. The fact that I didn't help my dying father, didn't even get tested to see if I could help, is one of those things. I struggled with it, even more so after Lola tried to tell me that Freddy might not have been so bad. I thought about what she had said. If he had tried to keep in touch and my mother had kept him away, she must have had her reasons. Knowing how he's treated Britt, maybe her reasons were just. Either way, I won't blame her for something that may or may not be true. But I did come home from LA still considering whether I should help him or not. Then he died a week later. I tell myself that God saw fit to make that decision for me; now all I have to do is live with it.

I grab a handful of worms from one of the hatches and sit at the picnic table under our bare red maple. It's not much right now, a thick trunk with empty branches, but by spring, it will look alive again. I'm already anxious for spring.

In the past month and a half, I've discovered I have a brother and a sister that I never knew about, and I've learned where my father has been all these years. I also connected with my brother-in-law, who has become a surrogate dad, and found out I'm going to be a father. It's been a crazy six weeks, and although I've managed it, I can't say I look forward to many more changes in my life for a while. Except one.

I spread my hands wide and let the worms curl around my fingers, contracting and retracting their bodies, inching their way along my palms. "I'm going to be a daddy," I say. They seem to respond with a collective sigh. It's not the first time they've heard me say the words, and I doubt it will be the last. It's still something I'm trying to wrap my head around.

Of course, I've been a daddy for several years, but Shaylene is different. I became her daddy after she was already walking and talking. Sure, she's mine, at least as far as the court says, but I didn't make her. Roland did. I took responsibility for her when he was too much of an asshole to step up.

But this is for real. A newborn baby will be my charge, mine from the minute it comes out of Cassie's body. I'm excited, and I'm scared to death.

I'm forty years old, and although I'm in pretty good shape, I'll be damn near sixty when my child graduates from high school. What kind of shape am I going to be in then? "I guess I'll have to take better care of myself," I say to the worms. They are easy to talk to, and I've done it so much that I seem to understand their motions better than some people's words.

"Are you talking to your worms?" Maryanne's voice startles me. I didn't hear her car pull up out front, and I didn't hear her walk around back. It's two in the morning, and the last thing I expected was her in my backyard. Well, that's not entirely true. I expect anything these days.

Maryanne is dressed in a slinky red dress, her dark-brown hair loose and hanging down. She has that freshly fucked look, and knowing Maryanne, that's exactly what she's been doing.

"No, I knew you were standing there," I lie. "What the hell are you doing out this late?" I hope she doesn't tell me. I know what Maryanne does with her late nights.

"I saw the light on when I was driving home and thought something might be wrong. Where's Cass?"

"She needed to get out by herself."

Maryanne stretches her arms over her head and bends to one side, then the other. "I understand that."

No. Your idea of getting out means finding some swinging dick for the night. Cassie's idea is a bit different. "I doubt that."

Maryanne and I haven't always been friends. She's the mother of my child and Cassie's friend, so I feel I have to be nice these days. It hasn't always been that way. I have been mad at her for eighteen years, ever since I realized Shaylene was Roland's kid, and Maryanne wasn't going to tell anyone. I'm still mad that she wasted so many years on my brother, but didn't we all?

She lays her hands flat on the table and cocks her head to one side. "So Cass goes for a walk in the woods, and you sit out here and talk to your worms. You two are a perfect match, you know."

"She's getting in her time at the Hill before the sale is final." After Cassie found out about Roland's vasectomy, she decided to get rid of everything that was part of him, including the land on Booker Hill. Angus is buying it from her, and he told her that she is welcome to come out whenever she wants to, but it's still hard for her to let go. Some people have such a hold on you, they can reach you from beyond the grave. I understand that.

I get up and give my reds one last squeeze then put them back in their container. I wipe my hands on my pant legs and sit back down at the table, across from Maryanne.

She scrunches up her forehead. "Can I show you something, and you won't freak out?"

How bad can it be? "What?"

She stands up, hikes a leg up on the table, and starts lifting her skirt.

"Whoa," I say. "No, I changed my mind."

"Oh, stop." She points to a small area on her upper thigh, which is covered with a piece of plastic.

I have to get closer to see it, but I don't want to get too close. I see a hummingbird. "You got a tattoo?" I don't know why she thinks that would freak me out.

"That's where I've been most of the night," she says.

I raise my eyebrows. *That's not where you've been most of the night.*

"I was at a bar, I saw Angus, and he saved me from some asshole who was getting too grabby. He has a black belt in something I can't pronounce. You should have seen the look on that guy's face." She starts to giggle, and I try to picture Angus going all Rambo on some drunk who was trying to feel up Maryanne. "So we went back to his shop, and he gave me this."

"And?" I don't care to know about Maryanne's personal life, but I know there's more to this story than a tattoo.

"And I gave him something too." Yeah, I should have seen that coming.

"I thought you didn't like him." Cassie told me how rude Maryanne had been to Angus, and how he stood strong and teased her at every chance. Cassie knew I would enjoy someone putting Maryanne in her place.

She shrugs. "Well, I've always wanted one. And you know me, I'm always up for a new adventure."

"Always wanted one what? A tattoo or an Angus?" I couldn't resist. She threw it out there, and I had to hook it.

She rolls her eyes, but she's smiling. "He's nice. We're going out to dinner tomorrow. A real date. Stranger things have happened, right?"

"Stranger than you having a real date with a nice guy? Yeah, stranger things have happened." In the past month, stranger things have happened. "But that's real close to the winner."

"How's Lola doing?" After coming back from LA, Lola went straight into the hospital and had all her female parts taken out. It's been rough for her, but she's a tough lady, and she's healing fast.

"She's going to be okay." And I am very thankful for that. When I first found out she wanted to donate part of her liver to Freddy Adams, I was so mad I could spit. But in every family, when it comes right down to it, there has to be one person who takes the lead and makes decisions. The rest of us follow. Lola is our leader.

I look up at the clear sky. Stars are blinking as if they are trying to talk too.

"You're going to be great, Clay," she says. I hate to think she knows what's on my mind, but I guess when a man knows he's going to have a baby, what else would he be thinking about?

"You know, I've been thinking about my own dad tonight." I didn't feel happy, or sad, or relieved by the news of my father's death. I felt nothing. I realize that Richard is right—if my dad had stuck around, I would be a different person, and I kind of like how I turned out. But it still bothers me. I worry about what parts of him are living in me, waiting to jump out.

"Clay, you are not your father," Maryanne says.

"I know. He was a chickenshit. What kind of man doesn't live up to his responsibilities?" Even in the dark, I can see Maryanne flinch. I wasn't referring to Roland, but the connection didn't go unnoticed.

"Clay, it has nothing to do with the man you are."

I have to laugh. It has everything to do with the man I am. Waking up one day at the age of five to hear my momma tell me that my daddy was never coming home had a way of molding me. If he had been killed in the war like Momma told everyone later, maybe it would have been different. But he wasn't. He left. "You know, I know I'm a better man than my daddy was, a better man than my little brother too. And I'm trying to live with the past. I know I can't change it. Cassie calls it my judgment. But here's the thing: I also know that the actions of parents weigh pretty heavily on a child. I don't think I had the chance to damage Shaylene much since she lived with you, but this one is going to be right here, twenty-four, seven."

"You aren't going to damage anybody. You are going to be the best father in the world. You've already proven that with Shaylene." She stops for a second, but she isn't done. "What about Cass?"

"What about her?"

"Maybe it's not you that you're worried about. Maybe..."

Of course, I've thought about that too. Cassie has a lot of problems, but between me, Babe, Lola, and even Maryanne, she'll be fine. "She's doing great with Dog."

"A baby isn't a puppy," Maryanne says. "She can't be dragging it out into the woods at two a.m. because she needs to walk."

"We'll figure it out." I don't know how, but we will. I love Cassie, always have, and the thought of her makes me feel better than a handful of worms.

"See? You are going to be great. You're a good man, Clay. Regardless of who or what your daddy was, you turned out fine, and so will your daughter."

"Son." I want a boy. I can't lie. I want to take him fishing, go to all of his ball games, and tell him how proud I am of him for just being him. I know I can do that with a daughter, too, but this family needs some more strong men to carry on the name, to reclaim it.

Chapter 32

Cass

THE LAST TIME I BURIED something on Booker Hill, it was raining and the ground was soft. Tonight, it's mid-December, and the ground is a little harder, mostly due to the cold weather. But thanks to the melted snow, it's not too hard for my favorite shovel. The police finally released it back to me a few weeks ago, five months after they took it for evidence when I was jailed for killing my husband. I like the way it feels in my hands.

I stop for a second. The hole might be deep enough, and I'm ready to get this over with. I grab the black cat clock next to me and throw it in. The white eyes stare at me, and the wide grin is reflected under the light of the moon. A large crack runs from the middle of its mouth to the top of its head, like a jagged scar. It looks creepy as hell.

A tiny flutter in my stomach makes me stop and put a hand on my abdomen. I know Peanut is too new to be moving around, at least enough for me to feel it, but every once in a while, I feel a flutter, and I think it must be her trying to say hello. She's obviously going to be a talker, which figures. "Hello, Peanut."

Movement at the tree line catches my eye. I wondered how long it would take Roland to show up. The sale of the land to Angus will be final in a few weeks, there's a big For Sale sign on the truck, and now I'm burying his clock. He has to know I'm trying to get rid of him. I guess his first clue should have been when I buried him in this same spot last summer. I wait, but it isn't Roland. It's Old Man Booker. He looks in the hole, then at me, and sits down to watch, just like he did when I was digging up Roland to throw him in the river.

Call Me Daddy

"You're pretty nosy for a dead guy," I say. He shrugs but doesn't say anything.

There's a chill in the air. I pull my coat tighter around me and decide I should take a break before I pile dirt on the clock. I sit on the damp ground next to Booker and look toward the river that runs behind our land. Soon, it will be Angus's land.

When I burned our shack down, I saved the clock and gave it to Clay. Roland loved the clock, so I figured Clay would too.

The night of the dinner party when Clay started throwing dishes, I realized he hated the damn thing. I was at the front door, saying good-bye to Lola, when the cat's hourly screech was followed by a crash. Clay left it on the floor. He told me later that as a kid, Roland used to wake him up at night and move his head back and forth like the clock, then Roland would tell him that the black cat was always watching him. It was Roland's clock, he said, not his mother's, and it only reminded him of all the times his brother had been cruel to him.

Maybe I kept it around for the same reason.

Clay likes to forget those kinds of things—maybe not forget, exactly, but he puts them in a place inside and locks them away. Although I have a lot of good memories of Roland, I have a lot of bad ones too. I needed to keep those so I could remember why I killed him. But it's time for Roland to disappear forever, so Clay, Peanut, and I can start fresh.

Booker points to my stomach. My hand covers it protectively. "Peanut?" He rolls his dead eyes.

"I want a girl," I say to the ghost sitting next to me, but he's looking off toward the river again. I would be happy with a little Clay, and I'll do my best with either sex, but I want a girl. I can't lie. I want to teach her to read and cook and know how to pick the right plants for Grams. But most of all, I want her to know how to love and teach her that she shouldn't let anyone take advantage of that. This family needs another strong, confident woman like Lola, but I hope this child never has to go through the hell my sister went through in her younger days.

The cat screeches from its grave, and the sound echoes across the Hill. I damn near wet myself and realize I forgot to take its batteries out. Booker slaps his thigh and opens his mouth wide in a silent laugh. *Very funny.*

I stand up, wipe the dirt from my behind, grab my shovel, and start filling the hole with hard dirt. By spring, the batteries should wear down, and the cat will finally be silent. Until then, Roland can listen to it every hour. *Don't say I never did anything for you, Roland.* I pat the land down and stand up, satisfied with my work. I turn to Booker, who nods his head and disappears.

When I look up, Roland is standing between me and the truck. His arms are crossed over his chest, and he shakes his head at me. My face goes hot. I raise my shovel, ready for a fight, and I see the beginnings of a smile. His dimples start to cave in on his face, and my anger is suddenly replaced with a feeling of pity.

I throw the shovel to the ground and move toward him. Holding my head up, I walk right through him. He becomes no more than a vapor around me. As his ether blows away on a slight breeze, I realize that as long as I don't acknowledge him, his power will run down, and he will eventually cease to exist. I don't know if I can do that all at once, but time will pass, and he'll be gone forever.

I gun the truck down the dirt driveway and don't look back.

Tick, tock, Roland.

ACKNOWLEDGMENTS

First and foremost, I want to thank my readers. Not only have they read, reviewed, and talked about my book, but they have sent me pictures of *They Call Me Crazy* from all over the world and shown their love of my work in some interesting ways. Having such an active group of readers has made this journey more fun than I thought it could be. You all rock.

Call Me Daddy is a story of family, and I couldn't write without mine. They are not only supportive but nutty enough to provide me with all the stories I'll ever need. A special thank you to my brother Kerry Stone and my cousin Steve Stone, who both had a place for me to go when I needed to get away, to my uncle Bob Rouse for "finding the mistake," and to my uncle Daryl Stone, for just being Uncle Daryl.

Rebecca Mahoney, Neila Forssberg, and Suzanne Warr are my amazing editors. Thank you for visiting Deacon, Kansas, with me, and leaving it a richer and more grammatically correct place.

Having a support group when writing is so important. I have several. My Red Adept family, the Kuskateers, the BaBB's, and as always, my subgroupies who never run low on crocks of pork.

The value of readers at every stage of writing a book can't be overstated. Thank you to Stephanie Raines, Michelle Dake, Avria Myklegard, Ashley Porton, and Randy Martin for reading the first draft of *Daddy* and letting me know what worked and what didn't.

Brandy Vaughn, you are the best UVI ever!

Beth Garland, Jen Badamo, and Carrie Rago for making me laugh, making me cry, and keeping it real.

Mike Hancock, for having a beach house and a welcome mat at the exact time that I needed beach therapy.

My mentors: Merle Drown, Richard Carey, Robert Begiebing, and Craig Childs. You are still stuck with me.

The faculty, staff, and students at Southeastern Oklahoma State University have welcomed me into their family with open arms. I couldn't be more appreciative of their support while writing this book.

For Troy, because a good bartender is hard to find.

And finally, to my muse, DeeDee. I miss you, girl. Keep inspiring me, until we meet again.

About the Author

Kelly Stone Gamble was born and raised in a small Midwestern town but, as an adult, became a city girl. As a member of the faculty at Southeastern Oklahoma State University, she now moves between her homes in Henderson, Nevada, and Idabel, Oklahoma, allowing her to enjoy the best of both worlds.

If you would like to stay in touch with Kelly, sign up for her newsletter at www.kstonegamble.com, www.facebook.com/KStoneGamble/, or follow her on Twitter at twitter.com/KellySGamble.

Made in the USA
San Bernardino, CA
25 November 2017

"A tale of passion and secrets, overcoming loss and finding redemption. Call Me Daddy is full of twists that will keep readers guessing all the way to the finish."

— Claire Ashby, author of NYT Bestseller When You Make It Home

Cass Adams comes from a long line of crazy, and she fears passing that on to her unborn child. Also, she's run over Roland and Clay's surprise half brother Britt, landing him in the hospital. With her inner demons coming out to haunt her, she doesn't know if she should keep the baby.

Clay Adams has his own decisions to make. His half brother shows up to tell him their father, Freddy, is still alive but needs a liver transplant. When Freddy blew out of town thirty-five years ago, secrets were buried. But it's time for them to be dug up, because only then can Clay hope to lay the past to rest.

Call Me Daddy is a story of family, the secrets they keep, and to what lengths someone would go to protect them.

This sequel to *They Call Me Crazy* can be read as a standalone novel.

Kelly Stone Gamble was born and raised in a small Midwestern town but, as an adult, became a city girl. As a member of the faculty at Southeastern Oklahoma State University, she now moves between her homes in Henderson, Nevada and Idabel, Oklahoma, allowing her to enjoy the best of both worlds.